Ravaged Land

a post-apocalyptic
novel.

By
**Kellee L.
Greene**

First Edition December 2015

For B, E and S.

Chapter one.

I think I took it all for granted. I had become accustomed to my daily routine and to be totally honest, I liked it. In fact, there was nothing I enjoyed more than sitting still, reading a book, soaking in the bathtub, watching a movie, or other simple things that some people think are monotonous. They are always on the go, scheduling the next event, sending text messages and taking quick showers, but I didn't mind being slow. I relished it. I thought everyone should take a more leisurely approach to life, what was the rush anyway? Had I been able to see into the future, I may have thought differently. I might have changed how I had lived my life.

There had been something drastically different in the air that afternoon, but I couldn't quite put my finger on exactly what it was. The whole day had been hot and humid, the weatherman had predicted a thunderstorm, and we were under a tornado watch. My clothes had been soggy from dripping sweat all day in the unpleasant, claustrophobic classrooms they refused to air condition. I had felt gross and was eager to change into something dry, ideally right into my pajamas. This day had been draining, and I was exhausted. Maybe I'd curl up in bed after a cool bath, read a book and listen to the storms pass by. That sounded like heaven.

I wanted to put a name to the smell floating in my nostrils. It was salty and musty, making me think of under-cooked French fries. Both the smell and the feeling in the air had been unsettling and I couldn't wait to get home. I walked faster hoping I'd beat the rain since my clothes were already wet enough. I crossed my arms in front of me and let my backpack hang off my shoulder as I walked fast with my head down. After the bell had rang letting school out I had practically sprinted out of the building leaving a little earlier than I usually did. Since it had been the last day before summer vacation, everyone else was lingering and making plans for the summer with their friends. They had all apparently been oblivious to that unusual fragrance in the air.

"Have a great summer Roslyn!" A tall girl shouted to me from across the street, waving at me altogether too excitedly as she opened the passenger door of a beat-up blue corvette. I couldn't remember her name, so I smiled awkwardly and waved at her. Then as if I felt weird about my hand up in the air, I dropped it down to gather up my dark blonde hair letting it fall down over my left shoulder.

I was probably about halfway home when I looked up from the sidewalk. Across the street was a boy in my class I didn't really know, but I recognized him only because he was often the object of discussions I'd overheard the other girls chittering about. He was cute, dark hair, dark eyes but guys like that don't have an interest in girls like me anyway. He wouldn't want someone who was as boring and low-key as I was. A boy like that is only interested in the most popular, the most beautiful and the most interesting girls. In front of me was another boy from my class, Ryan I thought, kicking a stone as if it were a soccer ball. Another one of the boys all the girls went crazy over, he was absolutely gorgeous, but he didn't know it, or at least if he did, he didn't care.

There was another group somewhere behind me. I could hear them talking, making plans for the night, and next they'd probably plan out the whole summer. After I rolled my eyes, I was hit smack dab in the middle of my forehead by an abnormally large drop of wetness. I wiped my skin dry with the back of my hand and tilted my head upwards. The dark ominous clouds looming ahead traveled at what seemed to be an unrealistic speed. Only moments ago the sun had been shining but now a darkness akin to night was setting in, the feeling made me shiver even in this heat.

I looked to the others to see if anyone else had noticed the extreme raindrops but the boy across the street still had his head down and was even further ahead of me. The other boy, Ryan, who had been in front of me had turned off and was walking into what I assumed was his house.

The drops of water started to fall quicker, each one smacking against my face and the exposed skin of my arms with small but annoying stings. I swung my backpack in front of me to look for something I could put over my head. Before I even got a chance to unzip my pack there was a loud thunk followed by the clanging rattle of a street sign. It had made such an unusual high pitched noise that my ears started to ring.

Another chunk of hail hit the ground a foot in front of me with a thud, crashing so hard it broke into countless smaller pieces on impact. They scattered all around my feet looking like little chips of glass. This was by far the largest and most dangerous hail I'd ever seen in my entire life. Within thirty seconds of each other, another two large pieces fell only a few feet away from me, and thankfully not on my head. How many more of these large ice blocks would fall? These pieces of hail weren't the small and smooth pebble-like hail I'd seen a hundred times before, instead they were rough and thick, jagged like chipped and broken rocks. I put my backpack over my head hoping it would at least protect me from the falling shards, but in all reality they probably weighed several pounds and the backpack wouldn't do much of anything to soften the blow.

Down the street a car window shattered with a loud pop and crack. I hadn't been expecting it and I jumped backwards startled by the sudden noise. My house was still a fair distance away, and the hail didn't seem to be letting up. If anything, it was getting worse. I needed to find a place to hang out temporarily until this lethal storm passed. The girl in the group behind me let out an awful howl. I whipped around to see watery blood streaming down her face. Her crystal blue eyes were wide with surprise. I guessed that she'd been hit by the small chunk of hail that rocked to a stop near her feet. Had it been one of the larger pieces she wouldn't have been able to let out her painful cry.

The house Ryan had walked into had a covered porch. I called over to the group behind me, pointing as I ran up the walk. "Over here, come this way!" I said, and they followed. I didn't think he'd mind... considering.

A car barreled down the street and I realized what was about to happen only seconds before it did. The driver didn't have a chance. The girl next to me with the gash in her forehead let out a scream that made my bones ache. It had been like something out of a horror movie. The boulder of hail which had been the size of a large watermelon smashed through the windshield. Copious cracks sprouted out from the hole that had been left by the chunk of hail further weakening the glass. The car slammed into a parked van, and the driver was ejected from his seat. The broken windshield had slowed the drivers exit and his body was sprawled out on the hood of the car like a rag doll. Blood pooled out from his middle and oozed out of his nose and ears. He laid there staring blankly towards me, his body motionless. Oh crap, was he dead?

The boy who had been ahead of me on the other side of the street was running towards the car, but he stopped suddenly when he saw the body spread out on the car. He put his hand on his forehead and then both hands over his eyes. I guessed it had been someone he knew. The winds picked up and the booms from the thunder and lightning shook the earth so much I worried it was an earthquake. It was terrifying.

The tall boy who was with the girl spun her around so she was facing the house and the guy with black hair stood in front of me to block my view since I had been unable to turn myself away from the gruesome scene. The front door to the house flung open, partly from the wind and partly from an aggressive push. The bang startled me and I jumped into the bigger guy grabbing his arm way too tightly.

"You guys have to come with me," he said. "Please, follow me." He gestured for us to follow him and it took me a few minutes to understand as my brain hadn't worked the same way it had before seeing the crash. Ryan was trying to get us to go with him somewhere. I caught another glimpse of the guy across the street, he was looking at us, he didn't say anything he just stood there. The others hadn't noticed him, I was about to say something when I was jostled by the guy with the black hair whose name I couldn't recall.

"But—" I managed to eek the word out in an attempt to alert them to the guy across the street.

"Go!" he said, his eyes begging me to make my feet move. And I did. I glanced back after a few steps and he was gone. We followed Ryan like lost puppies. The guy with black hair yelled through the howling winds, "Where are we going?"

We looped around the side of his house

going into the backyard, "My grandpa has an underground shelter. We'll be safe there!" We ran through his backyard jumping over broken tree branches and random things that had blown into his yard— trash bins, a grill, even a little pink tricycle.

"How far?" the tall boy shouted as a brick-sized piece of hail landed about a foot away from him.

"Not far," Ryan said, "this way!" He weaved between a garage and a small shed and onto the sidewalk of the next block. "That one," he said pointing to a green house across the street and three houses over.

We splashed through the puddles on the roadway running as fast as we could. A gust of wind almost knocked me off my feet, but somehow I managed to regain my footing without falling or blowing away. I saw a car rolling top to bottom and side to side through the air about a block away and then I noticed the twister that was propelling it. Another gust of wind came and lifted me for a full second off the ground. It happened so fast I wasn't even sure it had been real or if I was imagining it until I felt a hand grab onto mine pulling me along.

"Here?" I asked when we were in front of the green house.

Ryan turned around the side of the house. Boards from the roof were being lifted off, and the siding was peeling away towards the twister that I could feel was even closer than it had been before. The winds were stronger, and the air was filling with dust and dirt, and it was getting harder to breathe. A large piece of siding from the neighbor's

10

house zipped past my face and pierced itself into the side of Ryan's grandpa's house. It stuck out like an arrow that hit its target. A target that had only been inches from my face. We were finally in his grandpa's backyard when I realized I hadn't been breathing.

Everyone was holding onto one another. I grabbed Ryan's shirt as he flung open the doors to his grandpa's underground shelter. We all piled in — the girl with the gash on her head first, then the tall boy, then the pale boy, followed by the one with black hair and then it was my turn. I turned around to help Ryan inside when I saw a tornado weaving back and forth heading right for us. There was a second one the size of a full city block not too far behind it also heading our way. I wanted to scream but instead I gained a burst of extra strength and yanked Ryan inside. Together we pulled as hard as we could to close the doors, but I wasn't much help with the wind's ever-increasing strength. I could feel myself rising above the ground. My feet were no longer touching the floor, and everything felt like it was moving in slow motion as I was gradually being pulled out of the doorway. Ryan grabbed one leg while the boy with black hair grabbed my other. I felt like an out-of-control kite as they yanked me inside and threw me against the back wall. They hadn't intended to be rough with me, but they had to act fast so they could get the doors closed before we were all whisked away. The double doors had a huge lock that slid into place, but the wind outside was so strong the doors rattled aggressively, causing them to shake and bow outward.

I could hear the windows shattering in the house above us, it sounded as if the whole building was being torn apart at the seams. "This way," Ryan said as he grabbed a radio off a nearby shelf and a flashlight which he instantly flicked on. It was almost as if his grandpa had made him do test runs to make sure he'd know what to do should he ever need to come here in an emergency.

We followed him down a cement hallway. The thudding of our feet turned into booming as the hallway turned into a metal corridor, something that had been added somewhat recently by the looks of it. I wondered if his grandpa had been one of those people that prepared for the end of the world, what were they called? Preppers? Thinking of everything going on outside right now, I kind of hoped he was. I was thankful, I knew how lucky I was to be here. Even being in this hallway I felt somewhat safe, that was until I felt a sudden breeze and heard the whistling of the wind. The doors must have been pulled off their hinges. Ryan grunted as he opened the next set of thick metal doors, he passed the flashlight to the boy with black hair, "Go down, I'm going to wait for my family here."

It sounded to me as if the house above had been lifted off of the foundation and placed back down in the wrong spot. "Where are they?" I asked him, wondering at the same time where my mom was and hoping she was safe in our basement or somewhere even better. I questioned how safe a person would be in a normal basement with this storm. Ryan had saved my life and I didn't really feel comfortable just leaving him out here alone, especially with all the rattling and crashing noises. The wind was so strong I could feel it against my skin even at the end of the hallway.

"I'm not sure, work? School? Just… not home yet," he said shaking his head as if he was trying to sprinkle the worry that he felt out of his ears.

"They might be hunkered down somewhere not even trying to get here, you have to come inside, I don't think you are safe out here," I said tugging his arm gently.

"I have to wait," he said still shaking his head, because he knew better, he knew they weren't coming. He also knew that he should go inside and that the last thing anyone in his family would want was for him to wait outside of the shelter for them.

"Please," I begged, "if they come we'll just let them in." I tried to talk some sense into him, I hoped it wouldn't take much to sway him. I couldn't have timed it better, the wind picked up again with an ear piercing whistle. It was a forceful gust that shifted both of our bodies. At the end of the long hallway, I saw a piece of wood, maybe from a shelf, go flying up into the air and out of the basement with other pieces chasing after. Each airy blast was stronger than the last. The pieces of his grandpa's house were being plucked out like the loose pieces of a Jenga tower and at any minute it would come crashing down. He inhaled sharply and guided me inside, he tried to pull the door closed, but it was like a vacuum preventing it from shutting. Luckily we were able to get it closed working together, but we lost our footing and tumbled to the ground. Ryan vaulted up and slid several locks into place and pulled down a huge bar to secure it even further.

He offered me his hand to help me to my feet, I gladly accepted the help. I just stood there gawking at him, waiting for further direction, like I no longer knew how to function without guidance.

"Down."

"Excuse me?" I said looking at him as if he were speaking another language.

"Go down the stairs."

I pivoted and descended the approximately fifteen steps quickly, fearing the door would be pulled off its hinges and I'd be whisked back out into the storm, but the buckled down solid door didn't even rattle. It gave no signs that it was weak. The others were gathered by the door waiting for instructions from Ryan. He flipped some switches that caused air to start circulating, and I could hear the humming and buzzing of other things starting up. Once he was satisfied it was all working as it was supposed to, he closed the last door that would keep us inside and the nasty weather outside. We were locked inside. Underground.

Chapter two.

I was freaking out about what just happened. I held it all in mainly because I didn't know how to express it and I didn't want to cause everyone else to panic any more than they already were. I was worried about my mom, was she home? Was she OK? I wished there was some way for me to communicate with her so I could tell her I was safe.

"What was that?" The boy with black hair bellowed, "I've never seen anything like that!"

"I think I counted five tornadoes at one time, and that's just the ones I could see," the pale boy added.

Ryan turned on a small TV that was up against the wall centered within the living room. It was mostly cracks, whistles and gray fuzzy snow with little flashes of a grayish shadow of the newscaster who was overly dedicated to his job. He sat there spouting out everything that was going on outside, and for us, what was happening above ground. We all sat in absolute silence trying to make out what he was saying between noises and the static.

15

"Seek immediate sheltkrrrrrrrrrrrrrrr...
tornadoes, clusters of them...wizzzzzzzrrrr... here
is a look at the live radar...krrrrrr. Fwaappp area
covered in red, this is no joke folks...
whhhhhooooooooooo in all my years... fizzzz never
seen something like krrrrrrrrrrrrrrip." It started to
come in a little clearer for just a moment "We've
had reports of homes pulled right off their
foundation and thrown into neighboring states.
Hail the size of watermelons and as sharp and
deadly as axes falling from the sky. Downpours
that are causing major flooding and even landslides.
We've just, just...krrrrrrrrrip no end in sight, stay
safe out there krrrrrrrrrrr."

Ryan broke the silence, "I guess we'll be
down here for a while." We all stared at the fuzz on
the TV trying to make sense of it all. Everything
outside was being torn apart and we didn't know
where our families were or if they were even OK. I
couldn't stop myself from thinking the worst— that
our families hadn't found shelter in time, or a good
enough shelter. The storm came so fast. We barely
made it to safety. And why didn't the weathermen
know it was going to be this bad? How lucky I had
been did not escape me, I didn't know how I'd ever
thank Ryan if I survived this.

His grandpa's shelter seemed quite safe, I
couldn't even hear anything that was going on
above us. I wasn't sure how we'd know when it
was safe to leave this place, but the storm couldn't
last forever. We would have to wait for someone on
TV to come back and tell us it was OK, and then I
could go find my mom.

Ryan held out a bottle of water in front of my line of vision, "Drink?" he asked in a low voice. I nodded a thank you even though I had no intentions of opening it. I wasn't thirsty even though my mouth felt like sandpaper. I'd drink when I got home. The water at my house was great.

I had forgotten about the girl's wound until I heard her making little gasping noises as she dabbed her shirt sleeve against her forehead. "It really hurts," she whispered to the tall boy with a sniff, and he put his hand on her shoulder.

I hadn't noticed Ryan had left the room until he returned carrying a mirror and a first aid kit. "That's a big scratch," he said handing her the kit. Her bleeding had slowed significantly. She was lucky it hadn't been worse.

"Thanks," she said taking the kit and handing it to the tall boy.

I watched the radar on TV and tried to see if I could make anything out. With everything so jumbled and fuzzy it was hard to tell what was going on, but it appeared as though the whole state of North Dakota was covered in the colors red and purple. A small portion of our state had the yellow coloring but there wasn't a single area that had clear sky. Everything in our state and the surrounding states was currently experiencing severe weather. This was bad. The worst part of it all was that when they put the radar in motion it showed more coming. It was an endless storm of heavy rain, damaging winds, hail, tornadoes and dangerous lightning. They cut away to what appeared to be the map of the whole United States and parts of Mexico and Canada. I gasped.

"What's wrong?" asked the girl not even attempting to disguise her shaking voice. She now had a large piece of gauze taped to her forehead with a red dot in the center where the blood was soaking in.

"It's just all red, that just can't be right." The words spilled out. I spoke before thinking. It hadn't been my intention to make anyone more scared or on edge than they already were.

"What's all red?" the tall one asked.

"Everything, I mean, it's not even possible! It's everywhere, the whole United States, Canada, it's all covered with these storms, can that be?" I flapped my arms at the TV and looked at the others waiting for any kind of logical answer, but they stared back at me as if I had the answers, which I didn't. I wasn't even sure this was all really happening. Everything we had been through to get here seemed like it had to have been a bad dream. Only it wasn't.

"We are safe down here," Ryan said trying to keep everyone calm. "I know you're worried about your families, I am too, but there isn't much we can do until this all passes. We are several feet underground, this place has been flood tested, nothing can get us. It was designed to keep my family safe if there was some sort of end of the world disaster… like bombs or whatever. My grandpa was a prepper, he knew what he was doing, he was a little crazy about it…" he stopped himself, swallowed hard, "thank God he was though. I just hope my family…."

His words were getting stuck in his throat, it seemed as though he was having trouble talking after he said his 'grandpa *was* a prepper' as in past tense. I wasn't sure if that had meant his grandpa had died since building the shelter or if he was just assuming that his grandpa wouldn't have survived the deadly storm outside. But I wasn't going to ask. I already felt guilty that it was me down here and not his family.

Everyone was silent probably thinking of their own families. I refused to think of all the things that could have happened to my mom, at least not right now. She had survived a lot of hardships in her life, losing her mother to cancer, my dad cheating on her with a 24-year-old stripper, a horrible divorce, a stint with an abusive boyfriend and that was only the beginning. If anyone would get through this storm, it would be her. I didn't need to waste time thinking about it, I'd go to her as soon as I could.

"KrrrrrrrOHMYGOD! Krrrrrr… wizzzzzzzz…." The newscaster screamed and the station blacked out completely. There was no sound, no picture, not even any gray snowy fuzz. TV was gone.

"I'll try the radio," Ryan said, "Uhh by the way, I'm Ryan for those that don't know me." I already knew him, I had a few classes with him but he was quiet, I didn't really know anything about him other than his name.

"Owen." He and I were in study hall together but I couldn't ever remember his name.

19

I'd see him and think his name was Evan, he had shiny black hair and he was all muscle, solid and outgoing. I think everyone in school liked him.

"I know who all of you are but anyway, I'm Dean, and this is my little sister Sienna." She forced a quick smile but I could tell she was trying to hide the fact that she was scared out of her mind. Dean was tall, I'd seen him around before, mostly hanging around with Owen, and he was crazy hot. His brown hair was messy, but that kind of messy that probably takes a half hour of styling to perfect. What stood out to me most of all were his eyes, they were the color of chocolate syrup. I wondered how I hadn't noticed him more in school, but I never cared about things like that. Under other circumstances I might feel shy around someone this attractive, but considering what we had just escaped it didn't seem to matter.

"Seth," the pale boy with the blonde hair said. I knew of him only because he stood out at school, it was nice to finally put a name to his face. There was a short time where some of the other kids tried to get the nickname 'albino' to stick but he didn't let it get to him and it was short lived. I couldn't even remember the last time I had heard anyone call him that.

"I'm Ros," I said lifting my damp tangled hair in a pretend ponytail.

Ryan turned the radio dial so slow you could barely see his hand moving. There were a few stations had that annoying buzz but instead of them saying, "This is only a test," they were saying "this is not a test" and to stay tuned for further instruction. But those further instructions never came and Ryan continued searching. When he hit the end of the dial, he switched the power off out of frustration and hit the table with his fist causing a few stacked coffee cups to rattle.

"How will we know when we can leave?" Sienna quietly asked the group.

"Cameras." That was all Ryan managed to spit out after his frustrations with the radio.

"What do you mean?" I asked not understanding.

Ryan flipped a switch on the wall and clicked a button on the remote control. The picture on the TV worked but what it showed wasn't what any of us wanted to see.

"Jesus Christ." Owen choked and swallowed hard, "Is this some kind of joke?"

The screen was divided into four panels, one for each of the cameras that had been placed in various strategic locations outside. Camera with a number one appeared to be underwater, I couldn't quite figure out where it was located outside and why they'd need an underwater camera. Camera two wasn't working and showed just a solid black box. The third camera showed what the weather was doing the best. It was difficult to see but there were huge chunks of ice falling from the sky. It looked like it was snowing jagged melons. Dancing along the background was a bouquet of several tornadoes. It wasn't just a tornado or two, within the frame of this particular camera, it was at least four, and what looked like another two or three even further back in the distance. I wasn't sure if the ones further back were actually tornadoes or not due to the low visibility from the rain, hail, and misty fog. I wondered how many more there might be outside the viewing range of the camera. Was the whole state just covered with tornadoes? The thought was terrifying.

Camera four was my least favorite. It was the camera that I assumed was pointed at the shelter, or more accurately, the ground above the shelter. It was the worst of all three because it showed the ground above us wasn't actually ground, it was a large pond. We appeared to be at least four feet under the water by my guess. Not only were we already trapped underground, but now we were also trapped under a small body of water, and the rain didn't appear as though it had any intention of letting up anytime soon.

Sienna plunged her face into her brother's shoulder and sobbed. He almost looked as if he could do the same.

Ryan quickly flipped the switch. "OK, so who wants to see the place?" He hopped up on his feet with half a grin. He seemed proud of this shelter, or perhaps he was just good at hiding how terrified he was from the rest of us, for our sake.

* * *

He started the tour, "as you know, this is the living room... couch, chairs, DVD player, books and games." The room was about the size of your average living room, spacious enough considering. It was a long rectangle with a big, fluffy couch against the wall opposite the TV. There were two chairs also pointed towards the TV, and two wooden chairs, one on each side of the bookshelf which rested against the short wall. On each end of the couch was a cheap looking end-table holding matching lamps. The lighting wasn't great, but I wasn't going to complain.

"There is a generator that powers most everything, and most things have backup batteries," he said when he noticed me staring at the lamps. "We should conserve power when possible of course, but we'll be OK for a good while. Next room!"

He led us to the perfectly square kitchen which had a small dining table with four chairs. There were two stools pushed up to the counter so seating wouldn't be an issue. On the counter there was an impossibly small microwave, matching fridge and freezer and tons of cupboards. Ryan walked over to them and opened them displaying the assortment of goods they held. The shelves were fully stocked as I imagined the fridge and freezer probably were too. He opened a door at the back of the kitchen and we all took turns peeking in. It was another room, almost the size of the kitchen stocked top to bottom with anything you could possibly need, kitchen-wise or otherwise. It was a kitchen-sized general store.

There were small doors scattered about the entrance and living room. Ryan didn't open them but I assumed they were closets and storage areas, probably stocked with things one might need in an end of the world type situation.

Next there was a little hallway that ran between the living space and the kitchen space which I had to assume led to the bedrooms. "Door on the left here is the bathroom, sorry one toilet and one shower," he said grimacing, "and these are the bedrooms." He stretched his arms out as if he were presenting the top prize on a game show.

There were only two bedrooms. We walked into the first room which was fairly large and looked incredibly cozy. It had two full sized beds pushed against opposite walls made up with clean sheets, or so I assumed, and a large, plush comforter. One with a pink and white dot design was calling my name, even though I had no idea how I could even consider sleeping right now. My body was craving it, but my mind was still high on adrenaline. I needed rest, but with my thoughts going every which way I didn't know how I would be able to actually settle down enough for sleep.

There was a nightstand beside each bed and a closet on each side. In the middle was a stiff curtain divider you could pull out for a privacy wall.

The second room was even bigger than the last but it too only had two full sized beds. I wasn't the only one thinking about the math, Sienna was fidgeting next to me and I could tell she was nervous about the sleeping arrangements. Ryan walked over to the closet and pulled out a cot, "and with the couch in the living room, that's six," he said glancing at Sienna hoping she'd be satisfied.

"Ros and Sienna can have the other room, you guys can figure out who gets what in here and I'll take the couch." He glanced around looking at each one of us, and then crossed his arms, "well, that concludes the tour, so with that, I guess everyone should just go ahead and make yourselves at home. Please."

"Anyone know what time it is?" Seth wondered with a yawn.

"I don't know how anyone will be able to sleep!" Owen said seemingly surprised by Seth's yawn, "I still want to know what the hell is going on!"

I nodded in agreement but I knew we weren't going to know, at least not tonight.

Ryan pointed to a clock on the nightstand, "I think that's probably accurate even though the generator hadn't been on in some time, the clocks have backup batteries."

According to the clock it was 9 p.m. The running from the storm, getting in the shelter and the tour all took approximately six hours. It had all passed by in what felt like minutes. We'd missed dinner, but no one asked about it and I didn't even feel the slightest bit hungry. I just wanted this night to pass so we could hopefully find out tomorrow what the damage was and how we were going to get out of here. I wanted a little space from everything and everyone so I could mentally process what just happened and if it was a dream, make myself wake up.

"Oh, there are supplies in the bathroom, like toothbrushes and toothpaste, deodorant, towels, and all that stuff, if there is anything else you might need check the pantry in the kitchen. At the end of the hall is the laundry but we should limit using that as much as possible since all the running water is on the same line here. Full loads only, please."

"What about clothes?" Sienna asked picking at her fingernails. "You know, like a change of clothes or something to sleep in? I don't want to wear the same thing every day." She let just a little of her inner diva start to emerge.

"Right. Well, there should be some things in the closets, but it'd be my mom's or sister's things so I don't know if you'll find anything," Ryan said with a frown. "You are more than welcome to use anything you find though." I guess that was a problem with the stocking up of the shelter, they hadn't anticipated helping anyone other than the family, but why would they have even considered that? "My mom's things would be in this closet and my sister's in the other room."

"Let's see what we can find," I said putting my hand lightly on Sienna's shoulder as I guided her out of the room. She didn't protest or shrug me off, so we got a little space from the others. I wanted to be alone but since that wasn't likely to happen, I figured being with Sienna was almost as good as being alone. After all, we were about to be roommates, I might as well try to be her friend. We entered our new room, "Which bed do you want?" I asked not really caring all that much but secretly hoping a little for the bed with the pink comforter. Both beds looked inviting, my body desired to lie down even if my brain was a bee hive of thoughts, but it didn't matter, so why not let her choose? The other bed had a comforter striped with various shades of blue, the pink one must have been intended for Ryan's sister and the blue one was his. He was giving up his bed for us.

"I'll take the pink one," she said looking away from me.

That meant I'd be taking Ryan's bed. He was giving up his bed for me. That selfless act didn't make me feel so great. I didn't want to be the one to take his bed from him. I would have taken the couch but I knew Sienna wouldn't be comfortable sharing the room with Ryan.

"OK. Let's check out the closet."

I opened the door and I could feel Sienna's eyes peering around me attempting to get a glimpse of our future wardrobe. I pulled the string that clicked the overhead light bulb on in the small walk-in closet. It was filled with girl's clothes. The other closet by my bed likely was filled with Ryan's clothes which I'm sure he will want access to, but he hadn't said anything about it. His sister's clothes were close to my size, but they were a little big for Sienna, so unfortunately she had little choice. I found a nightgown which I handed to her because I figured the size difference would be less noticeable in gown form. For myself, I found a plain gray T-shirt and some yoga pants with pink zebra trim. They were not my style at all, but it was a change of clothes and for that I was thankful. We'd all have to make do when it came to certain things. Owen wasn't as small as Ryan, he was bigger and more muscular, athletic. And Seth was a little overweight, neither of them very likely to fit into Ryan's things, so they'd probably have to wear his dad's clothes and they likely wouldn't complain about it. We didn't know how long we'd be down here, it could be until someone came looking for us, or the water drained away. Our choices in most matters were pretty limited. Maybe tomorrow Sienna and I could go through Ryan's mom's things, perhaps she had items that would work, and it would give us something to do to pass the time.

I started to change hoping that it would help Sienna feel more comfortable with me, I didn't want to close the room divider afraid she'd take it the wrong way. Flipping the fluffy blankets over I crawled inside the soft bed not bothering to turn out the lights. I was so exhausted I felt like I was melting into the mattress.

"What do we do now?" she asked.

"I'm not sure," I said my face twisted, "Do you want to go get a book?"

"No, I think…" she paused for a yawn, "I think I'm actually tired."

"Yeah." I copied her by letting out a yawn against my will, "somehow, I am too." I glanced through half-closed eyes at the clock on the nightstand next to my bed. It was closing in on 10:00 p.m., only about two hours earlier than I usually go to bed, but today wasn't a normal day by any stretch of the imagination. Today was a lot different. That's the last thought I remembered having before I drifted off into a dreamland where things hadn't changed. The storms hadn't raged and destroyed everything in its path. We weren't trapped underground, or under water. I was at home and I was happy. Yes, today had been a lot different.

Chapter three.

I woke abruptly. I wasn't sure what had caused me to jolt up in bed. I was sitting upright and wide-eyed, almost frozen, and for a split second, absolute terror washed over me. My bones filled with a chill I didn't understand and my eyes didn't recognize my surroundings. I was about to scream for help when it came flooding back all at once, like a movie on fast forward. I gradually peeled myself off of the bed as if I had been glued to the mattress. I glanced at Sienna. She was out cold wrapped in her new pink bed with a little smile on her cute rounded face. She must have been dreaming of another day and some other place to look so serene. The light in our room was still on, we had both drifted to sleep so quickly neither of us had bothered to turn it off.

I tip-toed my way to the bathroom. It was so quiet in the shelter I was sure everyone must be sleeping and I didn't want to wake anyone up. We all needed our rest after yesterday, but of course I was wide awake. I must have had an awful nightmare, worse than the one I was living in to wake me up so suddenly, but I couldn't remember it. What could I have been dreaming about that was worse than what I had just gone through?

I couldn't help but notice how sterile everything felt down here, so much cement and metal and any surface that was painted was a dull green or a dreary gray color. There was nothing welcoming about the place, no wallpaper, or bright colors and anything that could have been built using real wood was made of cheap particle board instead. The bathroom door was open, so I slipped in, locking it behind me. I hadn't brushed my teeth or anything before falling asleep. I would have to worry about finding toiletry supplies tomorrow. I was way too tired, and I didn't feel like searching alone in the middle of the night.

As I stepped out of the bathroom, I heard the muffled fuzz of the radio coming from the living room. I walked around the corner to see Ryan with his back to me, slowly twisting the dial, searching for something, any sign of life, news or information of any kind. He had the TV displaying the outside cameras, but it was too dark to make much of anything out. Any lighting structures they may have set up were blown away, probably several states over by now. The camera that showed us under water was completely black so I knew we were still trapped. I sighed.

Ryan turned around sharply.

"Sorry, I heard the radio," I explained. I was hoping he wouldn't think I was snooping, although I guess I kind of was, but that hadn't been what I intended.

"Right," he said turning back to the radio,

"sorry, if it was too loud?" He turned quickly meeting my eyes.

"Oh, no… no, not that, it's fine, I just happened to wake up. Have you heard anything?" I asked walking closer with my arms crossed in front of myself, feeling self-conscious about my, err, his sister's clothing being on my body.

"Not really."

"Yeah, I'm not surprised I guess."

"Me either."

He turned back to his dial and started slowly turning it once again, and for a split second I was sure I heard something. "Wait! What was that? Go back a little… here let me," I said reaching over into his personal space forgetting all about boundaries as I spun the dial backwards until I heard it again. It was a voice, but I was having trouble making it out. I shook my head as if that would somehow help it come in clearer. I turned the dial a little left and a little right until I could get it in as clear as possible.

It was a woman speaking as if she was reading from something. It was difficult to make out what she was saying with so many words disappearing into the crackles of the radio fuzz. But it was definitely the voice of a woman.

"The bible? Is she reading the bible?" Ryan asked squinting at the radio.

I wasn't sure, I wasn't familiar with the bible, it sounded like it could be religious literature, but I didn't know for sure. I waited and tried to make out her words but to me it was just gibberish, it made little sense. She stopped reading and spoke.

"We are here sitting in the church basement waiting for help. Oh dear Jesus, please send us the help we so desperately need at 48 North Church Street here in the blessed city of Orlando. Dear Lord we haven't much, some are hurt, many have passed and are on their way to join you in your glorious heaven above. If anyone hears this please send help, in Jesus' name we beg for some kind of assistance." Her voice was old or simply worn out from all her readings, it cracked as if she had been crying excessively and was in need of water.

"Orlando?" Ryan whispered.

"That's hundreds and hundreds of miles away, is that even possible?" I asked.

With that the woman started reading scripture again. I pictured her sitting there with others gathered around her holding hands, sobbing and praying for their lives and the lives of their loved ones to be saved. It made my stomach flop as my thoughts drifted to my mom, but I pushed the thoughts back down, deep into the part of my brain where they needed to stay hidden. Until I was ready to confront them. I couldn't go there, not now, not in front of Ryan. Not like this, even though he could relate, just like everyone trapped down here could, it wasn't right.

I wondered how many people were trapped with the bible woman and what their situation was like. Was it as bad in Florida as it was here? Was it this bad everywhere? They likely weren't in an underground shelter filled with food, comfy beds, and a warm shower. Maybe not even a toilet. The good news was that other people had survived, at

least for now. Hopefully it was just a matter of
time before help arrived for them, and for us too.
Just as quickly as the voice had come in, the voice
vanished back into the fuzz of the radio.

"There must be some radio towers that
remained standing through all of this," Ryan said
hopefully, "maybe we'll get more answers or help
soon."

"If only someone knew we were down here
under that stupid giant pond above us," I said
sweeping my eyes up towards the ceiling. I hoped I
hadn't sounded ungrateful.

"Well, if my family made it, they might
think to check down here for me," Ryan said,
sounding as if he was trying to convince himself.

"Sure, yeah, maybe," I said not sounding as
comforting or confident as I should have.

* * *

I guessed roughly a week had passed since
being down in the shelter. Every day we waited for
help, but the water above us hadn't evaporated.
Each morning we'd argue as to whether it looked
like it was less or more than the day before. It
didn't matter, all I cared about was that it was still
there, because while it was there we were stuck
down here. And I was more than ready to get out
and breathe some fresh air, walk around or just to
be out of this little space. Each day the shelter felt
as though it was shrinking. The more I thought

about it, the worse I'd feel, so I made an effort not to think about it. When the claustrophobic thoughts crept in, I'd shove them deep down into myself. Into that dreary place you stick all the yucky things that would immobilize you if you thought about them too much. They were next door neighbors to the thoughts of my mom that I kept tucked away, and I had to be careful that when I was putting other anxious thoughts away I wouldn't let those sneak out.

When I was bored I exercised. I'd do crunches, squats and other things that would get me moving but wouldn't get me too sweaty. I wanted my heart to pump and it helped make me feel stronger instead of powerless, but I had to be careful so I wouldn't need a shower and waste the water we did have. I didn't know when we'd run out of water. We had loads of bottled drinking water, but as for the toilet, shower and sink water, I didn't know. We stopped using plates if we didn't have to so there was less dish washing. The trash was building up, but we'd be OK awhile yet. Thankfully the smell hadn't yet permeated the living spaces.

The tornadoes were less frequent, yesterday we hadn't seen any while the cameras were on. I hoped that was a sign these storms were losing steam.

Today when we turned on the cameras to check the water levels, none of us could believe what we were seeing. The rain had stopped. There were no flashes of lightning. No tornadoes and no hail pelting the ground and splashing into the pool above. The storm appeared to be over, but what was happening was both terrifying and depressing. What was visible of the water above was frozen solid and the amount of white fluff falling from the sky was unreal. Visibility was practically zero, just enough for us to realize it was an epic blizzard like nothing we've ever seen.

Ice sealed us in as if we hadn't been already sufficiently trapped. Now there was absolutely no way out, even though my thoughts of swimming out to the ponds surface were probably illogical anyway. Sienna dropped her face into her hands sobbing while the rest of us stared at the TV screen in disbelief.

"Maybe this is a good thing," Ryan offered.

"How can this be good?" Owen said pounding his fist against his leg so hard I had no doubt he'd bruise.

"Maybe it's a sign that it's all coming to an end."

"Or maybe it's only just the beginning, storm after storm after storm," Dean said putting his hand on his sister's back.

"We're trapped down here... forever!" Sienna bellowed.

"Well not forever," Owen muttered under his breath. I guessed he was hinting at the fact that eventually we'd run out of food and water. It wasn't worth arguing about, but even dead our bodies would still be trapped. I kept my mouth closed and my morbid thoughts to myself.

"We'll get out. We just have to let these storms pass," I said trying to sound reassuring, but

of course I didn't have any idea what was really
going on. Hell, the temperature dropped to freezing
overnight— I was just as clueless as the others
when it came to understanding the storm. For all I
knew these storms could go on forever. Maybe
once the ice melted we could try to open the doors
and let the water flood the shelter so we could
escape. Or maybe we could chip a tunnel through
the ice, although if the whole pond wasn't frozen
and too much water got inside we'd risk drowning.
I shook those ideas out of my head. There had to
be something we could try. We'd have to talk about
it when the time came. It was probably best to
wait, since we were safe and had plenty of food,
water and other supplies.

The day passed with everyone pretty much
keeping to themselves. Everyone was depressed
and turning inward, the negative vibe made me
even more anxious than I already was.

Ryan continued to fiddle with the radio most
nights, but I think I was the only one that knew
about that habit and I never mentioned it to anyone
else. Once in a while I'd sit up with him listening
to the fuzz but I'd fall asleep pretty quickly on the
couch with the constant white noise. Sometimes,
very rarely, we'd catch the bible lady reading and
pleading for help. She'd report that the people with
her were dying, she'd mention when they lost
someone, their name. She'd say something nice
about them and ask for Jesus to take them up to
heaven and far away from their pain and suffering.
Their group was small now, she never said how
many were left and sometimes I wondered if it was

just her.

On occasion we'd all get together and watch a movie, those nights were almost fun. There would be smiles and laughs, and I think for just a little while we'd forget. The nights were never planned, someone would just randomly start up a DVD, and then everyone would siphon into the living room to settle in to watch the movie. Comedies were always the best. Even Ryan would smile once in a while. Otherwise the only other time he smiled was when he was trying to make everyone feel comfortable, but I think everyone had picked up on that and it wasn't working as well as it had at first. Sienna was getting more depressed, very depressed, with each passing day. She'd sleep a lot, going as far as to take some of the sleeping pills and pain medicines when she wanted to force her body to sleep when it wasn't tired. It bothered Dean, he was worried, and he had no idea how to deal with it. He tried to spend time with her when she was awake even if it just meant sitting with her until the next round of sleep found her. At first, him being in our room was awkward, I had a hard time falling asleep, worried I'd be breathing heavy or worse, snoring. Some of the time I'd wait in the living room until he left, but now I liked having him there, it helped me fall asleep too. Most nights it was him that turned out our lights as he slipped out of the room. I had fallen asleep one night while reading a book, but when I woke up it was on my nightstand and my blanket had been pulled up to my shoulders. It was kind of sweet but of course we never talked about it.

Owen was easily agitated, often he was on edge but I didn't blame him. You had to be really careful what you'd say around him, the slightest thing could flip his switch. He never talked about himself or his family, so I didn't know exactly what his trigger was, I assumed it must have just been the whole situation which was understandable.

Overall, Dean and Seth handled it the best. They were the caretakers, they'd cook, do dishes and even the laundry. They'd clean up after everyone and make sure things ran smoothly. I think Dean mostly did it for Sienna's sake, while Seth just did it to keep himself busy. The three of them, Seth, Dean and Owen, had been friends before all this happened, so I think that helped them. Sienna had her brother. That had to be nice, but you couldn't tell by how she acted. They weren't alone the same way I was alone. I didn't really know anyone other than seeing their faces around school.

* * *

I started losing track of time. I estimated it was approximately two weeks after having heard the bible lady on the radio that we heard someone new.

That night, when everyone was sleeping, Ryan was twisting his radio dials as usual, while I relaxed on the couch dozing off here and there. My back was to Ryan, and I was letting myself get lost in the white noise instead of watching him. The noise was something I almost needed to fall asleep, so I didn't hear the thoughts in my head. I was just about to drift off again when he stopped at the voice.

"Anyone out there?" the male voice said, "breaker, breaker."

"Maybe they are on a CB?" Ryan said, his words soft and fast, waiting anxiously to hear if there would be more.

"Anyone out there?" The voice repeated, this time with a touch of apprehension, "Well the snow is melting here... the roads are clearing. I made it out to town today. Didn't see a soul. Am I alone out here?"

Then the voice stopped. The fuzz was different, we knew the person was still there, they just weren't saying anything. If only we had a way to respond, we could let him know he wasn't alone.

Ryan hopped up and turned on the cameras but it was still too dark to really make anything out. Yesterday, the snow had still been coming down as fast and strong as ever, but wherever this person was, it was letting up. Perhaps it was changing. Where was he?

"Anyone alive out there?" the voice said sounding sad, disappointed and lonely.

"Say where you are, say where you are, say where you are...," Ryan chanted barely audible. But all we heard was the quiet awkward fuzz of someone hanging onto a line, and no one talking back. Then there was a click, and the fuzz returned to its normal no one's there crackle.

"That's good news… right?" I asked trying not to sound excited.

"God I hope so," Ryan said putting his head down against the table. Tonight he'd sleep, even Ryan could only go so long resisting before falling prey to the sandman. I guided him over to the couch, pulled a blanket over him and he was out before I even stepped away. This could quite possibly be the first time since we've been down here that he's slept. Before I walked away I looked at him, maybe the first time I've really looked at him. He was actually very attractive. All it took for me to really notice was him laying here with a relaxed, peaceful expression instead of his usual stressed out, intense, trying to make sure everyone was happy expression. His brown hair was messy, half flopped in his face, I almost wanted to reach out and swipe it away from his eyes, the eyes that when open, were an impossible shade of blue.

"Everything OK?" I jumped about forty feet into the air when Owen appeared standing in the opening that led to the kitchen. He was just staring at me and I had no idea how long he'd been there before saying anything. He yawned and blinked a few times.

"Yeah, yeah it's great. I was just ah… helping Ryan to the couch… Good night."

"Right…." He nudged me with his fist as I sped passed him and into bathroom. I ignored his tone and what he was hinting at. I didn't have a thing for Ryan if that was what he was insinuating. It was that I just happened to see him for the first time and couldn't help but be curious. We'd been

41

stuck in here for weeks together, but I didn't really know anyone, I hadn't really seen anyone or let them see me either. Maybe now, now that there was some hope in sight that we might actually get out of here, maybe I should get to really know them. This wasn't the end. Once we all got out of here we would still be together after what those storms likely did to our neighborhood... the city... the state... maybe the world? We were all going to need each other.

Chapter four.

I tossed and turned all night long with dreams of getting out, alternating with dream of never getting out and all the imagined horrors of both. Some good dreams were sprinkled in, I'd just go home and everything would be back to normal, like nothing ever happened at all. Others were nightmares where the world was something dreadful, one had no sunlight, it was always night time, and another the tornadoes started swirling coupled with never ending earthquakes. In yet another we spent the whole dream trying to get out of the shelter, unable to escape and eventually we ran out of air. After that one, I woke up nearly paralyzed and drenched in sweat while I gasped for air.

Knowing it was morning only because of the time displayed on the clock, I rushed out without dressing or brushing my teeth to check the TV. I was the first one up and I needed to know what was happening outside. My eyes frantically searched the room for the TV remote as if I were in some kind of timed competition. When I finally saw it, it was propped up on Ryan's chest. His left hand clutched it while he lay peacefully asleep on the couch with his feet sticking out the bottom of the blanket. He must have woke in the night and checked the cameras, or maybe he was anxious for morning so he could be the first to check them. If he had checked during the night and went back to sleep that either meant he hadn't seen anything or it was not good news. I crept towards him like the Grinch, ready to pry the remote from his clenched sleeping fist.

I wiggled it back and forth gently avoiding any sudden movement. It was sort of a three step process which seemed to be working, wiggle-wiggle-pause, wiggle-wiggle-pause. Right when it was about to pop free, he turned over onto his side taking the remote with him. Crap. I peeked over trying to find a way to get to it, but I'd probably be crossing some sort of line. I gasped audibly when he muttered, "It's still snowing Ros, go back to bed." I stumbled backwards, the heat that filled my cheeks felt like it was burning me.

I shook it off. No more Ms. Nice Girl. I reached down between him and the couch, ignoring any invisible line that may or may not exist and pulled the remote out, spun on my heel and clicked the TV on. It turned out I didn't actually know how to get the TV to display what the cameras showed. When the obvious power button didn't automatically display what I wanted to see, I started pressing random buttons. The TV came on blasting the fuzzy crackle of static, I located the volume control at record speed before waking everyone up. The next button took me to the DVD player, then the next I was back to the fuzz, everything but the actual camera display.

"Ugh, give it here," Ryan groaned.

"No! I want to see for myself, just tell me how!" I sounded way whinier than I had planned. I might as well have just stomped my feet while I was at it.

"I'll put them on for you."

"Promise?" I asked keeping in my childish character.

"Of course, why would I lie about that?" He sighed making his annoyance with me known.

It was a good point though why would he lie about that? I handed the remote back to him. Without turning around, he pointed the remote over his shoulder and turned the cameras on for me. He tucked it back against his body instead of giving it back. I wanted to sigh, but really what good was it to me when I had no idea how to use it anyway.

I couldn't stop the air from escaping my mouth. My body locked up before I fell to my knees and crawled towards the TV like a crab running from a pot of boiling water.

Ryan grunted, "What?"

For a moment I couldn't get any words to form, they were getting stuck in my throat, they were hot and burning but I couldn't make them come out. I felt a ridiculous grin spread across my face and there was no stopping my hands as they clapped against my cheeks. A squeak of a laugh leaked out like steam. I heard Ryan moving on the couch behind me. He was next to me so fast it seemed impossible, like he had used some form of

45

teleportation. He reached out and touched the screen. Was this for real? It was still snowing, but it was clear to both of us that it was slowing down, it was only a bit heavier than what weathermen would refer to as flurries. The sunlight filtered through the fluffy pieces of snow and made the untouched snow on the ground glitter. It looked magical.

"I hate to say it, but that's beautiful," he said shaking his head.

"The sparkling snow or the fact that we may actually get out of here?"

"Both!" he said with a bright smile plastered on his face. He pulled me in for a hug. He squeezed me but let go abruptly as if I had been soaking wet, "Sorry," he said, as I was about to let him know it was OK he blurted, "Let's get the others! I can't wait to see their faces!"

He bounced up, but I grabbed his hand to stop him, "Wait! What if this is just temporary? What if it starts back up? Do we want to get their hopes up? What is the right thing to do here?" I dropped his hand when I realized I was still holding it. He hadn't seemed to notice or care about my awkwardness, or perhaps he was too polite to let it show, but more likely he was pondering my questions.

"Jesus Ros! I have no idea." Ryan appeared to be in thought then asked, "Are you glad you saw it? I know I am. I would want to know if I was in their position, wouldn't you?"

My hands ran roughly through my uncombed hair tugging at the snarls, I must look like I stepped out of a Tim Burton movie. There was no doubt I was probably in desperate need of a shower too. It was no wonder why he let go of me. I shook my head, "I would. You're right, I just... just don't want to disappoint them, Sienna is already in bad enough shape, can you imagine getting her hopes up and then finding out we really can't get out?" I crossed my arms over my chest suddenly extremely self-conscious about being in my pajamas.

Before we could decide, the sound of a plate crashing into a thousand little pieces against the kitchen floor brought us back. Startled, I jumped reflexively towards Ryan, grabbing his arm.

"It... it's over?" Dean choked out the words. He stood there with his hand positioned as if he were still holding the plate, and the other pointing at the TV screen. He looked as though he had seen a ghost instead of potential freedom. "Is it fucking over?" he demanded loudly his voice cracking in as many pieces as the plate had.

"Dean," Ryan said calmly walking over to him. He lowered his arm, "We don't know. It appears as though the snow is letting up, but again, we don't know. Maybe another storm is coming, we just can't know. We have to remain calm and have patience." Ryan grabbed the broom and started sweeping up the pieces surrounding Dean's bare feet.

"Are we going to get out of here?" Dean asked again as if he hadn't heard a word Ryan just said.

"We aren't sure," I responded slowly using

47

as few words as possible, trying to keep is extra simple so his brain had time to process the words.

"What are we waiting for? We have to tell the others… Sienna! She has to know! She's got to see this," Dean said stepping into the broken glass, "Christ!" The mini shards stopped him from rushing off and gave him a moment to think, "Did you guys try the radio? Or search the TV for any sort of broadcast? Maybe they will start coming in now with the weather clearing up."

"Sure, we can try," Ryan offered, dropping the pieces of the plate into the trash. He got his radio out and started searching. Nothing. Not even the bible lady. Next he checked the TV but nothing came in except for the cameras. "The towers are probably still down from the storms, it'll take time for repairs," Ryan guessed.

"Unfortunately, we are still stuck under that layer of ice," Dean said stating the obvious.

"Yeah… but if this is ending, the ice will melt… right? And the water will just go away?" Ryan said scratching his head, "eventually," he added.

"How long do you think that would take?" I asked them like they were experts. As if this wasn't the first time they'd been trapped under inches, possibly feet of ice.

"No clue. Days… weeks?" Ryan said rubbing his hands together as if washing them with air, "It'll depend on the temperature I suppose. The warmer it gets the quicker the process, if it stays cold, it'll take longer, much longer I imagine. I don't know… it's a lot of water up there."

"Maybe we should open the door to see what's on the other side?" Dean suggested.

"I don't think that would be a good idea. We have heat down here, it would melt any ice around the shelter, in fact, it's probably water between us and the layer of ice. Opening the door could flood the place," Ryan said shaking his head vigorously, vetoing the suggestion.

"We have to wait." I didn't like it any more than they did, but it was really our only option. At least maybe now we had an end in sight. We had some hope. Maybe it would be all we needed to boost spirits for a while.

* * *

At breakfast we decided to tell the others, mostly because Dean had told us he was going to tell Sienna whether we liked it or not. When Ryan shared the news, Sienna cried. Owen and Seth looked like they wanted to join her. They asked questions we didn't really have the answers to, but Ryan tried his best and shared our speculations. Sienna wanted to know how soon before we could leave. Ryan explained it could be days, weeks or even months depending on the outside temperature which we didn't know. She told Dean she couldn't wait to go home. Dean's face crumpled knowing their home, as they once knew it, was likely gone. Blown away with the rest of our homes. I could see the effort he was putting into keeping his mouth closed, and instead he forced a small smile for her sake. After all, this was the first time in a few days she looked awake, animated… alive. She had gone days without talking, and this little droplet of hope had gotten her to talk. He couldn't take that away, not yet. He wasn't going to be the one to shoot a devastating word bullet into her paper-thin heart. What was out there would be a discussion for another time. We'd all have to cross that bridge eventually as none of us knew what was or wasn't out there.

The rest of the day everyone was exceptionally cheerful and optimistic. Sienna showered. Seth and Dean prepared a big dinner of spaghetti with tomato sauce and garlic breadsticks made from scratch. It was a feast! They prepared twice as much food as usual and we stuffed ourselves until spaghetti was coming out of our ears. We sat around the table for a long time after the meal was over fantasizing about all the things we missed and wanted to do again once we got out. We didn't talk about what we'd find after we got out, just how amazing it was going to be to actually get out and breathe fresh air. No one allowed any of the bad discussions to surface at this dinner.

"I don't remember what fresh air feels like anymore. I honestly cannot imagine a cool breeze against my skin," Owen said with a sparkle in his eye.

"I can't wait to feel the warm sun on my skin," Sienna said closing her eyes with a child-like grin, everyone nodded in agreement.

"I want to run. Just run and run and run!"

Dean said which reminded me that he had been on the school track team. He was always moving. All this sitting still must have been harder for him than he had let on.

"Ros, what do you want to do?" Sienna asked leaning forward to hear my response. The others looked at me, I felt all their eyes on me at once and it made my skin warm, and surely my cheeks pink.

"I don't know… anything. Everything and nothing all at the same time," I said nervously with all their eyes on me.

Ryan quietly snorted. He was mostly staying out of the conversation, and I hoped it stayed that way. He was pessimistic and always so skeptical. And he worried a lot about everything. He'd bring everyone down if he spoke, which is why I was happy he was keeping quiet for the most part. I wanted to roll my eyes at him but instead I found ignoring him was just as easy.

"God, with all those tornadoes I wonder what's left out there," Owen wondered out loud, forgetting about the unspoken agreement to not talk about the negative around Sienna. The pinched look on his face showed that he had regretted letting the words out, but it was too late they were out there dancing on the table, taunting us and waving their arms at Sienna.

"I guess we'll see when we get out of here," I said carefully attempting to steer the conversation back to the positives by reminding everyone that we might actually get out of here. That was what was important for now. The aftermath? That would be something to worry about another day.

"I'm going to watch a movie," Seth announced launching himself off of the barstool, "Who's in?"

Everyone picked up their plates and threw away their trash before heading to the living room. I lingered in the kitchen listening to them decide on a movie. I decided to stay and wash the plates and cooking pots since Dean and Seth had prepared the meal, least I could do was clean for them. There was no part of me that felt like I could sit through a movie, I needed to move. Like Dean, I wanted to run and run and run, my mind and body needed the movement.

"Aww Christ!" Owen shouted from the other room. I draped the washcloth over the faucet and started drying my hands as I went to the living room. I flipped the dishtowel over my shoulder, noticing they had put on the cameras. The snow had picked up again. It hadn't been as heavy as it was before, but seeing it thicker than it had been this morning was clearly heartbreaking.

I jumped when Ryan threw the book he was holding against the wall. It made a sharp snap against the wall and a soft thud when it hit the floor. He flicked the remote at Seth and stomped out of the room.

"It's OK, it doesn't mean anything," Dean said trying to diffuse the situation and keep everyone's hopes up even though his expression told a different story. He was doing it for Sienna's sanity which was probably already hanging by only a few threads. "Tomorrow will be better again, I

just know it. Don't you think so?" he said looking
around waiting for backup. His eyes locked with
mine, and he knew that out of the others here I had
the best connection with her. He hooked me with
his eyes and tried to reel me in, "Right Ros? Don't
you agree? Better tomorrow... right? You watch
the cameras all the time, you must think it's
different, changing, getting better?"

I looked at Sienna, we hadn't lost her yet,
she was still present, still taking it all in but I didn't
know for how long, "Yeah! Of course," I said with
a toothy, hopefully believable, smile.

"Yeah, it'll be fine, you'll see." Dean gave
a big-eyed look at Seth and then at the remote
trying to telepathically convey a message to him,
"Let's get back to that movie!" Dean reminded me
of a dad type sometimes. He was always there for
Sienna, caring and comforting her and keeping us
all in line around her. He didn't want us to argue
around her, he wanted everything to be smooth and
even though it was all for her, we needed it too.

I slipped back into the kitchen when they
turned the camera off. After I put the last pot away
I went back to my room to find Ryan sitting on my,
well I guess technically his, bed. He had his back
towards the door.

"Oh sorry I was just, I mean... I didn't feel
like watching the movie, I'll go," I said feeling
awkward even though this had been my room for
the last several weeks. It really should have been
his room from the start, I had taken it from him, and
he deserved to have as much time as he needed. If
it weren't for Sienna I'd have taken the couch

without hesitation.

"No, no stay."

"Really it's OK, I don't mind at all. I'll just go umm… check the pantry."

He let a small chuckle escape, "Check the pantry for what?"

"I really don't know. I can't even make something up quick enough that would even remotely sound good," I said with a smile. "I just was trying to give you space."

Ryan turned to me, his face ragged and his hair wild. Had he been crying? I couldn't be sure, but I could tell he was out of sorts, more so than usual. There was no other way to explain it. At this point I had spent enough time with him, and the others for that matter, to be able to read them to some extent. "I do want space, but not this space. I want the space up there. I'm getting claustrophobic. I feel like I can't breathe most of the time. Ros, I need to breathe!" His eyes were sad and his voice panicked. I wanted to run to him and hug him but I didn't think he'd like that at all. If a person is feeling claustrophobic, being wrapped up tightly in someone's arms was probably not the best solution.

"I'm sorry. I know how you feel. I was just coming in here to do jumping jacks or run in place or some crunches or something." And it was true, I still wanted to be moving even after having seen the snow starting up again. "Sometimes I just do exercises to feel like I'm moving somewhere." I started to do jumping jacks even though I was completely aware of what an absolute nut-job I looked like, "join me!"

He looked at me sideways. His lip curled in amusement and then the parts of his face returned to their normal position, "You sure are… unique."

"I will… take that… as a… compliment. Seriously… jump!" I said between breaths as I hopped and clapped my hands above my head. I smiled at him with big crazy eyes. When he didn't move I grabbed his hands and pulled him to his feet, "I bet I can do more than you can. I've been practicing, though I must warn you, I knew this day would come!"

"Yeah?" Now he had on a real smile and it was gorgeous. He was a different person with that killer smile. I had to swallow my heart back down when it threatened to do jumping jacks out of my throat. I shook away the sudden desire I had to touch him. His perfect arms or maybe his solid chest, or better yet run my fingers through his disheveled hair. He started doing jumping jacks, but he noticed that I had disappeared, "Uh hello? Ready? Let's do this!"

"Right!" I said popping out of my daydream. What had just happened? That wasn't like me to drift off into those types of thoughts, especially right in front of the person I was having them about. Damn that smile of his, I made a mental note to keep myself in check. Not cool Ros, I told myself, not cool.

We matched each other jump for jump up to 120 when a giggle fit erupted. No idea what even started it, I think it was the serious looks on our faces, but I smiled and he smiled back and before I knew it we were laughing. I dropped to the floor, sweaty and out of breath. He flopped down next to me stretching out on his back, his chest rising and falling quickly with each breath. "Oddly I feel a little better," he admitted.

"I'm glad," I said between heavy breaths, "and now I feel tired!"

He smiled again, and I looked away before getting lured in by that smile again. Ryan was such a serious person nearly all of the time, so much so that getting to see this smile was doing a real number on me. I liked when he smiled. I liked him happy.

He rolled on his side and propped himself up on his arm looking at me, studying me. I suddenly was very aware of how sweaty I was and my heavy breathing which I tried to get under control. I wasn't out of shape, I just couldn't seem to catch my breath, I wasn't sure if it was the giggling, the exercise, or him.

"Thanks Ros," he said before taking a deep breath and exhaling slowly. I smiled at him but moved my eyes to the ceiling and away from that gorgeous smile on his face. "No, really I mean it," he said, his face slowly changing back into serious Ryan.

"No problem," I said wanting happy Ryan to stay longer and for serious Ryan to get smooshed down deep inside him for a little longer. It's not that I dislike serious Ryan, I just really like happy Ryan.

He pushed himself up and reached his hand down to help me up to my feet. I took it and he

pulled me up swiftly. I was standing only inches
away from him and extremely aware of it, if he
noticed the closeness, he made no indication of it.
"See you tonight?" he said with a smirk.

"Huh?"

"You know, the usual… cameras…
radios…."

"Oh, right. Yeah I think so, unless I'm too
tired from all the jumping jacks," I said with a
strange bounce that allowed me to get back into my
comfort zone. Too close and my brain started to
malfunction. I don't know what was going on here,
but I couldn't let what I thought was happening,
well, happen. There were too many other things
going on and so many more important things to
worry about. No other drama was needed beyond
what we already had. And besides, I was probably
way off base, just because I was feeling these weird
feelings didn't mean he was too.

"Thanks again," he said nudging my arm
with his fist, and then disappeared from the room. I
jumped up and down three times trying to shake the
unusual feeling off my skin. It didn't work. I
would simply have to stop thinking about happy
Ryan. It shouldn't be that hard, after all, happy
Ryan has thus far only existed maybe a handful of
times. For all I knew he had a girlfriend anyway!
Any girl who saw that smile would have melted
right into his arms. He could probably have any
girl he wanted, he was absolutely gorgeous when he
was happy. And even if he wasn't with someone,
he sure wouldn't be interested in the smelly, sweaty,
awkward girl with snarled hair he'd been trapped

with in this small, crowded, underground space for the last several weeks. Without a doubt, the thought of me and him never crossed his mind.

I couldn't stop thinking about him no matter how hard I tried to push the thoughts of him out of my head, they just kept creeping back in, stronger and stronger. I had to stop the thoughts. There was no point. It must have been from being trapped down here, a lack of fresh oxygen that was making me go crazy. I grabbed a change of clothes and went and took a quick shower. We were all taking faster showers, in fact, we rarely took them daily since we were worried we were going to run out of water and we wanted to conserve as much as possible. I suspected Ryan knew how to check water levels, but if any of us asked about it he would tell us not to worry about it, that it was fine and we had plenty. It was basically the same when it came to electricity and the generator. To him, it was his problem and not ours, at least that's how he seemed to feel about it, unwilling to burden us with such things.

I sat on the bed and brushed my damp, towel-dried hair. The gray yoga pants from his sister's closet, and the over-sized T-shirt I had found in Ryan's dad's closet was probably not the most flattering option. But I liked it because the big, soft, comfy shirt reminded me of being snuggled up in my bed at home. Since most of the time I had to squeeze myself into his sister's pants, the bulkiness and length of the shirt helped to disguise how tightly they fit.

Sienna slipped into the room with a silly

grin. "Hey, what was so funny in here?" she asked with big, curious eyes.

I was glad to see her spirits were still up, "Oh, ah, nothing," I said, the corners of my mouth turning up against my will.

"Spill it!" Sienna said flopping on her bed like a nosy tween.

"There is NOTHING to spill," I said standing up doing my best to be nonchalant. I set the hairbrush we shared down on my nightstand. I picked out a few loose strands of my hair that had been left behind in the bristles and dropped them into the trash can, attempting to look busy.

"We heard Ryan laughing," she said looking at me sideways.

"Yeah?"

"What happened?"

"Nothing happened! Maybe I'm just funny?"

"Suuure Ros, you're a barrel of laughs, that's what we are always saying, just how funny you are. Well, that and how much I enjoy being the Queen of England."

I rolled my eyes at her and left the room. Each step I made was careful and calculated, paying close attention to my body language, so as not to give off any clues about what was really going through my head. I didn't know where I was going but I wanted to put distance between myself and Miss Twenty Questions.

No one was in the kitchen and no one was in the living room. That means the boys had gathered in their room, with Ryan. Odd. This was new. I wondered what they were talking about and I even considered eavesdropping, if only for a second, but I talked myself out of it. I grabbed a book, laid down on the couch and pretended I wasn't waiting for Ryan. I'd ask him about the secret boys only meeting, hopefully he'd tell me, but he never came even though he mentioned seeing me tonight for our usual nightly get-together. When I woke up in the morning with a sore neck from sleeping on the couch, my book was on the end-table and I had a blanket draped over me. Instead of going to my bed, I rolled over and feel into a deep sleep.

Chapter five.

The next morning it was snowing again. It wasn't nearly as heavy as it had been, but it wasn't as light as it had been yesterday either. The mood changed significantly and everyone picked up where they had left off being depressed and ready to give up. I could feel the claustrophobia burrowing deeper into my body. There was also a certain horrible sense of loneliness that was slithering around waiting to constrict the life out of any hope that remained.

The generator had started chugging randomly for a few minutes here and there but Ryan insisted it was fine and that there was lots of juice left. I didn't know if he was telling the truth or if maybe he was making a guess or saying what he thought we wanted to hear. The lights would dim in the whole shelter, but then they'd burst back on like nothing happened. A similar thing used to happen in my house when my mom would do the laundry, like the washer would suck up all the power but then decide to share it again with the other plugged in appliances.

We still had a fair amount of food left, but it

was noticeably diminishing. That was just another thing Ryan didn't want us to worry about. We had plain rice and noodles to last years, but the water wasn't in endless supply.

The days went by slowly, each day slower than the last. It was a solid week that had passed since the episode of hope, but this morning I decided to turn on the cameras anyway. I had asked Ryan to show me how when he had given up several days ago. He no longer saw the point in checking daily, he, like everyone else, was slowly sinking inside themselves, ready to implode. So I started checking them when everyone was still sleeping either at night or in the morning. But it was that day, that morning, the snow stopped. There was nothing in the clear, cloudless sky. Not even a single flake lazily drifting by. The sun was starting to rise in the distance and I could see that the snow still covered the ground. We were still under ice, but what I saw looked promising. I kept it to myself, quickly shut off the TV and with a hop, I went to get dressed for the day.

I passed Owen in the hallway after my shower and he mumbled, "What are you getting dressed up for?" Maybe I should have showed them that day, I thought about it, but I didn't. I waited three more days, painfully keeping it to myself. It was three consecutive days of no snow, nothing at all — in fact I actually saw snow melting — before I decided to show them what was happening.

Owen, Seth and Dean allowed themselves a bit of hope again, especially after I explained that

I've been watching and for how long I'd been keeping my eye on it. Sienna had fallen pretty far into her depression again, worse than before and showed no emotion whatsoever, no matter how much Dean tried. Ryan, no surprise there, was skeptical. He told us it would probably change back, only giving a small glance to Sienna, maybe wishing he could take the words back. He advised everyone not to get excited until we saw a puddle of water on top of us. And even then he wasn't sure.

　　I was up bright and early the next morning to check again, and this time what I saw was almost frightening. It was impossible. Almost all the snow had melted, a deep pond sat above us. How could all of the snow melt that fast? And it continued to melt throughout the night? What was the temperature out there? I didn't know what I was going to tell the others, so I decided I'd show them.

　　　　　　　　　* * *

　　Later that day, everyone had been busy in other rooms which gave me an opportunity to quick check the cameras again. I flicked them on. The sun was shining and parts of the ground showed signs of drying. There wasn't any grass on the ground and what remained of trees was just rough, worn down stumps. The only vegetation that remained was brown, dried up shrubs. The pond above us was a buffet of mud, dirt, crusty dried dirt, scattered dead plants and sticks all illuminated by a beautiful, bright glowing sun.

I wished I had a way to check the temperature. My fingers clicked the remote surfing through the channels looking to see if any of the TV stations were back up and broadcasting. As I suspected, there was nothing. I'm sure most, if not all forms of communication were gone, or at least temporarily under construction. I pulled out the radio and zipped through the stations, but everything was fuzz as usual. As I was putting the radio away, Owen and Seth stomped like zombies into the living room. I had left the TV on but wasn't sure if they had even glanced at it.

"Just checking the cameras," I said. I quickly flicked it off figuring I'd wait for everyone so I wouldn't have to show it multiple times. "Where is everyone else?"

"Ryan's in the sho—"

"Thank God," Seth muttered cutting Owen off.

I smiled.

"Dean and Sienna are talking or should I say Dean's trying to reanimate her, bring her back to the land of the living. They should have stocked this place with antidepressants," Owen said crossing his arms in front of his chest.

"No one probably anticipated anyone being down here this long," Seth suggested.

"Um… OK… I can't wait. I'm too excited. You guys really have to see this," I said, pushing them towards the TV too anxious to wait for the others. I flicked it back on enthusiastically pointing at the screen. Things looked to be even drier than they had when I first checked only a short time ago. It was like all the water was just being sucked out of the earth with a giant wet-vac.

"Holy shit," Owen said clapping his hand against his mouth. He folded himself in half leaning forward staring in disbelief.

Seth turned on me, "You've known about this? How long? Why haven't you told us?" He clearly wasn't too happy with me.

"Only a few days... I just wanted to make sure it was for real this time," I explained and it was the truth. "After it had stopped the second time, no one really seemed interested... so I just kept watch and then this happened. This is good though."

"A few days? That's not possible!" Seth shook his head, he was probably trying to think back to the last time they had checked the cameras, and the ground was still covered in snow. It really hadn't been that long. And it really was that unbelievable.

"I know it seems totally insane, right? That's why I didn't say anything. I'm still not sure I even believe it. At the rate things are drying up, we can try to get out of here in what? A day or two?" My face was contorted with confusion in my eyes and my mouth with a big silly grin. Even though I didn't understand what was happening out there, I was excited by the possibility of leaving our underground home.

"Let's tell the others, they'll piss

themselves!" Owen roared slapping his knee. "Go get them Seth," he ordered and Seth obeyed.

Moments later he came back. Dean was practically carrying Sienna, and Ryan was shirtless. I pretended not to notice, but I noticed. His hair dispersed droplets of water on his shoulders as if Seth had pulled him right out of the shower. His sweatpants hung low on his hips as if he'd barely had a chance to pull them on.

"What is it?" he groaned glancing at me standing there holding the remote and still donning my oddball expression.

"I know, so annoying," Sienna chimed in like she was having such a good time in her deep depressed state.

"As if you guys have better things to do?" Owen said pointing his thick finger at them.

"Just get on with it," Ryan insisted, "I'm cold and wet and tired."

With that Owen moved his big body away from the TV screen revealing the mud, crusty dirt and most importantly the bright white glow of sunlight lighting up the desert-like earth.

"Are you kidding me with this?" Sienna asked with an oh-so-tiny glimmer of hope seeping back into her voice. She was obviously tired of riding her emotional roller-coaster with all its ups and downs, and twists and loops.

"Nope," I said with that stupid grin still on my face. She smiled back, leapt towards me and hugged me as if I had been responsible for the sun coming out. I wish I could have taken credit for it, but I couldn't. If it would have been up to me, I would have put the sun out much sooner than this.

"How long?" Ryan demanded.

"Ros said a few days now, she wanted to be sure before telling anyone," Seth said. I was glad he said it without any indication that he had been annoyed about me keeping it from them.

Ryan started to pace back and forth while we all watched him. I tried working on making myself stop smiling but all I could think about was getting out of here and I believed it was really going to happen.

"Well…." Ryan's train of thought seemed to have vanished but after a few blinks he started again, "that's just not possible."

"That's what I said," Seth agreed.

"It seems impossible, but look," I shrugged, "it's actually happening, and practically right in front of our eyes."

Everyone started to get really excited, "We should seriously celebrate again," Dean said.

"No way!" Sienna said in a nervous squeaky voice, "that totally jinxed us last time! Let's ignore it until we can get out of this stinky hell hole!" She must have felt Ryan's eyes on her, "Sorry Ryan, it's not that I don't appreciate everything you did for me, I'm just in dire need to get the hell out of here ASAP!"

Ryan nodded. He seemed to understand, what he did for us, bringing us here, probably saved our lives. He didn't have to bring us here, he was extremely generous sharing his family's shelter with us. We owed him and sadly it was probably something we'd never be able to repay.

"OK," Dean said with a small chuckle, "no celebration this time."

"Christ, we are actually going to get out of here," Owen said putting his hand on the top of his head and pressing his hair down.

"It must be hot out there," Ryan said, "like really hot, maybe even too hot for us to be outside," he added shaking his head trying to understand it all.

I had considered that possibility myself. It was obvious it was hot but how hot we wouldn't know until we could open our door and feel it ourselves. I had to be hopeful we'd manage. People live in the desert where it's 110 in the shade, like in Nevada, or in Death Valley. It would be uncomfortable, especially after spending so much time in the cool underground. We would just have to be smart, stay cool and hydrated and we should be fine. At least that's what I told myself. I had to wonder if things dried up this fast in the desert? For all I knew what was out there could be far worse than any desert.

"I guess we'll find out in a few days won't we?" Owen grunted at Ryan's negativity.

And so we waited.

* * *

Each day was significantly drier than the last. I think it was five total days that passed before we agreed to try the doors, which I thought was a good thing since the generator's energy dips were getting more frequent. Ryan continued to insist that everything was fine. According to the camera display there seemed to be some lingering water above, mainly located at the doorway. That was where the water would have been at its deepest, but we figured it wouldn't be enough to flood the shelter. It may pour into the shelter a little but it wouldn't do any significant damage nor did we think it would put us in any danger whatsoever. We all agreed to risk it and it likely wouldn't make the shelter unlivable if it came down to us having to close the doors back up. I nominated Owen to do the doors if they needed to be closed since he was the strongest and could hopefully close them the fastest. He accepted the challenge without dispute.

Today we were all showered and dressed for the opening of the door which kind of felt ceremonial. We stood semi-circle around Owen and waited anxiously. My face was tight and my jaw was sore from clenching it tight, worried about all the things that could go wrong, the things we hadn't expected.

"OK, here goes nothing!" He stepped forward and opened the first door. Nothing. Which was kind of what I had hoped for. The first door had formed a perfect seal keeping all the water out. Owen inched up the stairway to the next door, released the lock and thrust it open. Seth and I peered around the corner watching while the others waited behind us for an update. There were a few drips and a thin ribbon-like stream of water that fell to the ground, and that was it.

Owen turned around and descended the staircase, "Fresh air ladies and gents, but it is a scorcher." I had felt the heat blast in the second he opened the door. "So what do we do now?" he asked mainly looking to Ryan for an answer.

"I'll go check it out. Watch on the cameras just in case, and someone stay near the doors... just as a precaution," he said, but he didn't say what he was worried could happen.

Owen stayed to man the doors and the rest of us filtered over to the TV. I overheard Ryan talking to Owen, "Should something happen to me, do not hesitate to close this door with me out there. Keep them safe." With that, he was up the stairs and in a matter of seconds visible on the cameras. He spun around in a slow circle. I couldn't read his expression other than he was currently in his serious Ryan mode. He put his hand up to his forehead and wiped away sweat that had already beaded up. That wasn't a good sign. He stared a long time in the direction where his house should have been standing, the look on his face told me it wasn't there anymore. In fact, as he turned away, the look remained on his face which was enough to say there wasn't much of anything left standing, at least in this neighborhood. He walked back towards the shelter, he was coming back down the stairs, the door closed and locked behind him.

"So, it's hot then?" I asked the minute he was in sight, his hair a little damp around the sides.

"Yes. Very."

"What did you see?" Dean asked impatiently.

"Not much."

"What's that supposed to mean?" he pressed.

"The tornadoes... the storms were too much. My house is... nearly all the houses on this block are completely gone. There are parts of homes still standing, like a wall or two here and there, but I don't think there is a single house still intact, at least not that I can see," Ryan said hinting at the idea we should all assume the worst, that all of our houses were gone.

Sienna made a tight fist and hit her leg, "So we can leave, but there isn't anywhere to go?"

"Um...." Ryan didn't know what to say to her.

After things sank in, "Well just because things around here are gone, doesn't mean everything is gone. We can go out looking for help, other survivors, our families, there is a good chance there are others like us," I offered.

"That's right. Maybe folks gathered at the school or something. Probably holed up in the basement. We won't know until we go look," Owen agreed.

"So what do we do now? Do we have any kind of plan?" Sienna whined.

"We pack up supplies and head out," I said feeling a little bossy, but no one seemed to mind or argue with me, and no one offered up any other ideas. Maybe it was smartest to stay here and wait for help, I wasn't sure. I mean, we have a perfectly safe shelter and a nice thing going on with this running water thing, but I needed to know what was

71

going on out there. It was time to move on. I already knew from the radio that we weren't the only survivors, we had heard others. It was time to get out of this claustrophobic shelter, I wanted to at least try to find my mom. She's smart and strong, the toughest woman I know, if I survived, even by pure luck, surely she had survived somewhere too. "Anyone who wants to stay here obviously can, but anyone who wants to go out and search for our families or whatever, well, they can come with me. I'm leaving tomorrow morning."

"I'm with you," Owen said without hesitation.

"Me too," Seth said. I didn't imagine Seth and Owen would ever split up.

"We're coming too," Dean said answering for both himself and Sienna.

Ryan didn't say anything, he just walked off and shut the bathroom door behind him.

I don't think I could stop myself from looking a little disappointed. Owen put his hand on my shoulder, "Aw, I don't think it's you or anything. He saw what's out there, we haven't."

"Well, maybe he knows best and we should stay here," I said with a shrug and suddenly doubted myself. What if I was making a mistake?

"Maybe, but we won't know unless we go," Owen said curling his lips into a half smile. I smiled back, I couldn't have agreed with him more. "Besides he didn't say we shouldn't."

"Well, OK then. Let's pack and make sure we get a good night's rest?" Seth said sounding more like he was asking than he was telling. I hoped I wouldn't be looked at as the leader of this adventure because I wasn't a leader, far from it. I wouldn't know what to do or where to go.

Everyone agreed and went off in separate directions to take care of whatever they needed to take care of. I emptied out my backpack that I still had with me from the first day we came down here, it felt as though a lifetime had passed since that day. I filled it with the things I thought I might need, several changes of clothes, toothbrush and stuffed in as many water bottles as I could. There was a second bag in the closet which was smaller with a flap closure that was held in place with a thin strip of Velcro. This one I filled with snack bars, pop tarts and anything else I could find that would have a long shelf life. I realized we were giving up having a kitchen and pantry, warm food and having something to eat any time we wanted. Without knowing exactly what was out there for us, I worried it might be foolish to be giving up this luxury.

Before bedtime I had checked my pack at least six times before I could settle down in my cozy bed. It was another luxury that would soon be gone. Sienna was already sleeping and the boy's room was pretty quiet, they were either sleeping or about to be. I pulled up the covers and pushed my head against the softness of the pillow. It didn't take long until I drifted off into a dreamland where everything was perfect again.

Chapter six.

Ryan had his things packed and was sitting with his legs stretched out in front of him, waiting for us. He had decided to join us whether he really wanted to or not. Part of me felt bad for him, even if he wanted to stay here, it would have been hard for him to make that choice with everyone else leaving. It would have been too lonely for him to have stayed by himself. Heck, I wondered if he hadn't already been lonely even with all of us here. I couldn't help but wonder if the dips in power and dwindling food supplies, not to mention all the food we took, played a part in his decision making process.

"Morning," I said to him without making eye contact. The lights dimmed momentarily, and I felt a bit better about things, but Ryan didn't even seem to notice.

"Morning."

He popped up as if he had just remembered something and walked off into the pantry. Perhaps he was mad at me for being so quick to suggest we leave, without even a real conversation about it. He was probably right to feel that way, I should have put it up for some kind of vote or something. Not to mention he and I had sort of been a team down here, watching the cameras and listening to the radio. I hadn't even given him a chance, I just stomped all over his toes and made the call.

When we had all gathered together, we quietly ascended the stairs in single file. Ryan first, I followed close behind both nervous and eager to see everything for myself. Before we even got halfway up the staircase, I could feel the drastic change in temperature even with the door closed. He opened the door at the top of the stairs and the blast of hot air that hit my face was overwhelming. It felt like sitting too close to a campfire. My face felt like it was roasting and it had only been a matter of seconds. I took the hair-tie off my wrist and put my hair up. It was a sad attempt to cool down.

"Christ!" I heard Owen complain behind me, "I must be in hell, maybe this is hotter."

The others behind him all groaned when the wave of heat rippled towards them. There hadn't been much shade since everything had been uprooted and torn down by the storms. It had been too hot and with everything drying out, nothing was growing back. I spun around slowly just as Ryan had when we watched him on the camera. I was surveying this new world. The pure devastation was shocking. The cameras didn't even come close to showing how bad things really were. I felt a tear form in the corner of my eye, but it evaporated before I could even flick it away.

Ryan's grandpa's house was completely

gone. There was nothing left except for a few stray wooden boards, dirt, and twigs which covered what was once the basement. What was even more shocking was seeing dirt for as far as the eye could see. The roads were mostly gone, everything covered in a layer of rough, crusty mud. Crumbled parts of concrete were sprinkled around so you could still see where the roads had been. There were random structural parts of homes still standing, and across the street there was a single partial wall erect among the devastation. Just a wall. Nothing more, just a wooden frame with some peeling drywall and what appeared to be wallpaper hanging off the side.

Sienna was crying. It was a silent cry, but tears streamed down her face nonetheless.

I reached over and put my hand on her shoulder, "It'll be OK, everything will be rebuilt. It just takes time."

"It's... not... that," she said between sobs.

I looked at her my eyebrows scrunched together, I didn't know what she was upset about if it wasn't about everything having been erased away. She didn't explain and buried her face into her hands.

"That was where our house used to be," Dean said pointing down what was left of the road, "it's gone, nothing there," he explained. I couldn't even tell exactly where he was pointing because all that was there was crusty dirt.

"We should check out the area, maybe there is something there?" I suggested, "I think I'd like to see my house too if that's OK? You know, just to be sure." To make sure it was gone, even though I knew it was. I felt a flutter of sadness in my throat.

We walked towards the empty space that used to hold the Coats's home. Sienna and Dean paced the dirt searching for anything, a little trinket, or some kind of reminder, but there wasn't anything. It had all been blown or washed away.

"I'm sorry," was all I could offer them verbally. Dean nodded while Sienna swallowed a big lump of awfulness deep down inside herself. "Who's house next?"

"Mine would be, I think? Not exactly sure where you lived Ros," Owen said, and I flinched a little when he used the past tense of live. He walked across what had been the street and then several blocks further away from the shelter. Owen would have been a street over from Dean's house. They had lived close together, which I guess is why they had been walking home together. Probably also why they had been friends having lived in the same neighborhood.

There was nothing here either. Owen let the sand sift through his fingers for a while before standing and kicking at the ground, but just like the Coats's home, the Maitland's house was gone too.

"Seth where did you live?" I asked.

"Across town, lucky I was hanging out with these guys or I probably wouldn't be alive right now," he said with a nervous chuckle.

"We can go there next," I said, "Mine is just over this way."

I plodded towards where my house once stood, I was both anxious and apprehensive, I knew what I'd find, and what I wouldn't find. As I suspected, my house was gone as well, all except for a small part of the garage which was still standing. It offered us a moment of shade. It was still hotter than hell but at least the sun wasn't beating down on us.

Everything had been blown away, all except for a key that was still hanging on a hook. It was one of the keys for the moped that had been given to me by my grandparents. The other key must have fallen off and blown away, or maybe it was buried somewhere in the dried up muck. I had rarely used the moped, but I had loved it since it was a gift from my grandma and grandpa. I crammed the key into my pocket even though the moped was gone, it would serve its purpose as a memory.

A piece of paper floated down to my feet when I removed the key. I picked it up and saw it was a hand written note. Was it possible that my mom could have come back to leave me a note? Maybe she thought I'd come back and check on the house if I could. The problem was most of what had been written had been washed and weathered away. The paper was brittle, it had probably soaked up a lot of water and then in this heat had dried to a crisp. I was a little surprised it was still intact. On the note, the only word I could make out was 'going,' at least I was almost certain that's what it said. There was another partial word, but too many letters were missing to even make a guess, all I could tell is that it started with the letter 'A'. I took the paper and gently placed it in the front pocket of my backpack hoping it would be safe there. Maybe when I had more time I could look it over better and be able to figure out what it had said, but for all I knew it was just an old grocery list.

"One second," I said yanking out a bottle of water from my backpack. My throat was dry from the heat and air. Perhaps only twenty minutes or so had passed maybe a half hour, and I already was feeling dehydrated. I chugged the water so fast you could hear my swallows. "OK, ready," I said chucking the bottle against the garage wall. We started silently across town towards Seth's house.

Our area had been hit the worst, at least of what we'd seen so far. Once we got closer to the school, more of the buildings were in somewhat better shape, especially those of brick. But still most of it gone as if they'd never existed. Some of the school still stood but nothing substantial, it was still mostly shredded. The roof had been ripped clean off, there wouldn't have been anyone inside.

"This is just too hot," Owen said panting in the minimal shade provided by the school, "that was one good thing about the shelter, it was nice and cool."

I nodded in agreement, I too was not a fan of the heat, nor was Seth. I couldn't imagine anyone actually liked this temperature. Those who lived in places this hot must have done so out of pure necessity. At the same time, I was glad to be able to move freely, without being restricted to just a few rooms. I was no longer feeling claustrophobic, but now I was perpetually uncomfortable in my damp, sweaty clothes. At least I could breathe in real, albeit hot, fresh air.

After we took a five minute rest, we continued towards Seth's, which turned out was only a few more blocks. When we got there it was in the best condition of all the houses. The roof had been mostly torn off just like most buildings, but three of the four exterior walls were still standing. Some of the flooring wasn't coated in dried mud, and I could even make out which rooms had been the kitchen, dining room, and bathroom. We all leaned against the wall that provided us with the most cover from the sun while Seth roamed about, picking things up and then placing them back where they once had been. Most things were just shattered pieces of who-knows-what covered in mud. Not much of anything could have been salvaged, but he shoved a few things in his backpack, nothing he wanted to tell us about and no one asked. Just like when no one asked me about keeping the key that was clearly useless.

"Where to now?" Owen asked me as if I had a plan I hadn't shared with them. I wouldn't be able to lead the group anywhere, I was just as lost as they were.

"I'm not sure. To be honest, this is pretty much a disaster area," I said keeping the sadness out of my voice as much as possible. This had been my town. This is where I had lived and where I grew up. Everything I had ever known or cared about wiped away and all that remained were unrecognizable pieces of what had been people's lives.

Our searching for answers had taken up the

whole morning, and based on the position of the sun, I guessed we were well into the afternoon. The heat was blistering, almost literally, and unrelenting. We hadn't run into any other living soul, which I thought is what we all secretly hoped to do, find someone, ask questions, get answers and be saved. That didn't happen. It was just as lonely out here as it had been trapped in our underground hideaway, only up here we had more places to go.

"Let's find dinner, then a place to stay for the night," Ryan suggested.

"Sounds perfect," I said smiling at him thankful he had come up with a plan. It may have been a short plan, but it was a plan.

"Let's head to where the Target used to be," Sienna said. Even our small town had a Target. Where there was a need, there was a giant retailer willing to swoop down and fill it.

We were surprised when we saw the big bulls-eye still mostly attached to the building. The whole store was almost completely intact minus parts of the roof and the doors. The whole pharmacy department looked as if it had been sucked up through the roof and then spit back down.

"I'm going to go look for clothes," Sienna said skipping away on her own.

"Let's check the food situation," Owen said nudging Seth.

"And I'm going to go find the bathroom," Dean informed Ryan and me. I could see the bathroom, the doors dangled off their hinges and I'm sure the water wouldn't work, but it would still serve its purpose.

"Do you think Sienna's all right by herself?" I asked.

"Yeah, I think she'll be fine, its clothes what could go wrong?" he said with a handsome grin as he backed away from us, leaving Ryan and I in awkward silence.

I tried to keep quiet. The longer it went on the harder I found it to keep my lips pinched together, "I'm sorry if you think I overstepped my bounds asking everyone to come with me."

Ryan just shook his head.

"Oh, so it's going to be like that? Really?"

"You think I'd be mad about that?" Ryan said squinting at me.

I shrugged.

"Oh, so it's like that huh?" he said smirking.

The moment our eyes connected I wasn't sure if I was supposed to be mad or laugh. I didn't get a chance to do either. Our conversation was interrupted when we heard Sienna's shrill scream.

I ran as fast as my feet would move towards the clothing department with Ryan at my heels. There was another set of footsteps close behind us. I had a hunch it was probably Dean catching up, but there was no time to check.

I stopped dead in my tracks when I spotted her frozen in place. A big burly man had his arm wrapped around her shoulders and was covering her mouth with his hand. He hadn't seen us approach, we'd all ducked down under the clothing racks just in time, but he had definitely heard our stomping feet. He spun around in our general direction,

"Come out, or I'll ssslit her pretty little throat," he roared.

Chapter seven.

"Come out, come out wherever you are!" Spit misted out of his mouth as he spoke. He chuckled nervously, he didn't know who was hiding and it was apparent that he was a little skittish because of that. "I'm not going to wait forever!" he bellowed.

I looked at Ryan and he looked at Dean. No one said it out loud, but we knew at least one of us had to stay hidden. Before either Ryan or Dean could stand to reveal themselves, I popped up with my hands in the air. It had made more sense to keep the stronger of the three of us hidden in case things got out of hand. "Here I am. Please just let her go."

He snorted, "Don't tell me what to do, I'lls let her go if and when I'm ready. How many more of you little brats are there? And don't even thinkss about lying," he said pointing the knife at me briefly before putting it back to Sienna's neck. He had wobbled and slurred a few of his words. The bald guy with the bowling ball gut was probably here to loot the booze department although it sounded as if he already had. Maybe he had a drinking problem, or maybe all the devastation and destruction caused one. I'm not sure I could have blamed him for the latter.

"It's just me," I said trying my best to sound convincing.

"Now," his eyes narrowing, "that, my friend, is a lie." He pushed the knife against Sienna's throat and she stiffened. Her tears streaked trails through the caked-on dust on her cheeks.

"OK, OK, you got me," I said raising my palms up towards him, "there are two others, in the food department. But it's just me and her here, we were looking for new clothes."

"You sure make a lot of noise," he said with his eyes jerking around still skeptical. "End of the world and you two thought you'd do a little shopping? Using that five finger discount?" he smirked only amusing himself.

"Just wanting clean clothes, sir." I threw in a sir hoping to throw him off guard with my politeness, as if I could possibly respect this knife wielding jerk, which of course I didn't. "What is it you want from us?"

He thought for a moment, like I was a genie and this was his big chance to come up with his three wishes. It was clear he hadn't had a real plan when he grabbed her. He had probably just reacted thinking that maybe he was in danger and did the first thing he thought of, holding her hostage in case he could use her as a bargaining chip. He scratched his head with his knife hand.

Before I realized what was happening Ryan

flew out from a clothing rack near the big guy and knocked them both down to the ground. I hadn't seen or heard him sneaking towards them. I quickly scanned the area for Dean. He popped up from wherever he had been and was sweeping Sienna up and away from the drunk guy. Ryan's fist came back and then forward fast, and hard. The thud of him hitting the man in the jaw made me cringe. The man lifted his knife hand but Ryan was faster and sober, he swung again and the man dropped the knife. His chunky arm flopped to the ground. I thought Dean would grab the knife, but it was Sienna who scooped it up and crouched down by the man like she was some crazed Amazonian woman.

It was her turn to press the knife against his neck, "I should slit your throat you poor excuse for a human being!" she hissed. She angrily pressed again causing a little cut no larger than if he'd cut himself shaving, "But I'm not a bad person, so I won't. Get out of my sight before I change my mind," she threatened.

The man stood, wobbled and shook his finger at them, but then instead of saying whatever he was thinking, he changed his mind. He spat blood on the floor and weaved his way out of the store not looking back. It almost seemed as though he had already forgotten what had just happened. Sienna didn't put the knife down until he was out of sight.

"Um, whoa?" Dean said holding his hands up, looking both shocked and impressed by his little sister. He seemed to be wondering who this new girl was, and so was I.

"I second that!"

"You don't mess with the Coats," she said with an evil grin, "we need weapons."

"We do," Ryan agreed, "but this is Target. We can choose between a shovel and a bright orange squirt gun."

"Or... more knives," Sienna said still grinning. Instead of looking scared by what had just happened, she was proud of herself whereas I was just happy I was holding my panic attack in.

"Knives it is. At least for now. Let's go," Ryan said nodding towards housewares.

It was possible the knife section had already been ransacked, after all, the overweight drunk guy had been carrying one. Even he had at least, at one point, had enough wits about him to get a knife for protection, unlike us. Apparently we had been oblivious to the potential for danger. We grabbed a Guy Fieri knife set. Each knife in the set had a protective sheath. We also took a single packed up chef's knife. Ryan tore it out of its packaging and dropped it to the floor. He wrapped the knife tightly in a kitchen towel before placing it in the back of his pants.

"A paring knife? I think I deserve better than a paring knife," Sienna whined.

"It's all that's left," Dean said putting one of the larger knives into his backpack. The other two he held would go to Seth and Owen.

I could feel Sienna's eyes on me. My knife was already packed away, but she was probably thinking about how unfair it was that I had gotten the better knife. After how she had handled herself she probably figured that she deserved the real knife and that I should get the paring knife. I didn't offer her th better knife, after all she still had the pocket knife from the drunk man. She'd already threatened someone and won with the pocket knife, I would have been useless with either the pocket or paring knife for that matter.

"We'll get better weapons when we can," Ryan said trying to keep things calm and cool. "Let's get Owen and Seth and find somewhere to stay for the night."

Owen and Seth had gathered up two bags full of food before we'd found them. The rest of us filled our packs with as much food, Gatorade and water as we could fit inside. On top of what we still had left from the shelter, we would still have more than enough for the night. As we left the Target store, we talked about where we should go. We all agreed to leave our small home town behind and head over to the neighboring and much larger city. If traveling by car, which we wouldn't be, it was only about a ten minute drive. We weren't more than two blocks from Target when we heard the gunshot ring out.

* * *

The shot was so close that Seth dropped to the ground for cover. Ryan and Owen moved in front of me and Sienna protectively while Dean crouched down somehow already wielding his shiny new knife. Laughter erupted from a nearby barely surviving bush.

"Seriously? Who brings a knife to a gun party, brother?" A larger male, probably twenty-five or so stepped into view chuckling. He was going on the assumption, and rightfully so, that we had nothing more lethal than the knife.

The large guy loosely pointed his gun in our direction. He was twice the width of Seth and a good five inches taller than Dean. The beast was built like a truck, solid and he wasn't afraid of us. Even with a gun, there was still five of us and only one of him. I guessed he wasn't alone. As if he had read my mind he whistled and his minions emerged from seemingly random hiding spots.

They were quite a gang. I almost felt as if I was looking at a carnival freak show but for some reason that made me even more nervous. There was a girl who was even taller than their leader and toothpick thin. She was holding a shotgun lazily against her shoulder, the look on her face told me she knew how to use it and she would if she was told to. There were two short boys that appeared to be twins. Each one with a matching holstered pistol on the opposite hip of the other. They looked like a mirror image of each other right down to their matching leather vests and cowboy hats. If there hadn't been a gun pointed in my direction I would have laughed at the country-western version of Tweedledee and Tweedledum. The last gang member to reveal himself was perfectly normal looking which made him stand out even more than the others. He looked to be our age, with a black eye, and matching black hair that flopped down hiding his eyes. He looked familiar. Did I know him? I glanced at the others to see if they had recognized him but they didn't appear to. When his eyes met mine, it hit me. I knew those eyes. I recognized him and he recognized me too.

It was the boy from the day of the storms, the one I had made eye contact with when Ryan had pulled me to safety. He looked beat up, disheveled and depressed. I was happy to see he had survived, but he didn't seem as though he was. I wanted to ask him what his story was, but that wasn't going to happen. He was the enemy. He too was wielding a gun.

"This is going to be quick and painless if you do what I say. Then you folks can be off on your merry little way," the leader said breaking the silence after we had all sized each other up. "All you have to do," he said smirking at his pals, "is hand over your backpacks."

"Aww come on," Owen wailed frustrated. "Dude, the store is still full of all kinds of shit, go and take what you want!"

"I could do that… but you see, you've all already done that for me! What a time saver! It must be my lucky day!" He grinned showing his yellow, cigarette stained teeth, "Come on now, toss them over, one at a time to Shorty." Shorty, the tall girl, stepped forward a couple feet and gestured for us to get on with it and give her the bags.

"And if we don't?" Owen asked sounding ready for a fight. A fight we'd most certainly lose.

The leader stroked his gun like a pet cat. He then pointed it at a stop sign off to our right and let a shot ring out against the sign. He completely missed the sign but the loud pop from the gun was enough.

"They don't even know how to aim," I muttered under my breath.

"We can't risk it," Ryan said. I knew he was right, we were bigger targets, maybe Shorty or the other kids actually knew how to aim. I tried to think on my feet, there had to be a way to get out of here with all of our gear. Ryan must have heard my gears spinning. "We can just get more stuff, take out your knife when I go, put it in your pants and cover it with your shirt, do it fast," he instructed and stepped in front of me. He took his time pretending to fumble the bag before he ultimately tossed it towards Shorty. Sienna did the same with her paring knife. I slipped out the little piece of note paper I'd taken from my house, I fumbled and almost dropped the pack but thankfully no one noticed.

Owen and Seth tossed their bags over as well. When Dean stopped up to throw his, the leader coughed, "Wait, I want your knife too. But don't be cute, slide it over." He sighed and reluctantly did as he was told knowing that Target was out of knives.

Lastly, Sienna and I threw our packs over to the rag-tag gang. I was so frustrated to have to lose everything we had gathered, including my keepsake key.

Shorty slung a pack over her shoulder and

tossed the remaining packs to the others. My frenemy got my pack. He looked at me knowing it was mine. And just like that all of my things were gone. My key, my school notebooks, my water and my food, all of it, gone. Maybe this was some form of karma for me not having helped him, not that I ever had a real choice in the matter. But maybe karma didn't agree with me and it was going to hold me responsible. I had to pay the price until karma was satisfied. It decided I needed to make things right and the way to start was to give up my supplies to him.

"Thank you kindly boys and girls," said the gross leader, "Now, if you'll excuse us, we'll be on our way. Nice doing business with you all." With that they walked away down the street towards the broken down school.

"Let's get new backpacks and new stuff and get out of here," Dean said running his hand through his damp from the heat hair. He seemed both pissed off and nervous to be out in the open without anything to protect us. "There could be much worse people out here than those circus freaks."

So we went back into Target, staying together this time. They had enough backpacks and some over the shoulder bags. We stuffed anything we could carry with food, water, toilet paper, toothbrushes, clothing and anything we walked passed and thought we might need. Owen packed some over-the-counter medicines like pain relievers and vitamins. I saw him consider for a minute going behind the counter for the real stuff but he changed his mind.

We were in and out in less than fifteen minutes and heading towards the next town. The sun was setting, we were going to have to find somewhere to stay the night quicker than we had originally planned. The heat had only lessened a few degrees and we were all still dripping sweat from every pore. At least we no longer had to seek out shade every so often because the unbearable sun was beating down on us. It was only barely tolerable.

"How about that place?" Seth asked indicating a quaint house in the distance. It was far enough off the main road that maybe it would be safe enough for the night. "We can find something bigger and better tomorrow."

"Let's check it out," Ryan said turning the group towards the little home. The heat had made us all too exhausted to argue, even if anyone had wanted to.

The house was dark and quiet. We could see that there wasn't any movement inside because the curtains were open. We still called out asking if anyone was home when we opened the front door. Silence. The best part of this home was that the tornadoes had missed it almost completely. One window had been blown out, and the garage was missing its roof but the house itself seemed solid. It was made out of bricks which helped, but I figured it was mostly luck that it was still standing and with most of the roof still intact.

We slipped inside one by one. Sienna started lining up candles we'd taken from Target and lighting them. What we realized quickly was that the amount of candles we took was not sufficient even for this small home, but it would have to do.

"I'm going to look for a hammer and some wood to try to board up that window. Check the doors and windows, lock whatever you can, and anything we can't lock hopefully we can nail it shut," Ryan said walking out of the side door that led to the garage.

"I'll help you," Owen shouted as he stomped after him.

Seth had dropped down on the recliner and was sipping from a water bottle. He didn't look well. I wondered if he was suffering from exhaustion, dehydration or maybe it was heat stroke. I didn't know what to do for him except worry, and that didn't help anyone.

"We'll check the windows and doors, just take it easy Seth," I told him as I touched his shoulder briefly.

"OK, thanks," he said shifting the recliner back and putting his feet up with more effort than it should have taken.

I motioned for Sienna and Dean to get started while I stayed behind to look for a wash cloth. The bathroom was stocked with clean towels. I poured some water on it hoping it would be cool enough, but I feared it would be too warm after having been in the heat all day. "It's the best I can do Seth. I'm sorry," I said as I applied the cloth to his forehead. After a few seconds I removed it and lightly blew on the dampness it left behind.

He forced a weak smile, "It's great, I think my body temperature just dropped ten degrees."

"I'll get you another for your neck," I said walking off to get another wash cloth. I met Dean and Sienna in the small hallway and they informed me that everything was locked.

"But that won't stop anyone from breaking the glass should they want to," Dean said reminding us we couldn't drop our guard even when things seemed safe. We would probably never be as safe as we had been in our underground shelter.

"Breaking glass should be loud enough to wake us I'd think?" I said trying to offer some reassurance, even though it wasn't much.

"Most likely, but all we have is a couple knives."

I shrugged not knowing what else we could really do about it. Until it occurred to me that whoever owned this house maybe had things we could use, "Check around for a gun, or something else we could use. Check the cabinets, the basement if there is one, anywhere you can think of."

Dean nodded and took Sienna with him to search the house for weapons. Unfortunately, the house was getting dark rather quickly. I was putting the cloth around the back of Seth's neck when Ryan and Owen came in with several pieces of wood and started to loudly board up the broken window.

"Everything locked up?" Ryan asked.
"According to Dean everything is locked."
"What's wrong with Seth?" he asked when

95

he finished pounding in a nail. I opened my mouth to answer, but he bashed the hammer into the next nail before I had a chance. As he reached for the next nail I told him I thought Seth had just overheated and was exhausted. They finished boarding up the window, went back out to the garage, and after about twenty minutes, they returned and pounded several pieces of wood over each door.

"Close the curtains," Ryan ordered, "Someone might see the candles." I closed them as Dean and Sienna returned from their search.

"No guns," Dean announced, "but I found these." He dropped two wooden baseball bats in the middle of the floor.

"Well, it's something," I said.

Owen and Ryan finished their pounding just as I was about to ask Owen for one of those pain pills he grabbed. "Let's eat," Owen said, adding the hammer to the pile of baseball bats.

Everyone searched their packs for something to eat. I helped Seth with his and propped him up with pillows from the couch so he could eat more comfortably. I opened a can of cold baked beans and a small bag of potato chips and dipped the chips into the beans. Sienna stuck her tongue out and looked at me like I was crazy as she took a large bite from her chocolate toaster pastry.

Thankfully I had stuffed a novel into my backpack, so I had something to read as the night dragged by. The night passed by drama free. I found that reading by the candlelight helped me forget for a short time that I was holed up in a stranger's house, the world as we knew it was gone and that I was stuck in this miserable heat for the unforeseeable future.

Where were we supposed to go? Where were the relief services helping people like us? Where were all the other people?

Chapter eight.

The next day we headed out early before the sun was at its hottest. It felt hotter than it had the day before. If each day continued to increase at this rate we'd be in serious trouble especially without a permanent shelter. The look on Ryan's face said he had the same thought. I wondered if any of the others had regretted leaving the cool shelter behind for this hell.

Our first goal of the day was to find a suitable shelter and secure it. We wanted something big, so we didn't start feeling claustrophobic again. It had to be something with a good amount of shade, which would be hard considering so few trees remained. And those that were still standing were mostly bare, with shredded, broken branches. The shelter would also need to be close enough to the city so we could walk there but far enough away that we didn't get outsiders poking around. I hoped we'd know the right place when we saw it, but I wasn't sure if we even knew everything we'd need a shelter to be.

When we got close to the city we took the first country road we saw and walked out several more miles away from the city limits. It was sweltering, and we were moving slower because of Seth. I'd doused myself with our precious water at least twice already in an attempt to keep cool but it was so hot and sunny my hair was dry within minutes. Seth dragged his feet more and more with each rejected house. And then we saw it. It was like some sort of miracle. There was a two story house that had functioned as a farm, and it had been mostly untouched by the storms. I worried that it might be a mirage.

As we got closer we got excited because it was in exceptional condition, definitely livable and probably as secluded as we would get without a lot more searching. And we were all tired of searching.

The house was made mostly of dirty brown brick and it had some minor roof damage, but it was still intact. The garage was undamaged, and a large, like-new storage shed still stood in the back. A washed out dark gray wooden porch stretched around most of the house, and it was covered with caked on mud. We walked right up to the front door and turned the handle. It was locked. Ryan took out his knife, hid it from view, and knocked hard. I pressed my knife against my leg still tucked inside its colorful sheath. Owen and Dean had each taken a baseball bat from the last house and hid them behind their backs. We didn't want to look intimidating, we just wanted to be prepared if someone not so nice greeted us.

No answer.

He knocked again even harder, "Anyone in

there?" he shouted.

There were several large oak trees surrounding the home, even though they didn't have leaves they still provided a fair amount of shade from their thick entwined branches. They were brown and looked like they were dying but at least they were there and hadn't been uprooted like most of the other trees had been. It wasn't cool by any stretch of the imagination, not even in the shade, but it was cooler than being in the direct sunlight. Seth picked up one of the porch chairs that had blown over and sat down. His skin was a painful shade of red considering he was the palest skinned of us all. I hadn't known if he was sunburned or just running hot from the heat, heck, maybe it was both. We locked eyes, and I saw the pain in his.

I pushed passed Ryan and knocked as hard as I could. "Ding dong!" I yelled and kicked the door as hard as I could by the doorknob. The door shook but didn't pop open. I kicked again, fueled by my desire to get Seth inside, but this kick was far less powerful since I had used all my energy on the first blow.

"Let me try." Owen lightly moved me aside and with what appeared to be barely any effort, kicked the door in on his first try. He smiled as it popped open cleanly. The doorknob appeared to be a little wobbly, but he hadn't kicked a hole in the door or broken anything. I hoped the lock would still work.

"Secure the house, stay alert," Ryan instructed, "groups of two. Dean and Sienna upstairs and Seth and Owen take this floor. Ros and I will check the basement, garage and anything else. Lock all the doors and windows as you go through." He pushed the solid wood coffee table against the front door for added security.

After a opening a couple closet doors first, we found the door to the basement. I followed closely behind Ryan. It was one of those cool, dank and dreary horror movie basements, not a fun family room basement. The windows let in enough light so that we could see, and the cooler temperature felt nice, it was at least ten degrees cooler than it had been upstairs. There was no one down there, just boxes, storage and a wash machine. There was a pile of wood for a fireplace which certainly we wouldn't need, but there were also stray strips of wood that could be used for boarding up windows and doors.

"Let's check the garage," Ryan said heading towards the stairs. I followed him quickly, afraid something would jump out at me, even though I knew there wasn't really anything down there. Apparently I was following too closely and bumped into him. He turned to look at me, "Are you scared or something?" he teased, letting a hint of that super cute Ryan that I had only seen a handful of times before show.

"Umm no?" I said unconvincingly.

He laughed and put his hand on my back and gestured for me to go ahead of him. It was almost enough to turn me into absolute goo. He had that smile on, the one that makes me get all melty-goofy-stupid and he was acting protective which only added extra pizazz to the mix. It was either him, or the disgusting wave of heat I felt as I ascended the stairs that was turning me into taffy.

The garage was your average everyday garage. It had tools, a classic car under a tarp, gardening equipment, lawn chairs, bikes, all the things normal garages have. Ryan walked over to the large garage door and yanked upwards. It glided up a few inches, "Too easy to open." There was a window at the back that faced the shed, "Follow," he demanded.

I wondered if I obeyed him way too easily, but in this unfamiliar place I didn't really have the will or the desire to put my foot down. It was by far easier for me to just have him tell me what to do. By nature I was a follower, not a leader. It was just how I'd always been. The shed had a snow blower, riding lawn mower, rakes and some gas cans. The farm hadn't been used as a farm in a long time, or the storms had blown the barn away because there hadn't been one where you'd expect there to be one. It hadn't looked like they had grown crops either. But really there was no way to know for sure if they had or not, since everything had been flooded, frozen and then caked in mud. Any signs of things that once had been could now have easily been washed away.

"Ah! A generator!" Ryan said pointing at the back of the house. He lifted the gas can to find it only had a few drops left. "Of course," he said closing the shed and making his way over to the generator with me following behind. He tried to start it, but it was stubborn, it sounded like it wanted to go, which I decided was a good sign but it just wouldn't. "Needs gas," Ryan said communicating with me using as few words as he could and still conveying his message, "Might be too loud."

We walked around the house, checking it from every possible angle. We appeared to be well hidden… as much as one can hide a house that is. If someone came up the street they'd see it but it would look like every other abandoned house that was still standing. Of the people that were left how many of them would wander out this way?

"Hey um," Ryan said putting his hand on my arm lightly to stop me, "I just wanted to say that I was sorry for how I've been acting."

"It's fine," I said turning to head back inside to avoid any awkward conversations, like this one. One that I didn't think even needed to happen. Everything was fine, really, at least for me. With everything that was going on, this was pretty minor.

He stopped me by putting his arm up and blocking me so I had to turn to face him. "No, really I am. I'm just not good at this stuff," he said shaking his head. His face was only a few inches from mine. My heart raced and my mind stopped understanding the words that were coming out of his mouth. In fact, I had no idea what he was saying, I could see his lips moving but whatever was coming out made no sense. At that exact moment, I didn't understand whatever language he was speaking. All I knew was that he was so close to me I could feel his breath. "I just don't want you to get hurt, or anyone else for that matter. This new world isn't safe," he said ending the speech I'd only heard the beginning and end of.

"I'm fine," I said with a smile. I was mentally trying to put all the words I had heard back into some kind of decipherable order, trying to make sense of it.

His eyes were studying me. I wondered if he could tell how he was making me feel. Here he was just being normal and I was turning into a stupid puddle on the dry, crusty ground because I couldn't keep myself in check when I was this close to him. He put his hand out for a second as if he was going to touch my face, but I think I twitched, or made some kind of strange squeak, because he reeled it back in like a fishing line. I wanted him to touch me. I don't know what was wrong with me to even be thinking about him this way, to be thinking about anything other than survival. I was a horrible selfish person.

"Let's go back in," he said, still only inches from me. He looked down and touched his fingers lightly to mine. He took a breath and turned back into the other Ryan.

I followed him around the rest of the house and to the back door like a lost puppy. I could still feel his fingers touching mine although he had long since removed them. "Ryan," I said before I could stop myself. I had no idea what I was going to say especially now that he was back to being normal Ryan.

"Yeah?" He barely stopped, his brain was back to being focused on other things.

"I'm sorry too." It was the best thing I

could think to say. I wanted to slap myself across the face.

"For?" He turned to look at me.

"I don't know everything I guess."

"None of this is your fault, Ros."

I shook my head. Not helping that other kid was my fault. Leaving the shelter before we were really ready was my fault. It was probably my fault the circus freaks took our stuff. I was at fault for plenty. "Enough of this is my fault," I said as I lowered my head. We'd probably still be safe back in your grandpa's shelter if it hadn't been for me and my big mouth."

"I think we were all done with that place."

"There was this guy, the day everything happened..." I said, my eyes felt glassy. "He was across the street, I could have helped him."

"Or you could have gotten yourself killed."

I put my hands over my face. I felt guilty about the guy, even though he was alive and appeared to be surviving. He was with the wrong crowd, I hadn't the first clue about how he'd gotten to where he was but I imagined it wasn't pleasant, or he wouldn't be stuck with the circus freaks. I'm sure he had to do whatever it took to survive. It didn't matter to me, I should have done something. If I had, he'd be with us now.

"Come on Ros," Ryan said, gently pulling me in against his sweaty body, "It's going to be OK. We all just need to figure out how to live in this world. Things are different obviously, it's just an adjustment period." He put his finger on my chin and lifted my face up towards his. Our eyes met. Soft, delicious Ryan was back. Our faces only inches apart once again, "It really will be OK, I won't let anything happen to you," he said his voice sounding serious and intense. He blushed, or maybe it was just from the heat. I knew I was blushing too. I would blame the sun. Sunburn probably. Yup.

I tilted my head and looked at him sideways, "Why would you need or want to, for that matter, protect me?"

"It's not obvious?" He chuckled and narrowed his eyes.

I shook my head.

"I don't know how to say this, so I'm just going to say it. I sort of have feelings for you. For like a while now, but you know, with how things are. Well, it's just… different."

My mouth dropped open, and I looked like I was a fish desperately gasping for air, or water, or air and water. What did he mean by how things are? Things are with me and him? Or things with the world? "When did this happen?" I said a little louder than I had intended still quite surprised by the new information.

"Jeez Ros, I don't know exactly, it just did." He turned to go in and that was going to be the end of it. That would be all that he said about it as far as he was concerned, "Let's go in before I embarrass myself further." And with that he was inside and I was left staring at the opened door catching flies with my mouth still hanging open.

Inside Dean walked pass the opened door and was about to close it, "What are you doing out there? Come in! We still have a lot of work to do. I almost just locked you outside for Pete's sake!" When I didn't move he stepped out and pulled me in by my droopy spaghetti arm, "Are you OK?"

"Yeah. Yeah I'm fine." I blinked a few times and forced myself to come back to the real world where things like that just don't happen. The horrible new world we lived in where Ryan and I couldn't be any thing more than people trying to survive.

* * *

We all sat in the living room. Dean and Sienna reported their findings which wasn't much. They'd locked all the windows and doors and closed all the shades to help keep it cooler inside. Sienna had found a small stash of taper candles with a light pine scent that reminded me of the holidays and some holders. She had piled it all neatly on the dining room table.

Owen and Seth hadn't found anything either, but they had made sure the front door lock was strong enough to hold. Dean had gone around the first floor and closed all the curtains. That's what he was doing when he found me in my trance. What would the others think if they knew what Ryan had just confessed to me? How would they feel about it? What would they do? Worse, what would they think if they knew I was pretty sure I felt the same way?

107

"Ros and I located a generator out back and an empty gas can in the shed. Not sure if it'll work, we'll try to get gas tomorrow to test it out. For tonight we should have enough food and water, so I say we get to work on securing the house. Who wants to help me board up the windows? And someone can work on boarding up the front door. There is wood in the basement and out back, hammers and nails in the basement. The garage door opens too easily we'll have to figure out something for that too. In the meantime we'll our fingers and hope no one tries to get in through the garage."

Everyone stared at Ryan waiting for him to tell us to get to work. "Tomorrow… guns, gas, food and water. We start building up our supply," he said tapping each finger as if he were writing a list, "is that everything?"

"I think so boss," Owen joked.

Ryan rolled his eyes even though I knew how he felt about keeping us safe. For some reason he felt responsible, and he would not be dumb or take any chances about anything, especially our safety. "OK Owen you come with me, we'll board up the windows. Ros, Sienna and Dean, you guys board up this door, while you keep an eye on Seth. And Seth, just rest."

"Maybe if that generator works we could get a fan or better yet, fans," I said stressing the plural, "working in here."

"That would be fantastic," Seth groaned in his miserable state.

Dean went with Ryan and Owen to gather

the wood for our project. He came back with one hammer for the three of us. We were probably lucky that there were even three total hammers. Since the door opened inward, Dean started pounding the sturdy but irregular shaped wood strips on our side of the door. He almost had enough to cover the whole door, but there were a few places you could still see the door peeking through. He'd done the best he could with what we had. Ryan and Owen were boarding up the windows on the first floor. They left as few gaps in between each piece of wood as possible. Dean went to help them but moments later dashed up the stairs with more wood.

With each window that got boarded up, it got darker and darker in the house even though it was only midday. Sienna and I started searching for matches for the candles. It didn't take long to find a lighter stashed away in a kitchen drawer next to a hidden pack of cigarettes wrapped neatly in a dishtowel. Someone hadn't succeeded at quitting their nasty habit. We set up one candle in the living room and one on the kitchen table. It would provide us enough light for now, we couldn't risk burning out all of the candles before nightfall.

Seth had fallen asleep, and Sienna was munching on a toaster pastry. I decided to check out the house. The first floor had the living room and the dining area with the kitchen, laundry and garage off to the right. There was also a nice sized pantry that needed to be cleaned out. Down the hallway to the left was the first floor bathroom, and an office area that was piled with papers, mail, books and other junk. Further down the hall was the master bedroom and a slightly smaller bedroom that looked like it hadn't been used in years. The master bedroom had a small private bathroom and a large walk-in closet. Based on the clothing in the closet, it had been an older couple that lived here, which is perhaps why it appeared that it hadn't been used as a farm in a while. None of the clothing would be useful. I tried to imagine the couple, where had they been when the storm hit? What had happened to them? If they had stayed in their home, maybe they would still be here since the house had mostly survived the storms.

Upstairs was another bathroom and three bedrooms, two of which weren't used. The third belonged to a preteen based on the decor and the clothing in the closet. Maybe a grandchild stayed here often enough to have their own room, or maybe they lived with their grandparents full time. I didn't know why I needed to have a story for the family that lived here but for some reason I did.

It was several degrees warmer upstairs. I wouldn't be able to get any sleep with it being so hot, I would probably struggle with it either way, but I made it my personal goal to snag one of the downstairs bedrooms. That's just me being selfish. Again. The only problem with the master bedroom is that it had two windows so it felt a little less safe but once they were boarded up I imagined it would be OK.

I was heading back downstairs as Ryan and Owen were coming up the stairs to help Dean with the windows. Ryan and I made eye contact. I wished I could read his mind, so I knew what he was thinking. He was skilled at hiding most of his thoughts and emotions, especially when it came to the ones that were secret feelings he had towards another person.

I grabbed a granola bar, a bottle of water and my novel from my new pack. I lit the smallest candle I could find in the pile and went to the master bedroom, in a weak attempt to claim it as my own. Whether or not it would work was another story.

Chapter nine.

When I woke up, it was the middle of the night and I was alone in the master bedroom. Someone had come in, blown out the candle, and put my book on the nightstand. There was a light coming from the living room and a teeny bit of moonlight coming from the tiny cracks between the wood strips in the window. It was easy enough to see my way around. When I stubbed my toe on a chair along the way, it wasn't because of the lighting, it had more to do with not being used to the layout of the home.

I peeked into the room next to mine but I couldn't tell who was lying in the bed. It was far too dark inside the room to make out anything besides the general shape of a person. Seth was sleeping on the couch and a single candle on the table was providing the light. I had to use the bathroom, so I borrowed the candle off the table and put it back when I had finished. I tried not to make too much noise but Seth grumbled something, turned slightly and fell back asleep. Even with rest he wasn't doing any better with the heat. I had legitimate concerns for his health and I'm sure the others felt the same.

I went back to my room when a big crack of thunder startled me and I stumbled backwards and fell. I wasn't sure but I think I made a strange vocalization and it must have been louder than I thought because Ryan appeared in front of me. Behind me I could hear Seth hobbling closer.

"What happened? Are you OK?" Ryan asked looking me over in the darkness to see if I had been hurt. He helped me up while Seth held on to the wall and watched over us with a concerned expression.

"I'm fine," I said with a little laugh, "the thunder scared me is all."

"What thunder?" Seth asked, clearly it hadn't been loud enough to wake him up.

They both looked at me like I was crazy and listened intently. "Stay with her," Ryan ordered and rushed to the back door, our only door not boarded closed. We had to board up the door that led to the garage until we could figure out what to do about the garage door, so we left the back door alone, so we could come and go easier.

I watched him from the hallway, he kept himself hidden as he peered out the openings that remained between the boards. He looked all around and kept searching for the source of what I thought was thunder. He came back after making sure the back door was secure. "It doesn't appear to be storming, no rain, clear skies as far as I can tell. I'm not sure what you could have—"

And there it was again a big boom-like thunder, but now I had been paying better attention

I knew it wasn't thunder. Ryan ran to the front window, "Blow out the candle!"

Whatever it was, he spotted it, because he stared and didn't move, heck, I don't think he was even breathing while he peeked out between the slits.

"What is it?" Seth asked quietly.

"Should I wake the others?" I asked nervously.

"Shh!" Ryan said waving us silent.

I sneaked up to the window next to Ryan and peered out, at first I didn't see them, but when I did they were too close for comfort. About a mile down the road, out in a field, I couldn't tell how many were out there, but there they were, out in a field blowing up fireworks. Not just puny fireworks you can get at those little firework stands that pop up randomly around the fourth of July, but real, big, fireworks. They were booming and echoing like thunder. It would take them about ten or fifteen minutes to light one and then reset for the next. You could hear a faint cheer after the firework exploded and lit up the skies.

"Do you think they know we're here?" I whispered.

"I don't think so," he whispered back, his breath lightly dancing across my neck.

"I would have much preferred a rain storm," Seth said not noticing or acknowledging the new tension between me and Ryan. "Might have cooled things down." He was too busy thinking about the temperature.

After some time there hadn't been any more

fireworks, I figured they must have run out. A car
with bright lights was slowly coming down the
road. Outside of the passenger window someone
was holding a big flood light some people use to
shine for deer. They were using it to scan the
fields. But I didn't know what they were looking
for. People? Items they could use? Animals?
They were passing it back and forth from the
passenger side to the driver side slowly scanning.
The light brushed across the house briefly, this time
they didn't pass the light back to the passenger side.
There were definitely going to scan the house.

"Do they have a candle lit upstairs?" Ryan
asked.

"I'm not sure I was…." Before I could
finish he was running up the stairs to make sure it
was absolutely dark. I stayed at the window
watching them get closer and closer. "They are
almost here," I updated Seth as I heard Ryan
creeping back downstairs much quieter than he had
gone up them.

The car was going painfully slow but now
they were almost directly across from the window,
they lit up the house with the bright spotlight. Ryan
pulled me behind the wall so no part of me could be
seen through the crack of the window. Or so I
didn't make any kind of unusual shadow. We could
hear the car taking its good old time passing. The
flood light lit up the whole living room even from
as far back as the road. The light shined through
the cracks between the planks of wood making
strange shadows on the walls.

The car sped up, turned the light off and

drove down the road. Thankfully they weren't looking for a home of their own and were likely getting their supplies from town, they didn't have much of a reason to stop at this random home. Did they notice the windows boarded up? Would that be a clue someone was here? Maybe they'd just assume the windows were boarded up because of the storms. Maybe they hadn't noticed. Unless they'd been around here before and saw that the windows hadn't been boarded up until now. I really wished it would have just been a passing thunderstorm.

Ryan stood watching until he couldn't see the car any more. They were gone. "We really need to get weapons," Ryan said finally taking a noticeable breath, "and something other than baseball bats."

"Do we know they had weapons? All we know is that they had a car, a flood light and some fireworks," I said.

"Hopefully we'll never have to use the guns, but we need them for protection. Even if it's only to scare people off," Ryan said shaking his head, "It's not like only the good people in the world survived. I'd guess only the toughest, smartest and luckiest did. And even good people can turn bad in the worst kind of situations. Situations like this."

Seth had drifted back to sleep, he was just so worn out that any activity was too much. It being eighty-five degrees in the house, even in the middle of the night surely didn't help matters. There was no break, no chance to cool down.

"Let him sleep," I said nodding towards the

116

bedrooms, "He needs the rest."

We decided to leave the candle out, we'd have to test where we could put candles in the house so that they wouldn't be seen if you were outside. Maybe find some curtains or blankets we could put up to hide the light better. It would be morning in a few more hours, and there would be enough light to see your way around, or I so imagined. Even in the day with the windows boarded up it would still be dark. We would probably need to use the candles when it was light out and we assumed a candle inside wouldn't be spotted by an outsider during the day. The sunlight would drown out any light from the candle.

I turned to go into my bedroom. Ryan grabbed my hand stopping me in the doorway. His face was twisted, I couldn't read it.

"Will you be all right?" he asked

"Yeeesss," I said smiling at him. "I'm a big girl Ryan, I can take care of myself," I added trying to sound tough, when in fact I didn't know if I was OK. Heck, I didn't even know if I could take care of myself. The only reason I was even here now was because of them, I was one of the lucky. If I'd been by myself like the kid across the street, I surely wouldn't have survived to even join up with the circus gang. I hate to think what would have happened to me if I had been alone. But he didn't need to know that. It was better for both of us, all of us, if we all thought I was smarter and tougher than I really was.

"I don't know if any of us can really just take care of ourselves anymore," he said looking at his feet, "we all need each other."

"I'll be fine, good night." I squeezed his hand and gently pulled mine away before it got to the point where I wouldn't be able to pull it away. Or that I wouldn't be able to fall back asleep.

"If you need anything, I'll be right here, anything at all!" He was being protective, perhaps overly so, but at the same time it was really sweet. I'd never really had anyone, except maybe my own mother care that much for me before. He reached down and lightly brushed my dirty blond hair out of my face, the backs of his fingers lightly brushing against my cheek. That simple gesture overpowered the logical part of my brain instantly, the softness, the gentleness, my eyes lightly closed and I leaned into his hand. He turned his hand and slid his fingertips along the side of my neck, towards the back causing the hair on my arms to tingle.

I suddenly felt like I was floating on a cloud and not trapped in the bland darkness of God-knows-whose house. He tilted my head and slowly moved towards my face stopping only millimeters away, "is this all right?" he whispered. I nodded. His other hand found his way to the other side of my neck within seconds, and I waited for the kiss.

"Ahh… umm." Dean coughed.

Ryan dropped me like a hot potato and I stumbled backwards a half step. I glared at the back of his head. "What is it?" he sounded like an annoyed father. I left the scene and went back to bed, I turned my back to the door, but tried to listen to what they were talking about. Dean was asking what was going on outside and Ryan updated him about the fireworks and the car. Then I heard someone use the bathroom, and Dean going back upstairs. I sensed Ryan pause at my doorway, but I pretended I was asleep. I breathed slowly and held still until I heard the door creak as he partially closed it. Then I heard the creaking of his bedsprings as he climbed into bed.

I was frustrated with how he'd reacted when Dean saw us, I didn't even know how much Dean saw, just that he saw us close to each other. It was so dark there was no way he could have figured out what was going on, but the way he interrupted made it sound like he knew he was interrupting something. But for Ryan to just practically jump out of his skin to get away from me, well, it was insulting. For all I knew Dean just thought we were discussing what happened with the car because who would think something else would be going on?

This is what happens when you start letting yourself fall for someone. You get hurt, annoyed and just can't concentrate on the real things that need the attention, such as survival. It was time to forget about any kind of silly relationship and focus on what we needed to live. Survival of the fittest, isn't that what they say? Well, a relationship right now wouldn't really work now would it? Over it. The end. There was nothing to be over because nothing ever was. Thanks to Dean nothing happened. I continued repeating those things trying to convince myself until I fell asleep.

Chapter ten.

I peeked out of the window and guessed the time based on where the sun was in the sky. I estimated it had to be somewhere between 10:00 and 11:00 a.m. when I woke up. I must have had some sleep I needed to catch up on. When I walked out to the living room the others were already gathered around the kitchen table discussing the plans for the day without waiting for me. I was annoyed they hadn't waited for me. And now that I was annoyed about that, I was reminded about how annoyed I was with Ryan last night when he pushed away from me, which doubled my annoyance factor for the day. Not good considering it's still morning. This is what they mean when they say 'you woke up on the wrong side of the bed' I guess. It didn't matter which side I would have picked, either way it would have been the wrong side.

"Good morning sleepy-head," Dean said with a wink. Who winks? Yeah, I decided that was annoying too.

A troll-like grunt went along with the scowl I was now wearing, "So what are you all discussing?" I said trying to make it painfully obvious I was annoyed they were having this conversation without me.

"Not much, just listing what we need to accomplish today," Seth said. He didn't look much better than yesterday but he was sitting at the table participating so he had to be doing somewhat better.

"Right." Ryan jumped in not making eye contact with me, "First we need to make a run to town for gas for the generator, build up our food and water supplies but most importantly, number one on today's list, find weapons."

I nodded as if it mattered. "So who's going?"

Owen stepped forward, "Me for sure."

"First does anyone here know anything about guns?" I asked looking at them.

"I already asked that," Ryan said trying not to sound like a jackass but failing miserably.

"Yeah, I hunted with my dad," Owen said, "So I can shoot, although, in all honesty I'm not a great shot, and I've only ever shot at deer with a rifle. It goes without saying never at people with a handgun."

"We took archery at camp," Dean said gesturing at Sienna, and she beamed thinking she might have a skill that could come in handy.

"Oh," I said sounding disappointed. I wasn't really all that disappointed, but I felt left out and useless. Everything had already been taken care of and everyone seemed to have familiarity of some kind with a weapon. Except for me of course. Yet again, I was the weak link.

If the others picked up on my defeated body

language, they ignored it. No one went out of their way to make me feel included or bring my spirits up. I walked to my backpack and took out a bottle of water and chugged it. Water was going fast, at least mine was.

"Yeah, we need more water," Ryan said seeing me gazing at my empty bottle, "and soon, so we should go?" He motioned at Owen and they both started emptying their packs on the floor. "Hey Ros maybe you and Sienna could find a way to organize our stuff?" he added before taking Dean's pack and emptying it into the pile inconsiderately. He could have at least not made such a mess of things if he expected me and Sienna to clean it up.

"Uhh…." I rolled my eyes as big as I could manage, "Sure." I sighed and flopped down into the recliner. This is how I'd be useful, by being the housemaid. I guess I should have just been pleased I was being included in something.

"Maybe I should come too," Dean offered. "I'll know the bows, and I can come back with a pack of food and water while you guys find gas."

"Yeah sounds good, except I'm not sure you coming back here alone is a great idea," Ryan said scratching his head.

Dean grinned, "Well I'd have my new friend with me, I think I would be all right."

"Hmm… well, OK, I guess. If you're sure?"

"I'm sure."

The boys got ready quickly. Owen was going to carry two packs, Ryan one pack plus the gas can and Dean emptied Sienna's pack into the pile. They'd get a good haul of items as long as they could find the stores with supplies still left. Hopefully nothing too far away— they planned to be back before night.

"Don't forget you have the baseball bats, and your knife. Carry it with you at all times, you know, just in case someone should come poking around," Ryan said putting on a baseball cap and a pair of sunglasses he'd found in a drawer. "And lock this door once we are out. Don't go outside and don't open the door for anyone."

"We know," I said saturating the words with rudeness.

"Look," Ryan said, he was going to try to explain something until he realized everyone was waiting on him for the go-ahead, "Can we talk about this later?"

"I'm not going anywhere," I said and practically shoved the three of them out of the door and made a grand gesture to show I'd locked the door behind them. After I locked the door I made a mental note to search for a spare key so they would be able to get back in easily. That way they wouldn't have to wait for someone to open the door for them.

Sienna watched me stomp away to my bedroom, she called out after me asking if I was OK. I took a breath and shouted back, "I'm fine, just tired I guess."

After some time to myself, I came back into the room to find her organizing the pile of goods that had been dumped out of the backpacks. "I sort of felt like I was being excluded this morning. I should be a part of the group, everyone probably just thought I was being lazy," I said as if I need to justify why I had left the room.

"Sorry Ros that wasn't our intention. Ryan thought you were tired, and he said we should just let you rest," Sienna explained.

"Well, that's not his call," I said stiffening my spine.

Seth was watching them walk off through a crack in the window curtains making sure everything went smoothly for as long as he could see them. Instead of taking the roads, they walked through the dead and dry crusty fields towards town. Once they were out of view he came and sat at the kitchen table and helped us sort as best as he could. He was still exhausted and miserable. I didn't think he'd be better until he got a fan or some way to cool down. Although he was helping which certainly was a step in the right direction but he needed to cool down his body.

Today seemed like it was going to be even hotter than it had been yesterday. If it kept getting hotter every day, eventually we'd all get run down and none of us would get anything done. Maybe Ryan would be able to find gas for the generator, and it would work. Then we could get some fans running to help cool things down.

After we finished organizing the stuff from the packs we decided to clear out the cabinets, pantry and fridge of everything that was expired. We were going to make room for the new items they'd be bringing back that we could use. We'd found some garbage bags under the sink and threw out everything that was unusable for the cabinets and pantry. The dreadful rotting smell was overwhelming when I opened the fridge, and I started tossing everything into a bag. When we were finished we had two full bags of trash.

"That smell is only going to get worse in the house," Seth said.

"Yeah, you're right," I said scrunching up my nose and refusing to admit to not having thought this through. "Should I bring them out to the storage shed?"

"Maybe," Seth said. "I wish we could wait until the others got back."

I thought about setting them in the garage, but that door was boarded up too, I'd have to go outside and open the garage door to get inside. "Well, I'll just drop them outside the back door, we can figure it out later," I said hauling them to the back door. I looked outside to be sure it was safe and then I opened the door, gently tossing each bag against the bricks of the house. I closed the door and locked it quickly. Then I made sure the curtains on the door weren't swaying, paranoid that even the smallest thing could be a giveaway that someone was inside. We also had to keep them closed tight, leaving only the smallest peek hole, so we could see when the others returned.

* * *

I'm not sure how many hours had passed before Dean returned because I had fallen asleep in the chair watching over Seth. I was changing the cloth on his head, every ten minutes or so, whenever he'd start moaning and groaning in misery. Sienna was sitting at the table writing in a notebook she'd found. Eventually he fell asleep and then I must have dozed off as well.

There was a light knock on the door which startled me. It also made me think we should come up with a secret knock. That way we'd at least know when it was one of us, or maybe it would be easier to try and find a set of keys like I had planned. Sienna peeked out just enough to see, "Dean's back!" She popped up to let him in.

"Wait!" I said right as her hand touched the door lock.

"What?"

"Just make sure he's alone," I said sounding paranoid.

"OK!" she said looking around, "He's alone as far as I can tell."

She opened the lock and Dean slipped inside. He closed the door, locked it and checked to make sure it was secured. He had a backpack stuffed tight, a bag filled with arrows and two bows. How he'd made it back in this heat carrying all of it was impressive. He peeled off his shirt which was stuck to him like an orange peel. He yanked two half gallons of water out of his pack pushed one of them against me and ordered me to follow him. I think it was mostly out of curiosity that I did follow without asking any questions.

Sienna just shrugged and went back to whatever it was she was writing as I followed Dean into the bathroom. He shut the door behind us. "OK, I need you to pour this over me," he said as if this wasn't the most awkward thing ever. "Take your socks off," he demanded. It was weird to have Dean being so bossy when he was usually more of a sit back, take it easy, kind of guy. While I took them off, he laid a towel on the side of the shower, "Stand up here and hold on to the towel bar with your free hand."

There I was standing on the side of the shower holding onto a half gallon of water while Dean finished undressing. I looked away the second I saw everything was coming off. I realized why he wasn't able to ask Sienna for help and Seth would have been incapable, but couldn't he have just done this himself?

He was in the shower, "OK ready!" All the things I shouldn't see weren't really visible from my angle. Not that I was looking, but I had to at least watch where I was pouring. It would just be wasteful if I wasn't actually pouring the water on him. I poured slowly to make sure the water would last. Only about a quarter of the first jug remained when he asked me how much was left, "I'm going to try to wash my hair." He took the shampoo bottle off of the bottom ledge of the tub and quickly lathered up his dark sepia hair, "OK ready again." I started pouring again trying to make sure I got all the soap out while he tried to squish it out with his fingers at the same time.

"Hold on," I said as I grabbed the other jug,

"OK, ready?"

"Yeah," he said waiting with his hands in his hair.

It was important to get all the shampoo out of his hair. After I finished what was left of the first jug I started to pour from the second one being extra careful. I wanted to make sure to rinse every inch of his hair completely.

"That's it," I said when the jug was empty.

"Great, thanks Ros."

I carefully climbed down keeping my head down. I had safely made it passed him without seeing anything.

"Could you hand me a towel?" he asked as if he had waited to the precise moment that would be the most contrived. I could feel his eyes on me. I couldn't give him the one I had been standing on there had been too much splashing. Without turning I took another clean one out of the drawer and handed it to him over my shoulder. "Thanks," he said, I could sense the smile on his face based on his tone, this whole escapade was amusing him but I wasn't sure why. Dean must have had an odd sense of humor.

I slipped out of the bathroom to come face to face with Ryan, "You're back!" I said sounding more surprised than I would have liked, especially since Dean came out seconds after me with just a towel wrapped around his waist. Droplets of water fell off the wet peaks of his clean hair.

"Excuse me," he said squeezing between us. He bounced up the stairs leaving me there by myself to explain. This looked bad. Very bad.

Ryan didn't wait for an explanation, not that it mattered in the least since all words were currently being held hostage by my voice box. Ryan shut the door to his room. I stared at it for about thirty seconds before heading to the kitchen table to see what they brought back.

On the table they had all the food, water and other supplies such as candles, batteries and flashlights, towels, T-shirts and more that Sienna and I would have to sort through later. I stopped in my tracks when I saw the guns lined up on the kitchen counter. A lump in my throat started to form, getting larger and larger threatening to choke me.

"Do we have to keep those here?" I asked pointing a droopy finger. My voice vibrated due to my nerves. Before all this happened, I don't think I had ever even seen a gun other than on TV.

"Uh, yeah," Owen said looking at me like I was crazy or that maybe I had completely forgotten what the world was like now, and maybe for a minute, I had. It wasn't like all the guns were just going to start firing on their own, but it didn't matter I just didn't like them. Guns were dangerous but if it was a matter of life or death, well, I'd have to be more open to them. I knew relatively nothing about them, I saw big ones and small ones and various packs of bullets. "Ros, I'll show you how to shoot. You'll feel better then," Owen said.

"I thought you hunted deer?"

"Yeah but I had to learn to shoot to hunt those deer," Owen beamed, "now aiming and actually hitting your target, well that's another

129

thing."

"But with a rifle."

"How much different can it be?" he said shrugging.

I crossed my arms, not wanting any part with the guns but knowing I'd have to be able to protect myself or if it came to it, one of the others. The bow would be too complicated and I'd be too slow. My knife wouldn't be helpful except only at a very close range, and the baseball bat wouldn't be any better. I'd have to try and come to terms with the fact that life now included having guns around.

Dean came trotting back down the stairs and examined the gun collection. He completely ignored me and the fact that I'd just seen him, sort of seen him, completely naked. We were just not going to talk about it, and I guess there wasn't really anything to talk about anyway. It's not like anything happened. Dean hadn't been the least bit shy about his body, not even an ounce. If anything, he seemed almost eager to show it off and to be honest from what I did see, he didn't have anything to be embarrassed about.

Ryan came out of his room wearing a new set of clothing, his hair still damp from sweat. He'd grabbed a gun, looked it over and stuffed it in the back of his waistband, slid on his sunglasses and stepped outside. Owen grabbed a gun, mimicked Ryan and put on his own new pair of sunglasses which were far too small for his face, "We got gas, going to help Ryan with the generator," he said as he disappeared. At least he had told us where he was going.

* * *

After an hour or so, I heard the generator start up, and it continued to run. Sienna and I had finished organizing the take from today's run. Dean was in the living room chair tinkering with his bow, and Seth was watching him while he lay down with a wet cloth on his head and neck. I was dripping with sweat from all the activity of the day, my clothes were wet and my hair stuck to my face and neck. I had considered asking Sienna for help with a shower, but there wasn't any spare water jugs for me. Dean had brought his own special jugs of water back just for his shower.

The day was winding down when Owen and Ryan came back inside looking proud of themselves, "It works!" Owen cheered. "Let's see what else we can get to work."

They walked around trying lights and Ryan stopped to listen to the fridge which kicked in when the door was opened. "What happened to everything that was in here?" he demanded.

"I cleaned it out earlier. All the junk is outside stuffed into a couple of garbage bags," I said nodding towards the back door but not looking at him.

"Ros, what were you thinking?"

"Excuse me?"

"That couldn't be any more obvious of a sign that someone is here... trash! Think about it,"

131

Ryan said sounding like an absolute jerk.

"You didn't notice it when you were out there!"

"I wasn't paying attention! I was trying to get the generator to work," he said angrily. "For someone who was paying attention... well surely they'd notice trash bags appearing suddenly."

"I figured we could just hide it in the shed or garage," I shrugged.

"That's going to stink in this heat. Obviously we can't put it in the garage." Ryan sighed and tapped his foot as if he was dealing with someone who wasn't very smart. "I guess we'll have to put it in the shed for now and bury it or something," he said sounding exasperated. The way he was talking to me was rude and embarrassing and happening in front of everyone.

"Come on man, she was just trying to help," Dean jumped in trying to defend me. Obviously it was the last person Ryan wanted to hear talk right now. Ryan took a step towards him and glared, more than ready to pick a fight. Dean eagerly stood up and stepped into Ryan's personal space ready to accept the challenge. The shift in the air had to have been noticed by everyone.

Owen's radar instantly picked up on it and he stood between them like a brick wall, turning to face Ryan, "Hey man, you should hide that in the shed now before it gets too dark out." The sound of Owen's voice breaking the invisible force between them was enough to get Ryan to storm out of the dining room, slamming the door behind him. My body shuttered with the door.

"I can do——." I started to offer since I was the reason the bags were out there, but was quickly cut off by Owen's simple yet effective hand gesture.

"He needs the air." Owen took a deep breath and sighed trying to change the atmosphere. The rest of us were still holding our breath and our bodies were motionless.

"But it was my mess, I should take care of it," I said upset with myself. I should have thought things through before I cleaned out the fridge. The smell inside the fridge had been so putrid, it had only been a matter of time before it smelled up the whole house. At the time I hadn't considered the generator, but then again it wasn't like they were going to let it run all day and night. That would guzzle too much fuel and add too much noise. Right or wrong I still should have been the one to deal with it. I considered going out to help Ryan, but I was probably the last person he wanted to see, or at least the second to last.

"More importantly," he turned to Dean, "What's going on with you and Ryan? You guys were fine this morning. You both better get it together."

Dean sat back down and returned to busying himself with his bow, "Nothing man, it's all good." Dean glanced up at me just ever so quickly. It was so fast I wasn't sure it had even happened. He wasn't about to get on Owen's bad side, he and Owen were friends before all this happened. He trusted Owen and knew when to stop testing his limits. If Owen wanted him to cool it, he'd do it.

"Let's go upstairs and see if we can find good places to shoot from if we should need to defend our fortress," Owen joked attempting to lighten the mood. Dean followed him upstairs. Owen probably was just going to try to get him alone so he could find out what was going on. What I would give to be a fly on that wall.

Ryan came back and went straight to the basement. I debated about whether or not I should go after him, tell him I was sorry about leaving the bags outside in such a noticeable spot, but he was stomping back up before I could decide. He had been looking for a fan for Seth and found one. He plugged it in and aimed the slightly cool wind in his direction. I freshened up the washcloth on his forehead and it wasn't long before Seth was thanking Ryan.

"I feel better already," he said, "so much better."

"You should eat something," I told him. "Let me get you something."

I brought him a cereal bar and some water. He ate and drank slowly but he did seem to be improving. His eyes were open and his breathing more relaxed. "Too bad I won't be able to leave this spot," he teased but with a dash of truth mixed in.

"Aw Seth! You'll see once you recharge you'll be much better!" I smiled at him and went to the kitchen to put what water we had in the fridge so we could have it cold. I tried the stove top and was surprised when the burner started working, I'd be able to boil water if we could get some from the sink, rain or other sources. My mind went to worrying about whether anyone passing by would hear the generator and what that would mean for us.

After I'd grabbed something to eat I went to my room to read my book. It was getting dark and any light that filtered through the wooden boards was vanishing. I lit my candle and closed the curtains to help ensure the light stayed inside. I was sick of being in sweaty clothes so I darted out to grab one of the new T-shirts assuming they were for whoever needed one.

Back in my room, I undressed and put on the T-shirt that thankfully was an extra-large size. I may be swimming it in but it kept me covered, and it felt great to be in a clean shirt. My only wish was that I could have washed my hair. Maybe now that I can boil water I'd actually get to have a warm bath soon instead of just cleaning with a washcloth. I fantasized about soap, everything about it, the lather, the scent, and how clean I'd feel after rinsing it away. The thought made me smile.

I settled in bed and spent the rest of the night reading, daydreaming, and eventually falling asleep.

Chapter eleven.

As the weeks passed, the boys, and always just the boys, gathered more and more supplies of all kinds. We had started to clean out space in the basement to store and organizing all of our goods. Ryan would get gas cans and fill them whenever he could for the generator which we stored in the shed out back. We'd only run the generator at night and only for a few hours or if someone needed to cool down with the fan. The heat hadn't let up, we just got better at managing how we handled it and maybe a little more used to it too.

Seth was somewhat back to normal although he continued to be affected by the heat when he overworked himself. On the nights we decided to run the generator, he would be the one sitting by the fan in the living room. But at least he'd been able to be up and help out more often. He'd spent a lot of time in the basement building shelving for our supplies because it was cooler down there and he could accomplish more. I could tell he felt useful when he was down there helping with the shelving and organizing. His shelving design always had me feeling like I was in a little store when I went down to get something, everything organized, facing outward, shelves always stocked, it was actually quite amazing. People would kill for it.

They'd brought home a DVD player and were constantly bringing movies back which it turned out were pretty easy to find, it was something no one who was out there trying to survive wanted. We had all the newest movies, well newest back when there were people who were actually making movies. A few times a week we'd have movie night, everyone all together. Just like we had done at the shelter. Seth, Owen and Dean sat on the couch, Ryan in one chair and me in the other. Sienna always lounged on the floor. She'd lay there on her stomach with her face propped up on her hands. I'd pop popcorn on the stove for everyone and once in a while a rare treat of soda on ice. It was a night everyone looked forward to, even Ryan. After a while, repeating our daily schedule week after week, we all sort of fell into a nice comfortable routine, just as we had back in Ryan's shelter. Everyone did their job and everyone pitched in with something, we all wanted to, no one had to be forced. I think, at least for me, it kept me sane to stay busy and do things that helped.

Ryan had distanced himself from me, not that he had ever really been near me. I never said anything about any of it and assumed I had imagined the whole thing. He'd only tell me things he felt he needed to tell me, which wasn't much. Anything he needed me to know, the others needed to know too, and he'd tell us all at the same time. I would spend any free time I had reading by candlelight, and I really came to enjoy it since it helped me escape this dreadful world.

They wouldn't ever let me or Sienna go on runs. Ryan or Owen would tell us maybe we could go on the next one and then quickly change the subject and ask if I needed anything and to make a list.

On their runs they had picked out our clothing, and they were horrible at it. They never brought back anything that was my style, but they picked out things that were clean and durable and that's all I needed or cared about. Sometimes I'd just look down at myself and laugh, thinking they had to be doing it on purpose but I couldn't call them out on it, in case they weren't and I'd hurt their feelings. So I'd just wear it and be happy I had something that was new.

We had enough water saved that we could take very shallow baths. You'd want to plug the drain, soap yourself up and splash yourself clean. It wasn't fun or relaxing, but it worked. And with the heat, it didn't matter the water from the basement was cold, in fact it felt better when it was cold. You'd come out feeling refreshed and cool for a while until your body rewarmed which happened too quickly.

Everything was going relatively smooth albeit boring. Everyone seemed happy, well happy enough considering. Ryan and Owen even brought me home a new book to read on their last trip which I was excited to dive into. They'd bring me books whenever they'd come across one, books were pretty easy to find too, but less so, and many were damaged. Once they brought me one from a run that I really liked, I read it in two days. All except for the last twenty pages or so that had been smeared from some sort of liquid. I made up my own ending but still thoroughly enjoyed the story.

It was about dinner time when I heard the noisy car pull up in front of the house. A panicked look spread across the faces of the others the second they heard it too. We were prepared for something like this, but at the same time, we weren't prepared for something like this.

The noisy engine was cut and the car doors slammed shut as whoever it was exited their car.

Chapter twelve.

Dean dashed upstairs in what sounded like three bounding steps. He didn't come back down. I imagined he had his arrow pointed at someone. It was almost as if he had done drills where he trained for this and knew exactly what he would do. He had been prepared, I wished I could have said the same for myself.

Owen grabbed his weapon off the counter from where he usually kept it when he was downstairs. He always took it with him when he went up to bed for the night. Ryan pulled his out of the back of his pants, which was where he most often kept his for easy access. Seth took a baseball bat as Owen still hadn't shown us how to shoot. Ryan didn't want him to risk it, the noise would bring too much attention and maybe he was right but it left the two of us sort of defenseless. Owen had given us a brief lesson on how to use the gun, but we never actually got to practice shooting or aiming. Right now I wished we would have, then maybe I wouldn't feel as terrified as I did.

I felt like a ninja as I silently sprinted for my knife which I hid under my mattress.

"Shhh!" Ryan said waving his hands at us.

I needed to know what was going on so I went up to the window beside him and looked out from where I thought I wouldn't be seen.

Ryan motioned for Sienna to go upstairs but she was frozen just standing there in the middle of the living room. "Get down," he whispered aggressively, but she didn't move. He soundlessly dove towards her and yanked her back into the hallway where they were both completely out of site. If they came up to the windows and peeked in, they wouldn't see anyone. I hoped.

Seth was standing on the side of the door ready to swing his bat should anyone get through, which was unlikely, it was boarded up securely. I was pushed against the wall on the other side of the window behind the chair I usually sat in during movies. I wasn't exactly sure were Owen was but I was certain he was around and ready.

I peeked out of the window again, and I swear I heard Ryan sigh. In my quick glance I saw that it was four, possibly five people wandering in the front yard. One of them may have been a girl with her head shaved all except for her purple and black mohawk ponytail. They looked like they were in a punk rock band. They wore leather jackets and had dreadful hairstyles, dark eye makeup, and of course guns of their own. The one that I thought might have been a girl had her gun on her hip and followed a male with spiky hair as he approached the door.

Bang bang bang!

The door rattled but didn't budge even

though he pounded hard, as if he was hoping to accidentally pound it down by sheer brute force. He pounded again, and I curled up behind the chair watching the door jiggle with each knock. I couldn't stop seeing a scenario play out in my head in which the door was ripped into shreds and popped open with a kick.

"Anyone home?" he said followed by the laughter of his hyena minions. Did they already know that we were in here? Had they seen Ryan and Owen and followed them? The boys were way too smart for that, they'd have never led anyone back here at least not intentionally. I suppose it was possible they could have been followed without them knowing and tracked back here or was it purely a coincidence? Maybe it's just what this group did, going door to door searching for people or supplies. Or maybe they smelled the trash bags I'd filled. I never did find out if Ryan had ever buried them.

Bang, bang!

He pounded a third time. I saw them move to investigate the house. I knew they were circling around because they were dragging something, a stick or maybe their own baseball bat, along the window and it made a screeching noise against the glass. Then it scratched against the exterior wall where I sat. I hugged myself and buried my face into my arms holding my fear inside as tightly as I could. The scratching got fainter as they moved around towards the bathroom then my room and then I didn't hear it again until it was at the back of the house.

That's when I noticed the curtain hadn't been closed all the way and they'd see me and Seth clear as day. "Seth!" I whispered. He didn't hear me he was following the noise with his eyes, "Seth, the curtain! Move... NOW!" I whispered again only a hair louder. At the last second he crouched behind a chair that was barely bigger than him and I made myself into the smallest ball behind my chair. The bearded man looked inside, and I was terrified at seeing a stranger so close to our new home that I began to shake. I was worried I was shaking so hard the floorboards were moving and shaking everything in the house. And I worried that if I could see him, wouldn't he be able to see me? If he had, he ignored me and moved along the kitchen continuing to drag his scratchy thing. When they got back to the front of the house I could hear them discussing something, but I couldn't understand the mumbles. Only by tone could I tell they were trying to decide what they should do.

First I heard a rattling noise, and then what sounded like a weird grinding noise. I realized they had opened the garage door. Owen and Ryan must not have ever figured out a way to secure it or maybe they hadn't tried too hard with everything else they had been doing to gather supplies for us to live. They were in the garage now scrounging around. Ryan had put Sienna in the bathroom, I'd heard the faintest door click and he was crawling military style towards the kitchen keeping his gun pointed towards the door that led to the garage. Seth and I didn't move, and I still didn't know where Owen was. I hoped Dean would stay upstairs until someone came and got him, or if he heard he was needed for backup. I didn't know if he could hear them futzing around in the garage or for that matter, how much he heard of any of what was going on while he was up there.

"Open it," one of them said.

"It's locked."

"Try harder."

And there was kicking and pounding. My body jumped with each one. I felt a tear stream down my cheek and then a matching one on the other side. The second was because I was upset with myself for being such a coward.

"This one's boarded up too."

"Aw shit man we'll have to come back with something. Let's go, probably nothing here anyway."

"There is probably something in there, something good, since it's boarded up," a third person said.

Then they closed the garage door and walked out front. Someone threw something at the house and I jumped again almost letting out a noise but I stopped myself. Seth was back at the front door ready with his bat, so I peered up through a crack to see if I could see what they were doing. They were walking away. All except for the one that was at the window. He popped into view only inches from my face. I fell back covering my mouth with both shaking hands to keep myself from screaming. I prayed to everything and anything holy that he didn't see me. He tapped the glass with his fingernail where my face had been.

144

"Let's go!" someone shouted to him.

"Yeah I'm coming!" his voice so clear through the window.

Had his window tap been a message? Had he seen me? If he had he would have told the others. Maybe he was testing the thickness of the glass? I didn't know. Right now, I didn't care. I didn't breathe again until I heard the car drive off and could no longer hear the car engine. I was still unable to move.

"Are you OK?" Seth asked reaching his hand out to me. I couldn't take it, my arms didn't work. I was stuck, I felt paralyzed. This is where I was going to be the rest of my life, curled up into a terrified ball behind this chair.

I shook my head unable to respond.

Ryan returned to the living room with Sienna and sat her down on the couch. She was visibly shaken too, but she was movable. That made me angry. The freshman was tougher than I was. I wasn't exactly sure when it had happened but I was standing.

The stairs creaked loudly as Dean come down them rapidly. Owen was standing near the kitchen table. They were all looking at me, their mouths were moving but nothing was coming out. Everything started to spin and get fuzzy, and the last thing I heard was Ryan saying "Oh shit," as he took a step towards me.

* * *

When I came to, I was lying on the couch with a cool cloth on my forehead, Ryan was perched over me. Dean and Owen were at my feet, Sienna sat on the chair with her arms folded looking annoyed. I heard Seth dragging the chair I had been hiding behind back into place.

"You OK?" Ryan asked as he loosely pinched at my hand.

"Mmm… yeah. What happened?" I asked sitting up and removing the damp cloth from my lap after I noticed it had fallen off my head. I gasped at the pain I felt, and I reached back to feel a big goose egg had formed, "My head?"

"You fainted," Dean said walking around the coffee table and sitting beside me with a concerned look on his face. Then it all came rushing back at full force and I flinched at the memory. My whole body jerked thinking about the men coming and snooping around our home. In this heat, of at least 100 degrees, I shivered. "And you hit your head pretty bad when you did." Dean slid his hand to the back of my head feeling for the bump, "Jesus!"

Ryan glared at Dean but reached back and felt it too. "Do we have any ice?" he asked Owen. Owen shook his head. "Right… no freezer, I think we need to turn on the generator and make some ice." Thankfully we had the generator off when the men were here otherwise they would have known without a doubt there were people inside.

"What if they come back?" Sienna asked.

"I think we have to risk it…" Ryan said

lightly pressing the cool cloth against the back of my head. "Need anything? Something for the pain?" he asked quietly and kindly.

"Ibuprofen?" I asked wincing. Dean darted up and brought two pills and a bottle of water. I took them eagerly wishing they'd work instantaneously.

"It's almost dark, I don't think they'll come back tonight, they'd have to carry flashlights and why would they bother when they could just come back during the day? It's not like anyone would be calling 911 on them. Owen would you start the generator? Seth would you start the ice?" Ryan asked, his eyes wide with concern.

"I want to go lie down," I said trying to stand up.

"Here?" Ryan asked.

"No, in my bed, I don't want to be by the window, door or chair right now. Could you help me?" I asked Ryan. He carefully helped me up and when I wobbled threatening to fall on my face, he caught me and guided me, practically carrying me to my room. Dean stood watching the whole time ready to jump in to help if he was needed but it was Ryan's arms I wanted to be in. It was his protective body I wanted to be next to in order to feel safe again.

He started to help me into bed but I wanted to change first. Every night I'd slept in an over-sized T-shirt, it was comfortable and cool. "What is it?" he asked when I stopped moving.

"I want to change," I said not sure how to go about changing and have him here to steady me.

147

"OK what do you want?"

"That shirt," I pointed to the one haphazardly draped across the top of the dresser and he grabbed it while I held onto the bedpost.

"OK what else?"

"Just that," I shrugged.

"Should I leave?" he offered, but I honestly didn't think he could. I didn't know if I'd be able to hold myself up with this vertigo and remove and replace my clothing on my own without falling.

"No, stay… help," I said blushing.

"Right, ummm… OK, just tell me what you want me to do," he said aiming his eyes towards the ground.

"Not sure, I've never had to do this before," I said, "I mean, having to change while feeling like I'm going to lose my balance and fall on my face."

"I could get Sienna," Ryan offered.

"No, I'm afraid she'd drop me if I fell." I shook my head, knowing it would have been easier if she could have helped me, "Let's just do it, quick. Stand behind me." I started to take off my shirt but I couldn't do it one handed, and I let go of the bed post. My body started tipping forward and Ryan grabbed my hips to pull me back up. He held me steady while I finished undressing myself. When I got the shirt above my head I felt the stiffness in my shoulders and neck and struggled to get it off. I felt the shirt disappear from my hands as Ryan yanked it the rest of the way off.

There I stood in my bra and jeans, wobbling forward and backwards, at least it felt like I was. Ryan pushed the T-shirt against my hand and I

148

opened it and struggled to get it on. "I can't, my neck hurts too much," I said holding the shirt in front of myself covering as much as I could. I grabbed a hold of the bedpost again. "You're going to have to do it," I said, almost not even feeling embarrassed because I felt out of options and really wanted to just lie down. In fact, I started to seriously worry I might have a concussion.

He took the shirt and pulled it down over my head while I held on tightly. Once it was over my shoulders I was able to get my arms in one at a time, and he helped me pull it down. I felt as though that couldn't have gone any smoother than it had. After all, he saw my back, big deal everyone has a back and my back was a back he wasn't interested in any way. If he had been, he no longer was, so it was just a back.

"There!" he said as if we'd accomplished a great feat. I turned to him and smiled. I wobbled towards him and he caught me, "In bed," he ordered.

"Wait."

"Now what?" he said not sounding annoyed but more like he was wondering what else there could be.

"My pants," I said, "Help me sit down." He guided me down to the bed and once I was sitting comfortably, I covered with a blanket, undid my jeans and wiggled them down as much as I could. Ryan looked at me and placed his hand on mine holding it still. The look in his eyes was overwhelming and intoxicating. He lifted my hand off my leg and placed it on the side of the bed and did the same with my other hand making sure I was well braced. He slid his hands up my thighs to the waistband of my semi-pulled down jeans and slowly started to pull them down my legs. He wiggled them around my knees, then over my calves, slipping out one foot and then the other never taking his eyes off mine.

I had forgotten all about the throbbing pain in the back of my head. My heart was beating fast and I was extremely aware of each beat it took. He dropped my jeans to the floor and leaned forward against the bed one of his legs between mine. His right hand found my thigh and slid slowly upwards to the band of my underwear, but he thankfully kept going. I didn't want to stop whatever was happening, since whatever it was both felt amazing and it cured all pain. His hand was moving up my side over my shirt. The T-shirt was getting all bunched up and wrinkled as it exposed the bare skin of my stomach and part of my light blue underwear. I could tell the cover I had once been under was no longer on top of me, but Ryan didn't seem to notice. His eyes never moved from mine, watching me as his hand roamed. It almost seemed as though he was expecting me to stop him.

When he got his hand as far as my shoulder, he slid it around towards my back and gently guided me down into a laying position. He twisted my body so my head was on the pillow and turned me on my side so I was facing him. He was being careful so the big bump at the back of my head wouldn't have any pressure on it. He slid his hand out from under me carefully trying not to jostle me too much. He touched my cheek and let his thumb brush against my lower lip making my whole body tingle. Ryan took the light sheet and pulled it up over my hips, it was too hot to be covered with anything more than that. Heck, once he left I'd probably kick my legs out anyway.

He lowered himself down to my ear and whispered "Good night, Ros." He glanced at me for a brief second, "If you need anything just call for me." The bed bounced upwards as he removed his weight.

"Ryan," I said and exhaled.

"Hmm?"

And if I hadn't heard the words come out of my own mouth, I would have doubted they had been mine. I looked into his eyes, "Don't go."

Chapter thirteen.

When I woke up Ryan was sleeping in the chair with his head cranked to the side. He would certainly have a sore neck when he woke up. Speaking of hurting, my head was throbbing, and I had the headache of a lifetime, but the bump felt as though it had gone down. I felt something behind my head and pulled it out. It was a plastic bag full of water that had been wrapped in a towel. They had made me ice and someone must have placed it under me while I slept. It hadn't even woken me, I must have been out cold.

That's when I had the flashback of what happened with Ryan. Had it really happened or had I imagined it? It was far too real for it not to have been real. I was staring at my feet feeling embarrassed, and I'll admit a touch happy. A tingle surged from the top of my head to my toes about the incident, when Ryan coughed. It startled me at first, but I played it cool. I smiled my best smile and said, "Good morning."

"Ugh, yeah...." He pressed his fingertips deep into his neck muscles, "Sorry Ros, I'm a real ass in the mornings," he forced a small smile in return. "I slept in this chair all freakin' night," he said sounding as if he wasn't sure. Yes, I had asked him to stay, but I didn't ask him to sleep with his head cranked to the side all night in that uncomfortable chair. I wanted to ask why he didn't sleep in the bed, but decided against it.

I hugged my legs to my chest, "Did you apply the ice to my bump?"

"Sienna made the ice," he said. His head darted back and forth from me to the open door, "I told her I'd stay in here through the night in case something should happen, you know, like a concussion or something."

"Sure." Maybe I had dreamed our intimate moment, I did bump my head pretty badly. It wouldn't be that out there to have actually dreamed it even though it had felt so real.

"Ros I have to ask you something," he said looking at the door again. It was bothering him having it open, he got up and closed it quietly. It hadn't sounded like anyone else was even up yet.

"Shoot," I said feeling a little sick to my stomach.

"It's about that day, with Dean." He sat at the edge of the bed with his back towards me. I could tell he was uncomfortable and that something was bothering him.

"What day with Dean?"

"The day you'd both come out of the bathroom," he said taking a sudden interest in his feet.

At first I couldn't think of what he was talking about but then, I remembered. It stuck out

like a sore thumb. This whole time, this is what
had been bothering him and why he mostly had
been avoiding me. "Oh," I said trying to find the
right starting point to explain and assure him he
was worrying about nothing.

"If you're interested in him, you know, I'd
get it, I'd back off. I can see how he looks at you,
and ever since that day, he's been different towards
me, so I just want to know what happened... and
where I stand?"

I shook my head and moved forward onto
my knees, "No, no, no! It's nothing like that! Dean
and I... there's nothing between Dean and I! He
needed help getting cleaned up and he asked me."

"No one else could help huh?" I could hear
the smirk on his face through the words, "Or do it
himself?"

"Sienna is his sister and Seth was out on the
couch suffering from his heat stroke or whatever it
was. It really wasn't a big deal! You are totally
wrong about how he feels about me, we are just
friends. He's never said anything or tried
anything."

He turned to face me, "That's really all that
happened?"

"Yep." I'd seen maybe more than I should
have, but it had been completely innocent. That's
all he needed to know, is that it was innocent and
nothing happened.

"God Ros! My stomach has been tied in
knots since that day and he's been so smug."

"You could have just asked sooner...."

He leaned closer to me, "How's your head?"

"Mostly fine, I mean, it is throbbing like you wouldn't believe, but the lump feels smaller. It's nothing a few pain pills won't fix." I was suddenly embarrassed again about what had happened yesterday when those men came snooping, and what a big baby I had been. I shouldn't be so weak. How could he even be interested in someone he'd have to worry about every second of the day if I couldn't pull it together when I needed to?

"What's wrong?" he asked noticing my mood change.

"Nothing, just thinking about yesterday."

"Yeah." Was all he mustered to say before he put his hand on my arm, "So, where do I stand with you? You are so hard to read."

I laughed so hard I fell backwards onto the bed, "I am not! You're the one with the poker face. I haven't been able to read you since day one! I'm an open book, heart on my sleeve, all those sayings… that's me!"

He was smiling at me when he came down on the bed beside me and propped his head up on his hand. His staring at me silenced my laughs and his gorgeous, mysterious blue eyes reeled me in. The whole mood in the room changed. It was more intense, and more sensual, that was until I opened my big mouth. "What about you?" I asked unabashedly.

"Huh?" he said startled out of the moment.

"That night, you and I, were, well, with the fireworks guys driving by shining the light. We were, very, umm… close and then Dean came down."

"And?"

"You let go of me so fast I stumbled backwards, you were totally embarrassed being so close to me and being seen!" I said remembering how quickly he had let go of me.

"I was not! That's not... he just startled me is all," Ryan said his face serious. "The car driving by was intense, then being with you was, well, intense, then he just interrupted in the middle, umm, at the start I guess and it just caught me by surprise."

"Really? That's all it was?"

"Um. Yes. And then I was coming back to you but you'd went back into your room, and had your back to me, I figured you'd come to your senses or something. That I'd lost my chance."

I laughed again, but this laugh was more of an uncomfortable one, thinking how things could have been had we just talked to each other instead of ignoring everything. "You haven't," I said, my voice less than a whisper, I had barely heard myself speak but I had felt my lips move.

He slid closer to me and rolled halfway so that his face was inches from mine. Ryan grabbed the back of my neck carefully avoiding the bump, his movement was smooth and swift. He seemed to be holding onto me tightly as if he feared I might just pull away or change my mind at the last second. I didn't. He slowly put his lips against mine, letting them lightly touch as if I was a delicacy he was trying to savor. It was soft and amazing and when neither of us could stand it any longer, he pulled me harder to him and was actually kissing me. It was a real kiss, nothing like I'd ever experienced before. We were like soft magnets drawn to each other with force, our lips would attract and then slightly resist and then attract even more.

He pulled away and placed gentle kisses on my chin. Then he placed several little kisses down the side of my neck. I pushed into him as I arched my back. My body was on autopilot. It was doing its own thing, and I felt like I had little control over myself, but in a good way. He pulled the shoulder of the large T-shirt down exposing my shoulder and covered my skin with kisses. His other hand glided up the other side of my shirt. I could feel the warmth from his hand against my bare skin. His hand drifted further upwards until his thumb curved against the side of my breast.

In the time it took to blink my eye, I had become very self-conscious about laying there so exposed. My shirt all bunched up just below my breasts, my exposed shoulder, but more importantly the fact that I was in nothing more than a T-shirt and my underwear. I pulled my shirt down and the blanket up over my legs in one quick movement.

"I'm sorry!" Ryan said quickly pulling away.

"No! No... it's OK."

"I don't know what I was thinking, I got carried away, I didn't mean..." he rolled over onto his back, "Shit, shit, shit-shit! I screwed up!"

"No!" I turned to look at him. I hadn't meant to hurt his feelings or make him feel bad, it was me who got nervous and shy of my own body. To be completely honest, this was the first time I'd done anything more than just a silly passionless kiss that had no real feelings behind it. The kind you do because you feel like you should. Because everyone else was doing it and doing much more than that for that matter. I was just overwhelmed, the intensity of it, it all just overcame me, but all in a good way. "It's me. I suddenly felt stupid and ugh, inexperienced," I groaned wishing I could take that back.

"Why? What do you mean? You never need to feel stupid with me, you aren't stupid," he twisted his head to meet my eyes. He was lying there on his back, his body stiff.

"Well, OK, here I am, practically lying in my underwear, you're fully clothed, and I've never really done anything like this before," I said feeling like a complete moron.

"We can do this at whatever speed you're comfortable with," he said, "and you're beautiful. You don't have to hide yourself from me."

"Yeah?"

"Yeah. You have two people who are crazy about you, in this house alone."

"Well, I am one of the few girls left in the world, that isn't saying much," I said only half joking.

He laughed, "Guys liked you before all this. The end of the world has nothing to do with it."

"Listen, if I do something wrong, let me know," I said, as I rolled over resting against his warmth and placing my hand on his solid chest. I planted a soft single kiss on his cheek.

"You won't." He copied me and placed a kiss on my cheek smiling that amazing Ryan smile at me.

"Don't be so sure about that," I said kneeling on the bed so I could look at him stretched out on my bed, smiling and relaxed.

"I'm positive you won't," he said.

He sat up and took my hand into his. Right now we were on some magical cloud where the only things that existed were Ryan, me and this bed. The heat wasn't there, and in the outside world there was grass and it was green. The trees were back to normal, and there were flowers everywhere. Right now it was a fairytale instead of a nightmare.

I leaned towards him for another kiss and he met me halfway. This was officially happening and actually real. I didn't know what the others would think, but at this moment I didn't really care either.

We spent some time just enjoying this and each other. It was perfect. I never wanted to leave this room.

"What will they think if anyone sees you leaving my room?" I asked, curious to hear his response.

"What? You're embarrassed of me?" he teased.

"Of course I'm not, but I'm not sure I want the whole house knowing our business just yet either. Or wondering what we are doing at any given time," I said moving over to sit next to him. "What will they think?" I asked nervous about how

159

this was going to change the whole dynamic of everyone in the house.

"I'll go out and get your headache pills. Sienna knew I was staying in the chair all night anyway they won't think anything new, at least not today." He opened the door slowly so the hinges wouldn't creak and slipped out. Sometimes he's so present in the moment and other times he seems so lost in himself. He came back after a minute or two, "Seth is snoring on the couch and the others are still upstairs."

There he was at the foot of the bed looking absolutely amazing. His eyes sparkled crystal blue and hair all messed up as if he had just been fooling around with someone, and the most unbelievable part of it all was that that person was me. Standing in front of me was the guy I just had a make-out session with. I had run my hands over his solid chest and his perfect stomach. I could still imagine what he felt like, smelled like and tasted like.

He moved within inches of me as if he could read my mind. I tugged at the bottom of his shirt, he smiled down at me. I slid one of my hands inside to feel his warm skin under my palm. He leaned down to kiss me.

"We should probably get ready for the day," he said, "not that I want to, but the others will be up soon. We have to run to town… more gas, food, you know, the usual."

"Right," I said pulling my hand back as I stood up. Our bodies were so close to one another you couldn't have fit more than a piece of paper between us. He let out a little sigh like he didn't want to go, like he wanted to stay in this room all day. So did I. But that wasn't an option for us, we had things to do. We had a responsibility to the other people with us who were stuck in all of this too.

"Tonight? Can I spend time with you again tonight?" he asked holding me tight against him and kissing my neck.

I shivered and pushed into him, "I suppose," I said playfully, of course I wanted to spend time with him again. I didn't want this moment to end because I wasn't sure it would ever happen again. Ryan could be very fickle. I worried by tonight he'd forget all about me.

He left tearing off his shirt as he did so, either because he was hot or maybe he was leaving me something to think about. I heard the door to his room close, and I flopped down on my bed smiling. We hadn't really done anything, I mean we had, but not what the others would have imagined went on if left to their own devices. No one needed to know how far it did or didn't go. That was my business, and Ryan's too. I giggled thinking how maybe now it was officially Ryan and me, and that we were a thing.

Chapter fourteen.

After lounging around on my bed for far too long daydreaming about Ryan, I got up and changed my clothes. I popped the pain pills — although I didn't think I needed them anymore now that my pain problem had lessened due to Ryan's kiss — and went in search of food. Seth and Owen were in the living room playing chess and Ryan was at the table drinking a bottle of water. Sienna sat across from him writing in her notebook. Dean hadn't come down yet.

"Good morning," I said cheerfully, realizing as the words left my mouth how out of character it was for me to be this lively in the morning but no one seemed to notice. They all grunted their good mornings to me and it made me smile. I searched around for something I wanted to eat and decided on a packaged muffin. I washed it down with a big gulp of bottled water. Ryan caught my eye and raised his eyebrow at me, I guess he noticed the hop in my step. The eyebrow seemed to say "play it cool man" but I shrugged it off, whatever, it was a good day... for once.

"What's that noise?" Sienna asked.

It sounded like rushing water, then I saw the flash of light followed by a boom of thunder that made me jump, it was real thunder this time. "It's rain!" I announced running to the back door window. It was coming down so hard a foggy mist was forming low to the ground. There was another bolt of lightning that struck so close the whole house shook. "And I was just about to say I was going outside to dance in it," I said moving away from the window.

"Ryan! Owen!" Dean shouted from upstairs. "Get up here!"

They both rushed up so fast they almost tripped over each other. I followed at a more reasonable pace. When I got up there Ryan was putting a pail down under a ferocious leak. There were six leaks and so far only one pail.

"Run down and look for buckets," Ryan ordered. Owen and I dashed down the stairs. He continued down to the basement, and I looked under the kitchen sink, the bathroom sink, the closets, the pantry, anywhere I could think of where a bucket might be. I found a large mixing bowl in one of the kitchen cabinets and brought that up. They put that under the smallest leak. Owen came up with two buckets that looked to have been used for mopping. We had four of the leaks taken care of, "There's gotta be something we can use!"

I went back down with Owen close behind me. We moved slower this time as we tried to think of other places to look. Seth and Sienna were now helping us look. Sienna found a storage bin filled with clothes she dumped out and brought up, and

Seth found a gallon sized ice cream pail holding golf balls he handed to Owen. The storm raged on and the rain showed no sign of weakening.

"Oh my God it's starting again," Sienna whined. "What are we going to do?"

"We won't be safe here when the tornadoes come," I said as I started to pace nervously. I was trying to think of what we would need to do. My eyes darted to Ryan, but he looked calm and unconcerned. I pinched my eyebrows and shook my head at him.

Dean flicked the back window curtain open and looked outside, "I don't think this is like before. There's no hail. I don't see any tornadoes."

"I agree," Ryan said not noticing Dean rolling his eyes at him. "I think this is just a good old fashioned thunderstorm."

Every five minutes or so the smaller buckets were emptied. The mixing bowl overflowed a little a few times but we put towels around it to help from future spills. We had been quite lucky that there wasn't much of a mess from the water before we had the water receptacles in place.

"Wish we could save the water and boil it. Seems like such a waste," I said when we were all sitting in the living room listening to the storm. Unfortunately, we didn't have any empty bottles to collect and store the rain water. I made a mental note to put it on the list for next time. Maybe they'd be able to get some of those big water jugs people used to use with water dispensers.

I was sitting on the couch far away from the window and chair that I had my breakdown in.

Seth was next to me and Dean on the other side of him. Owen sat in the chair by the window and Ryan sat in the chair next to me, which had sort of become his chair. Sienna was lying on the floor with her pen in hand and notebook resting on her lap.

"Maybe the rain will cool things down," Seth said ignoring my desire to start saving water and thinking only of his wish for things to cool down. Not that I could hold it against him.

We waited and waited for the storm to let up, taking turns emptying the buckets. The trip to town was postponed, and Ryan and Owen didn't know what to do with themselves having the extra time. After a while they decided to go into the garage and see if they could find a way to lock down the garage door thinking no one would be venturing out today so they'd be less likely to be noticed.

They had been out there for hours. Sienna was scribbling away in her notebook and would glance towards the window every so often with a worried look on her face.

Seth went outside and turned on the generator after running it by Ryan first to make sure he wouldn't mind. He had been sure to point out that no one would likely be out today to hear it. Ryan had agreed. Seth sat down by the fan and started watching a movie.

"What are you writing about?" I asked Sienna while munching on a pop-tart. We had lots of food and water stored up so missing a trip to town wasn't a big deal. In fact we were set, they could have missed a lot of trips to town. But we never stopped worrying about how we would eventually run out of supplies. The more we had the better we had all felt. Our pantry was full, the basement was filling up more and more each day. But with every item we brought into the house and stored away a little bit of the anxiety went away. It would be nice to not have to rely on going to town. There could be a reason, like what had happened today, that would stop us from going to town and we'd need that stockpile.

"Keeping a journal. Documenting the new world… and writing some fiction. This is the third notebook I've filled." She flashed me a drawing of a landscape of what our world used to look like. Below it was what things looked like now. "Just keeping myself busy I suppose," she smiled.

"That's amazing!" It really was. I was impressed, she was very talented. "You need more notebooks! Why don't you write down some art supplies for their next trip?"

"The other things they bring back are more important, besides what would I do with it? Art isn't necessary," she shrugged.

"That's arguable! You're talented and one day things may go back to how they were if people rebuild." She just shook her head at me as if I was being foolish but she had a small smile on her face happy about the compliment.

Dean had joined Seth in what appeared to be a movie marathon based on the amount of movies they had stacked on the end-table. I went upstairs to empty the buckets. It hadn't been my intention to snoop but when I went into Dean's room to empty the one in his room, I couldn't help but notice his stack of survival books and a fairly large collection of fiction books. He had a backpack filled with survival supplies, probably things he had read about in his books. Was he planning on leaving us? Or was it just in case something happened to all of us and he was left alone? I obviously couldn't ask and I wasn't sure if I should say anything to Ryan about what I saw. Maybe he already knew and then I'd just look bad for being so nosy. It wasn't like Dean would ever leave without Sienna.

I took the pail, emptied it in the upstairs bathtub, and returned it to his room. When I turned to go to the next bucket I'd bumped right into Dean's chest. He put his hand on my back to steady me. I gasped and let a strange squeak escape from my lips. Dean had been so quiet I hadn't even heard him come up, a new skill he acquired from his books perhaps. He hadn't been there when I dumped the bucket, so thankfully he hadn't seen me snooping. "Emptying buckets," I explained as I took a step back and twisted my fingers together nervously.

"Yeah I figured." His words were slow as he slid past me and spread out on the bed. He folded his arms behind his head, crossed his ankles and raised his eyebrow.

"Movie over?" I asked in the doorway.

"Yup. He's starting another but I'm done, I don't have movie stamina like Seth does," he smiled, "But no one does."

167

I disappeared into Sienna's room where the smaller of the leaks was located and dumped out the bowl. Dean was so stealthy he'd gotten out of bed, grabbed a bucket and was at the bathroom ahead of me right as I got there to pour out the bowl. "How rude of me not to help," he said brushing passed me, making sure our bodies made contact. He looked down into my eyes with an adorable grin that made my cheeks warm. Could Ryan have been right about Dean having feelings for me? I started to feel uncomfortable, Dean was tall and attractive, and I didn't fail to notice that. The truth was I just didn't know much about him. It wasn't like he was quiet and mysterious, I just didn't know him, not from school and not even that well from our time together after the storms. I knew he cared about his sister, I knew he was good with a bow, or so he said, and that he was a decent cook. He had these brown eyes so dark they almost appeared black. They were captivating.

"Thanks for the help!" I looked up at one of the leaks, "We will have to get up there and fix these."

"Yeah, I'm sure we can find something at a home improvement store for it, I can't imagine a product like that is in high demand right now. We are probably the only ones looking to fix a roof," he said again smiling at me. His smile was magical, I think my cheeks were at a full on blush. It was just the thought of him possibly having feelings for me that made me feel different when I was around him. Of course his feelings hadn't actually been confirmed, it was just Ryan's theory. And feelings

168

or not he was still really hot. No matter, I was with Ryan now, I mean I think I was, I'm not sure it was official, but I hoped so. Dean would just have to deal with it and I wagered he'd manage to be just fine, it's not like he knew me that well either.

"Ha! Yeah, you're probably right. Well, thanks for the help," I said as I walked down the stairs and he retreated back to his room probably to study his survival books.

When I came down into the living room, Ryan and Owen were in the kitchen re-boarding the door that led to the garage. Ryan saw me coming down so I felt I needed to explain since I figured he would still be uncomfortable about Dean and I being alone together. At least he had been the time before… that whole shower thing. At the same time, I also felt like I shouldn't have to explain. That I should be trusted, but just to be safe I did it anyway, "Emptied buckets, this rain will not let up! Going to be a busy night of bucket emptying."

I left for my room to throw myself into a book. Seth waved to me with powdered cheese coated fingers from his cheese flavored puffy snack as I walked passed him.

Ryan knocked lightly before coming into my room. He sat down at the end of the bed to take his shoes off as if this was something he had always done. I had folded my novel in half across my knees as I listen to him tell the story of how they tried, but failed to secure the garage door. After he was finished talking, he leaned over to give me a kiss, just a normal kiss. I loved it. Then he asked about my day but I grinned stupidly at him since he had been present for half of my day. "What?" he asked.

"So, is this just how it is with us now?"

He smiled, "I hope so!"

"Me too," I smiled back. "But what about the others?"

"I'm not sure yet," he shook his head. "You have any ideas?"

"Not really, I'm not even sure it matters."

"I think it will with at least one person."

"Dean?"

Ryan nodded as he started to undress. He whipped his shirt off and tossed it on the chair and started to undo his pants, standing there only in his boxers. Then he climbed into bed with me and pulled the sheet half way over himself. Because of the rain the house was a little cooler, the sun hadn't been beating down on it all day which gave us a slight break. I set my book down on the nightstand and curled up next to him. He kissed the top of my head, "What a day huh?"

"Sure was." I snuggled closer. Being in this spot was peaceful, my mind was quiet and I felt completely safe. His skin was warm, soft and smooth, I wanted to feel it against every inch of my skin. We lay there listening to the rain pound into the window and the rolling thunder. It was incredibly relaxing and before we knew it we were both sleeping.

Chapter fifteen.

Dean was sitting at the kitchen table looking miserable. His hair was messed up, and he had dark circles under his eyes. I had asked him if he was doing OK.

"Yeah, Owen and Sienna slept through the night, I had to empty those buckets like every hour on the hour and that damn bowl overflowed several times. You know you could have come up to help," he said only half teasing. In his sleep deprived state he hadn't bothered to hide the ounce of truth he left lingering in his words. His agitation seemed focused on me which I guessed was because I had been the one to ask him about it.

"Oh God Dean, I'm sorry! You're absolutely right!" I said feeling terrible.

"Ah, it's over and done with now," he said quickly as if he noticed how bad I felt. "The rain stopped about an hour ago, I'm just going to tell Ryan I'm not going to town today. I need to stay and catch up on some sleep instead."

"Oh, OK. Sorry," I said taking a long drink from a bottle of cool Gatorade. Having the generator on so long yesterday chilled the fridge

171

well enough that some of the things inside were still cool. Although, I wasn't sure when the generator had been turned off since Ryan was with me the whole night. "If you want I can tell him and you can go up...," I said as Ryan exited my room and came to the kitchen. I was positive Dean saw where he'd come from but he didn't say anything and his expression hadn't changed.

"Tell me what?" Ryan asked. At least he had put his jeans back on and hadn't come strutting out in his boxers.

"Dean's not going—"

"I'm skipping the town run today," he said interrupting me. I ignored it and chalked it up to his lack of sleep or maybe it was a guy thing, a power thing, a 'he just came out of your bedroom what the hell' thing.

"How come?" Ryan asked raising his eyebrows.

"I'm just not, shouldn't that be good enough reason for you?" Dean said sounding as if he was trying to start an argument. "I don't have to tell you everything all the time, man." He got up and slammed the chair against the table. His feet pounded hard against the stairs as he sprinted up to his room.

I waited until I heard him close his door. "He was up all night emptying the buckets," I whispered.

"Shit."

"Yeah, he'll be OK," I said sounding more sure of myself than I was.

"I don't know about that."

"Why do you say that," I asked squinting up at him as if his face was as bright as the sun.

"He saw me leave your room," he said as he slipped around me and gave me a well hidden pat on the behind. I popped up on my tip-toes as the little gesture had taken me by surprise. I smiled at him fully enjoying our little secret.

"He'll be fine!" I said trying to convince us both. I left the room to go change my clothes and get ready for the day. I washed up with a bottle of water and brushed my teeth. Then I walked to the room I now practically shared with Ryan and put on a light weight button down shirt with a striped pattern and a pair of skinny jeans. It was one of the outfits I had that looked good, at this point I had lots of clothes to pick from and could manage to find a decent outfit every so often. I pulled my hair back into a loose ponytail and thought I looked all right considering I hadn't been able to pick out any of my own clothing.

When I came out Owen and Ryan were discussing the trip to town they were about to go on. First, they were going to the home improvement store, then to fill a pack with food from whichever place had the best selection left, and finally to the gas station to fill up our gas jug for the generator. They wanted to replace an extra day's worth of food since they'd taken yesterday off.

They approached the runs as if it was a nine-to-five job, except it was a job that they never wanted to take a day off from. It would be a relatively quick and simple run for them. They'd be back before noon and could get started on patching the roof.

"Can I come with?" I asked not even sure I wanted to go, but I knew the answer would be a big fat 'no' as it had always been before I'd given up asking.

"You don't need to," Owen said.

"Well I know, but Dean's not going, and you said it'll be quick so I thought maybe I could be of some help," I said looking to Ryan hoping for some support.

"It's safer for you here Ros," he said not making eye contact. He must have found it easier to tell me no if he wasn't looking at me.

"It's safer for you here too," I countered.

He had been trying not to, but he looked at me, and I could tell by his expression he wanted to tell me to stay, that was until he saw me. "Fine, but you stay close and do what we say. You'll carry both your knife and a gun."

Sienna had come down and heard that I was getting to go with, "No fair! I want to come too!"

"Awe Christ," Owen muttered.

"If she can do it, I surely can," Sienna said taking a verbal jab at me. I had to assume she was referring to when we had the visitors and I'd lost it. Not that she had been that much better, but she hadn't passed out and injured herself.

"Well, maybe another time," Ryan said. "Four is too big of a group, we can't draw attention to ourselves and I already told her she could come this time."

"Fine, but I get to come next time!"

"Next time Dean isn't able to come it's your turn," Owen corrected.

When we were outside, Owen and Ryan showed me how to protect myself from the sun. They wrapped their heads with a light cloth, wore sunglasses, slathered sunblock on any exposed skin. They triple checked their guns and put them in their waistband. Owen gave me a quick run-down on the gun, how to use it, how to point and how to turn the safety on and off. He told me to leave the safety on, and only if it was a true emergency should I turn it off, because, and roughly in his words, 'it would be safer for all of us since I had no idea how to use it.' I would just be using it as an intimidation tool should the need for one arise. I slid it into my waistband just as they had done and pulled my shirt over it so it was hidden. Owen handed me an empty pack, if I was coming it was to help, not to just go for a walk. Ryan grabbed the gas can, and we started out.

We went towards town wrapped in our protective clothing and shades, with our weapons hidden. It all made me feel tough, until I remembered how I wasn't. I followed two steps behind at all times. It was smart to let them lead the way. Every so often one of them would glance back to make sure I was still there and not passed out from overheating or something worse. We'd get the gas last, they told me, because it was the heaviest and hardest to carry. First we'd go find the roofing supplies. Going around town was far easier than I had imagined, they took back streets and stayed hidden as much as possible. We hadn't run into another living soul, we did however run into some angry dogs.

"What are those?" I asked. They didn't seem like normal dogs. They were some kind of cross between a pit bull and a greyhound. Beefy and solid like a pit bull but long and tall like a greyhound. They were mean, they snarled and growled, even at each other. Each time we'd seen them off in the distance they were too busy to notice us, tearing something stringy and bloody apart or fighting with each other.

"Some kind of dog, a cross-breed I think," Owen said, "We avoid those. Always."

"Right." The last part was obvious. I hadn't failed to notice that when the dogs were anywhere in sight — or even the couple times we heard their harsh bark — that the boys would be more than ready to pull out their guns and shoot the dogs dead. I almost wanted to ask how many dogs they've had to put down on their runs but I decided I didn't want to know.

We picked up a medium sized pail of roofing sealant, two brushes, some shop rags and left. Next we headed for their usual stop for the water and food supplies. They took me to what used to be a family run grocery store. It wasn't quite as large as your typical chain grocer, and the food was noticeably diminishing.

"It's not just us taking stuff from here is it?" I asked knowing what they came back to the house with and noticing how much appeared to be gone from the shelves.

"Nope," Owen said.

"Have you ever crossed paths with any others?"

"Nope," Owen said lifting his crossed fingers at me.

They helped me fill my pack with things that weren't expired. We were now able to take things that needed heating like soups, noodles or rice. But before we had the ability to heat stuff either microwave or stove-top, we'd only take things that were edible even cold.

There was a display that held all kind of seed packets which appeared to have never even been touched. I grabbed a bunch of packets, a brochure and a booklet that was on the display when no one was looking. The seeds would be my secret since I didn't want to get teased about how nothing would grow in this heat or on the land. I thought maybe one day we could figure out a way, maybe even in the basement somehow. It seemed silly to just leave them behind when maybe one day we could try. So I slid them in the front pocket of the backpack. The juicy red tomatoes and the bright orange carrots pictured looked so amazing I almost felt like I could taste them. I fantasized about being able to grow and eat fresh fruits and vegetables. It would be a welcomed change from the canned and boxed junk packed with preservatives that we have been surviving on. Which I suppose, all things considered, I shouldn't really complain about since it was better than nothing.

We turned to leave when the pack was full, "Wait!" I said looking at what signs remained above head until I found the aisle that said 'Office Supplies.' I found a sketchbook, pencils and crayons that I was going to carry until Owen reminded me I needed a free hand. He shoved them in with the brushes and rags from the home improvement store looking at me as if I should explain the art supplies, but he packed them away even though I hadn't said anything.

The nearest gas station was dilapidated. The paneling was shredding off the sides, paint was peeling away from surfaces, the sign was missing and the door of the main entrance was hanging by a single hinge but at least the tanks below still had gas inside. Ryan pried one of the heavy metal covers off and lowered a tube into the tank. He put the tube in his mouth and quickly pulled away when the gas started flowing. Ryan quickly placed the tube into the gas container and let it fill while Owen looked around. Being at the gas station was easily the most nerve-wracking part of the run since we were out in the wide open with no cover. It was not the safest but luckily it was the fastest stop. Ryan put the cap on the red jug and we turned around the side of the building to head back home.

We spun around quickly at the sound of the whistle, "Hey beautiful," he said in a deep, raspy voice.

Owen and Ryan both stepped in front of me instinctively and protectively. There was a rough looking man leaning against the side of the building. The new world hadn't been kind to him, then again it was likely the old world hadn't been either. He had on a leather vest all patched up and a cigarette hanging out of the side of his mouth. He had a black and white bandana with skulls wrapped around his head, with his sunglasses propped on top revealing the baggy skin under his eyes. His skin was wrinkled and crispy not from age but likely from spending too much time in the sun, but somehow he had avoided being burnt. He rested one foot against the side of the building, his body relaxed, as we stood there tense.

Ryan had his hand on the handle of his gun, but Owen kept both hands out in front of him balancing the heavy pack with the sealant over his shoulder. The pack itself could probably be used as a weapon if need be, but I figured Owen was keeping his hands visible to the stranger so he wouldn't be suspicious of them. Although I imagined we weren't the first people he'd run into that carried guns. He would probably just think we were some stupid kids with some guns we didn't know how to use, and as far as I was concerned he had that right about one of us.

"Relax boys," he said giving them a little peak at the shotgun he had been hiding behind his leg, "Just saying 'hi' to the lady. Being friendly is all."

"All right then, we don't want any trouble. You've said your hello, now we'll just be on our way," Ryan said taking small, slow steps away from the man and the situation we had found ourselves in.

"We haven't finished our conversation yet have we gorgeous?" he walked over to us with a small limp and his shotgun over his shoulder.

179

"Come here," he said wagging his finger at me.

I shook my head side to side, I didn't want to leave the safety of being behind Ryan and Owen. This guy gave me the creeps. Not just because he was significantly older than I was, there was just something about him that screamed prison escapee.

"Don't be shy, love, come here," he said pointing the shotgun at Ryan. He completely picked him at random as far as I could tell. Truthfully, it wouldn't have mattered which he'd decided to point his gun at. I would have done whatever I had to for either of them.

"Christ," Owen muttered.

"Don't," Ryan whispered not taking his eyes off of the man.

I forced my feet to move, I wasn't going to let anything happen to Ryan or Owen because I had made them take me with them. I had practically forced it on them, they told me not to. This was entirely my fault, this was exactly why they wanted me to stay home. It was just my luck that this happened the time I came with. This piece-of-crap, former inmate, just happens to be hanging out at the gas station.

He kept the gun pointed at Ryan while he slid my sunglasses off with his other hand, and slowly hooked them over the top of my shirt his fingers lingering against the sweaty exposed skin of my lower neck. He pulled my headwrap off awkwardly slow and let it fall to the ground, "Let it down, love," he ordered trying to make it sound like I was just as into this as he was. If he believed that he was insane, which seemed quite possible.

I yanked out my hair tie pulling out a few strands of my stringy, dingy hair with it. I thought about grabbing my gun and pointing it at him, but I worried I wouldn't be able to do it fast enough and he'd pull the trigger. Ryan wouldn't have time to get out of the way, by the time he realized what was happening it would be too late. I wouldn't even have the time to make a threat of any kind, but then again it would take him by surprise. It would probably be the last thing he was expecting from me. I wasn't going to do it now, but if I had to I'd try it. Maybe it would work, maybe it wouldn't, but not yet.

He ran his fingers through my hair, but they were sweaty and they got stuck and pulled. I felt violated even though it was just my hair, but I kept my eyes on Owen and Ryan waiting for the right time to make a move. Their worried and tortured expressions were enough to make me feel nauseated. I needed to do something to get us out of here. "Is that your bike?" I asked motioning my head towards his bike.

"It is, love. Do you like it?" he asked, his gun still pointed at Ryan. Much of his eye contact was focused on either Ryan or Owen, even though he was talking to me.

"I do, I'd love to go for a ride sometime and feel the wind against my face. Must feel real nice in this heat," I said flicking my hair to the other side, "I know this is probably asking too much but could I sit on it?" I said trying to keep my body movements relaxed and my voice calm. Everything about this man repulsed me, but I pretended I was in a movie, if I played this part perfectly maybe I'd win an Oscar.

"Yeah you can, baby." He walked backwards, keeping his gun aimed at Ryan while I strutted runway style towards his bike. I climbed on the bike as slowly and as seductively as I could. I hoped that maybe it might give the boys an opportunity to take over the situation. I straddled the bike and let my head fall back as if I was trying to imitate an intimate moment, some kind of motorcycle ecstasy. Thankfully it was enough for him to let his guard down, he lowered his shotgun and bit his knuckle. He took two steps towards me, ready to drive off taking me with him on all his bike adventures. Except for the fact that I had pulled the gun from my pants and had it pushed up against the side of his head. The safety on, but he didn't know that. I kicked his shotgun loose and it stirred a small cloud of dust when it hit the ground.

Owen reached down and picked up the shotgun while Ryan pointed his — likely with the safety off — gun, at the man. I climbed off the motorcycle keeping my gun pointed at him.

"Here's what's really going to happen," I practically spit in his face. I didn't like how he had made me feel, so powerless, and in front of Owen and Ryan. Maybe I was done being powerless, or maybe having had Ryan's life threatened helped put me in a different mode, but I was ready to kick some biker ass. I don't know what and it didn't matter. "You're getting on your bike, and you're driving away. I'm keeping the shotgun to remind myself every day that there are disgusting old

182

perverts out there." When he didn't move I pushed the gun as hard as I could against his head, "What are you waiting for?"

"This isn't over," he spat back. "I'll find you. A tough mama like you with a real man like me, not some stupid little boys," he said actually spitting on the ground near his feet. "That's who will be repopulating a world like this. I'll find you!"

"Get the fuck out of here before I lose my patience."

"You heard the lady," Ryan said backing me up. I could tell he wanted to pull his trigger, he didn't want to let this guy out into the world where he could come back. Maybe by doing so he'd be saving another girl out there, but that just wasn't the kind of person he was.

The man got on his bike, kicked it to a start and sped off on his excessively noisy bike. I re-wrapped my head and put my sunglasses on as if nothing happened. I couldn't tell if I was in some kind of shock or if I was just proud of how I handled myself for once. All I knew was that I didn't want to pass out again.

"Are you all right?" Owen asked.

"I'm fine."

"Are you sure?" Ryan said in mild disbelief.

"Yes," I said holding my head high, but my hands were shaking uncontrollably. I hadn't realized how bad it was until I couldn't even manage to get my gun back into my waistband. Owen gently took the gun, checked the safety and carefully tucked it into my waistband.

"I'm sorry I made you take me with you, I didn't mean for this to happen," I said wondering exactly how angry they were going to be with me, it had been entirely my fault after all.

"Ros, this could have happened without you here, he would have just bothered us about something else, maybe threatened us for our guns or supplies. Just happened you look the way you do, a noticeably beautiful woman, heck, he probably hasn't seen a woman in a while is all and couldn't help it. After all he let his guard down pretty easily," Ryan said.

Owen smiled at him and then at me, he chuckled, "Aww shit, how did I not see this sooner," he grinned and hit Ryan on the arm.

"Shut up," I said.

Ryan grinned back.

"No, no, no! It's great you guys really it is!"

"Seriously?" I glared at them both. "I was just almost kidnapped, raped and kept as some biker mama, and you guys are like mental high-fiving? Really?"

"Sorry," Ryan said walking over to me. He wrapped his arm around my shoulder and planted a kiss on my forehead, now that Owen had figured it out, he didn't have to hide it around him. "I'm very lucky," he added on a more serious note.

"You know what? Good for you guys." Owen half hugged us both and started leading us off towards home taking an alternate route just in case the biker was watching us from a distance. Or because maybe the noisy bike could have alerted someone else and they'd come poking around. I didn't think the biker was watching or we would have probably heard his bike a mile away. The route he took was longer and seemingly random. We weaved in and out of yards and through various structures hoping that if anyone was following we'd lose them pretty easily, keeping our group and home safe. I started breathing normally again when I saw the back door to our house.

"Really are you all right?" Ryan asked.

"I mean yeah I am, but he had a gun pointed at you, I didn't have much of a choice about any of it," I said sounding sappy.

"I get it," he said probably thinking about how badly he wanted to have pulled that trigger, "I'd have done whatever it took too."

When we got to the house Owen went inside closing the door behind him giving us a moment of privacy. Although I wasn't sure if he had done it intentionally or not, either way I welcomed the moment with Ryan because of what happened. Maybe some time with him would help me relax and feel safe.

Ryan and I moved closer to the house so we wouldn't be seen if someone was peeking out. I rested my back against the wall and he had his hands pressed against the wall on either side of me. He took his glasses off revealing his beautiful blue eyes which sparkled in the sunlight. I took mine off to look at him, but the instant mine were off my face he was pressing his lips to mine passionately.

"I can't let anything happen to you," he said in one quick breath. He smoothly slipped his hands behind my neck taking care to avoid my almost completely gone bump. He tilted my head towards his and kissed me again.

I wanted to say something in return but the kisses erased all words from my mind, I couldn't think of anything to say, it would have just come out gibberish. But I felt the same, I'd protect him with my life. He took a small step backwards letting his fingertips trail down my shoulder and then my arm, taking my hand into his.

"Want to help us with the roof repairs?" Ryan asked.

I nodded excitedly. Ryan had probably just wanted to keep an eye on me, but I was happy to be helpful regardless. I figured he was just anxious about leaving my side right now after what happened with the biker. At least I could feel useful, and I doubt I'd find a way to screw it up.

Chapter sixteen.

After we had re-hydrated and gotten something to eat, Ryan, Owen and I had made our way up to the roof to try to seal the problem areas. Even though I was still sweaty from earlier, I hadn't bothered to wash up since I knew we'd be out in the heat for awhile. Owen brought up the supplies. Seth and Sienna had helped by holding the ladder and being our lookouts in case someone came along, but they probably just wanted to be outside for a while. If anyone came our way they were on strict orders to quickly remove the ladder, hide it as best and quickly as they could, alert us and lock themselves inside. We'd hide on the roof until it was safe again.

Most of the problems with the roof were noticeable and likely a result of the tornadoes that had passed by in what almost seemed like a lifetime ago. The others we had to guess at and we put down extra sealer in random spots that looked questionable for good measure. It only took us about an hour to complete the repairs. We wouldn't know if they would work or not until the next rainfall. Ryan was half way down the ladder when

Sienna screamed.

I looked down over the edge carefully to see two of those dog beasts ferociously lunging towards her, she had no protection whatsoever, no gun, no knife, nothing. "The dogs," I said to Owen, and he started down the ladder as soon as there was enough room so he wouldn't be climbing down on top of Ryan.

She screamed again. I watched everything from over the edge of the roof wishing there was something I could do. I drew a blank, even if I had my gun I didn't think I would have been able to even use it well enough to help. One dog stood back as if watching the back of the more aggressive dog while he threatened Sienna with his sharp teeth. It snapped at her, but missed. Ryan was almost off the ladder and he already had his gun in hand. It all had happened so fast. The bigger, more wild dog leaped at Sienna. All she could do was cover her face with her arms, but Seth had dodged out in front of her. He saved her by blocking the dog and taking the blow himself. After a minute she uncovered her eyes wondering why the dog hadn't slammed into her, only to see what I had seen. The big dog was on top of Seth, biting and pulling at the flesh on his arm.

I covered my ears after Ryan shot the dog the first time, the second shot was muffled through my hands. I scrambled down the ladder, "Stay up there," Owen scolded when he noticed the ladder shaking and me descending. The dog wasn't giving up on Seth, Ryan shot again and again, the dog whimpered and stopped, it cried out in pain looking at the other dog. The second dog stood there watching the first dog, growling but not moving. Owen and Sienna rushed to Seth once Ryan pointed his gun at the second dog.

No one had been holding the ladder when I resumed climbing down and it started to tip with me on it. I fell maybe three feet and blacked out for maybe a second or two when I hit my head on a small rock. Like the clumsy girl I am, I re-injured my previous head lump. Ryan turned to help me up and in the brief second he did, the second dog leaped at him knocking him to the ground. He bit him hard in the forearm and Ryan yelled out. I picked up Ryan's gun, got the safety off and pulled the trigger. The first bullet grazed his ear and the second got him in the shoulder and the third in his foot. My hands shook a little but I just pointed at the dog and shot. I didn't aim at anything in particular. My only thoughts were to hit the dog and kill the dog.

"He got you?" I said knowing the answer.

"Not bad, just a scratch," he said grinning. He stood up, took the gun from me and shot the injured dog point blank. He sent me inside to tell Dean what had happened. Owen, Sienna and Ryan helped Seth inside since he couldn't stand on his own. After I told Dean, we gathered various medical supplies we had stocked up in the basement and some clean towels.

I opened a first aid kit and spread out the bandages, gauze, peroxide and a bottle of water on top of a clean towel. When they brought him in they put him on the kitchen floor, since he was

189

bleeding pretty badly. At first, I was overwhelmed with all the cuts, I didn't know where to start. I felt frozen in place and no one else was moving either. But then something in my head clicked and I started to act even though I felt a tear trickle down my cheek.

"Scissors?" Someone handed me a pair of small scissors from the first aid kit and I cut open his shirt. "Cut off his pants," I said handing the scissors to Owen.

I carefully pulled the cloth away from his torn up skin, trying to avoid touching the wounds. Seth was in and out of consciousness, when he was present he was muttering gibberish, he looked to be in shock or something. "Seth? Seth! Are you OK? Do you know where you are?" I asked loudly as I started cleaning the first and the worst cut I found. The cuts in his skin were unusual but honestly I wasn't all that familiar with wounds, they were bubbling as if he had carbonated blood. I didn't say anything, but I looked across his limp body at Dean who was working on his arm copying what I had done. The confused look on his face showed he too had noticed things didn't look like they should.

After Dean and I finished up cleaning his front side, Owen helped us gently roll him over. We started to work carefully and quickly on his back. The wounds on his back were bubbling the most as they'd been open the longest, that seemed to make some kind of difference. The skin around the wounds were so dark and bruised that they were almost black. Once he was all washed and bandaged up Owen, Ryan and Dean carried him to the couch trying to keep him as steady as possible, then he passed out. I looked at Ryan's arm in the kitchen, it wasn't nearly as bad, but he had a cut a few inches long, not all that deep but it still needed tending to. The blood he had seeping out wasn't bubbling that I noticed, but I cleaned it just as well as I had cleaned Seth's.

"His wounds need to be looked at, treated somehow, stitches and antibiotics," I whispered to the others in the kitchen when they gathered around to see how Ryan was doing, "Like from a professional," I added.

"And where would we take him Ros? The ER? Everything is gone. Most people are gone. The odds of even finding a doctor or a nurse are astronomical," Ryan said throwing his hands into the air frustrated with the situation.

"I know all that, but that doesn't mean that there isn't a doctor somewhere!" I was almost shouting at him. Everyone knew he needed a doctor the problem wasn't convincing them, the problem was actually finding one and soon.

We all turned when we heard movement on the sofa. Seth had woke abruptly, his eyes were stretched wide open and his pupils were abnormally dilated. He started screaming and clawing at himself and the bandages. Owen rushed to him and held down his arms while Ryan and Dean held his legs but he was strong. They struggled to keep him down. I tried looking at him to make eye contact to calm him, try to talk to him so he'd relax and realize where he was but he never looked at me. Even when his eyes had appeared to be focused on me, it was more like he was looking through me as if I wasn't even there. Wherever his mind was right now, it wasn't in this living room. Maybe somewhere inside he could hear me, so I kept trying to calm him telling him it would be all right.

He dropped back down almost as suddenly as it came on. I brought the supplies over to the couch and treated the wounds he'd reopened from his clawing while he was out. Every few minutes he'd whimper or try to say something, but never fully woke, thankfully. I happened to rest my hand on his head as I got up and noticed his temperature was too hot, well hotter than Seth normally was even when he was hot.

"Do we have a thermometer anywhere?" I asked.

"I'm not sure, Seth organized all that stuff down there, but it is possible we grabbed one at some point," Owen said.

We'd checked the bathrooms when we first went through the house and organized what we wanted to keep so we knew there wasn't one here unless the boys had brought one back.

"Let's go check," Ryan said and everyone went down leaving me alone with Seth.

I sat there holding his hand stroking the back of it. I figured it had to be my fault that this happened, "I'm sorry Seth."

His eyes popped open at the sound of his name. He didn't blink, nor did he freak out. Seth just stared straight out passed the ceiling it seemed. I didn't let go of his hand but my heart-rate increased with every missed blink. Then he slowly turned his head so he was staring at me.

"Seth?" Still he didn't blink, "Stop it Seth you're scaring me." But he didn't stop, he kept staring until I dropped his hand and shakily started to back away from him. He didn't seem like himself at all. He didn't seem like he was even there, he looked like Seth but what was in there didn't feel like Seth. I felt like I was stuck in this room with a stranger, one that was really creeping me out. His eyes followed me as I slowly backed out of the room. There was nothing I could do to stop the scream that escaped my lips. I swung my arms wildly when I back into something. It was Dean who was coming up with a thermometer they had found.

He grabbed me in his arms and looked at me, "Ros, it's me! Stop screaming!" and I collapsed into his arms while he held my shaking body tight against him.

"Christ, what was that about?" Owen asked but he wasn't specifically asking me. He had no doubt heard the screaming and seen how terribly shaken I was. He wanted some answers.

Ryan peaked around the corner at Seth, who must have returned to his original laying down position. He hadn't said anything about how creepy it was for Seth to be staring like that, so he must not have seen. "Ros what happened?" he asked putting his hand carefully on my back. Dean held me tight. He didn't offer me to Ryan. If he had any guesses about Ryan and I being together, he didn't care and right now I didn't either as long as whoever had me didn't let me go. If they had, I felt as though I might just melt into a pool of water and seep through the floor until I soaked into the earth below this house. While the tornadoes and hail storm had been scary this had been bone chilling in a completely different way.

"It's going to sound stupid," I said, knowing I could never retell it with the same eerie quality it had as experiencing it first-hand.

"Tell me what happened? Are you hurt?" he said talking slowly as if he was talking to a child which only briefly infuriated me before I shivered. All I needed is more people thinking about how incapable I was at handling things. I just shot a feral dog-beast for god-sakes, I can do stuff.

"No, I'm not hurt," I said and told them all what had happened, trying to imitate what he did as best as I could, but surely it did not suffice. "It was like a horror movie, he's not himself," I added.

Ryan handed the thermometer to Owen and gestured for him to go take it. When Owen came back with the results a minute later I was still in Dean's arms my face pressed into his chest. He held me so tightly I didn't think he wanted to ever let me go.

"104.9," Owen said, "I don't think that's good."

"Wet cloth on his forehead, and one on the back of his neck. It might bring him down some," I said finally pulling myself from Dean, "I can get them." I offered since I had done it hundreds of times before, applying the wet cloths to Seth just felt like my job even though I didn't want to do it.

"I'll do it," Sienna said rushing to the

bathroom before I could argue. I couldn't decide if she was trying to be helpful or if she was trying to prove something. It didn't matter.

"He's lying there in his boxers, not sure a wet cloth will make any difference," Owen said with a frown. Owen and Seth had been friends for a long time, I could tell the weight of what had happened was finally settling in for him. He paced nervously.

"It's something to try," I said shrugging then crossing my arms in front of me. "Maybe give him two aspirin too, if you can get him to take them, oh and antibiotics, do we have any of those downstairs?" Not that any of us would even have the slightest idea of which ones to give him.

"We can check town tomorrow," Ryan said.

"You can't leave us alone here with him," I said sounding frantic. I didn't think Seth could do much in his condition but I was still fearful of that small chance I was wrong.

"I can stay, I'm sure Ryan and Owen can manage it," Dean said rubbing my shoulder. Ryan was starting to look annoyed. Now that I had stepped back and composed myself somewhat, Ryan wanted Dean to back off. It was subtle, but it showed in his eyes.

Owen stopped pacing, "Or I could just go now, I know the way, I'll be fast!"

Ryan looked at him for a minute contemplating but realizing how dangerous that would be, he'd never agree to it. Owen could handle himself, but it was almost night, he wouldn't be back in time. They had never went out at night not even together, no one knew what it was like out there at night. "Not going to happen, we can't afford to let anything happen to you Owen, I'm sorry."

Owen opened his mouth to argue, but he didn't say anything. He knew Ryan was right. He grabbed a box of pop-tarts off the counter and threw it at the dining room wall, it popped open and the packets of tarts sprinkled the ground. "Arrrrgh!" he growled in frustration.

Ryan reached out and put his hand on Owen's shoulder. Owen's head bowed. I wanted to hug him and tell him things would be OK, but I didn't know if they would be. I just let him have his moment.

"Let's put him in my bed, I'll stay on the couch, until he's well," Owen offered, his voice raspy. They carried him upstairs while Sienna and I waited. Seth didn't wake, but I heard a few whimpers as they climbed the stairs.

"Ros, can you bring up the fan?" Ryan yelled down to me after a few minutes.

"I got it!" Sienna shouted back as she unplugged it and dashed up the stairs.

I didn't wait for them to come down, I went to my room and I went to bed.

* * *

Lying in bed staring at the ceiling, I wished we would have at some point stashed a car somewhere nearby for quick trips to town, like in the case of needing medicine. Or perhaps even for a fast getaway, I mean who knew what could happen, we should plan for anything and everything. It would have been smart. I made up my mind to suggest it to the others tomorrow, but there was no point in doing it tonight, it wasn't like someone would run out and search for a working car now.

I heard someone starting the generator. I assumed they were going to use the fan to try to cool Seth down, Sienna probably put new cloths on him by now. Hopefully he would be feeling better in the morning and if not they'd go out to find antibiotics if need be. And Dean would stay here with Sienna and me... just in case.

Ryan came into my room what felt to be an hour later but I didn't really know how long it had actually been. I was just happy he was finally here.

"Come here," I said sitting up crossing my bare legs in front of me.

"Gladly," he winked and tore off his shirt.

"I want to see your arm." He held his arm in front of me while I slowly peeled back the bandage. It looked OK still, maybe a little redder than it should have but I was happy to see it wasn't bubbling and that there wasn't any pus. I didn't think it was infected, heck, the bandage had barely soaked up any blood.

"How does it look doc?" he asked jokingly, "Am I going to live?" Now he was just being over dramatic. I rolled my eyes at him, not really thinking this was something to joke about, but he was probably just trying to keep the mood light. We'd had enough stress for one day, more than enough to be honest.

"Looks all right I think. Not even on the same spectrum as Seth's, thank God."

He moved close leaning in to kiss my neck. For a second I was going to object, after everything I was worn out, but when the tingles shot through me, I decided this was exactly what I needed to take my mind off of things. He eased me down positioning himself lightly on top of me. While I was enjoying it and attempting to let my thoughts go, my body must not have caught up to my mind. I must not have been responding how I should have because he abruptly stopped, "What's wrong Ros?"

"Nothing," I lied with an insincere smile. I leaned into him and kissed him once on the mouth.

"OK, now really, what's wrong?" He backed off waiting for the truth, or an answer he'd accept to be the truth. He was already able to tell when something was bothering me and I guess that shouldn't be surprising considering all the time we had spent together. Practically 24 hours a day for months, I supposed I wasn't much of a mystery at this point.

"Why do you even want to be in here with me? I'm such a baby. A coward," I whined.

"What are you talking about?" He took my hand, but I pulled it away and shook my head. My eyelids started to flutter and my eyes felt warm as they threatened to fill up with salty tears. "You saved my life today. And what about with that biker creep? He wanted to kidnap you, probably rape you and maybe even just leave you for dead when he was done, but you pulled your gun on him. You saved yourself. Ros when it comes down to it you become aware, you're present and you are more than capable."

"I'm a big baby who's scared of everything. I was, I mean, I still am scared out of my mind about Seth's crazy episode before and I've been living with Seth now for how long? Months. He's never once hurt a fly. The worst thing he's done is back at the shelter he cooked that pasta dinner and it was a little too salty for my taste. And how do I treat him when he needs me? I back away from him. And now I'm afraid of him," I said flopping all the way back on my pillow not completely unaware of how childish it must have looked.

"You're too hard on yourself," Ryan said propping himself up on his arm next to me. He slid his other arm around my middle and lightly stroked his thumb against my side. "We'd have probably all reacted the same way if it would have been us instead of you, don't worry about it." He kissed my arm, my shoulder and then to my neck.

"Whatever. We need a car," I said as he continued to kiss my neck and shoulders, his hand began to wander more freely. Touching my skin as he ran his hand down to my thigh and then back up tugging on my underwear as his hand glided up my shirt and to my bra. "What if we have to get out of here, or we have to get something to save someone's life, like something from a pharmacy," I said forcing myself to ignore what he was doing until I could get my thoughts out. "We are so unprepared for emergencies."

"We'll get a car," he said kissing my chin then my lips. His hand was at the back of my neck holding me to him. He tilted my head so my eyes were looking right into his. He was only inches from me and with serious yet lust filled eyes, he whispered, "We'll get a car, we'll get the meds, everything will be fine."

With that his hand was back to roaming, and I felt a little more relaxed. I touched his arm, then I let it slide down his chest absolutely loving the feel of his warm skin. He was caressing every inch of my skin and it was driving me insane. I didn't want this moment to end. It was quiet moments with Ryan where I was able to completely forget everything else, which was good for my mental health. These parts were easy and far more pleasurable.

I was lying there wearing only my over-sized T-shirt covering my underwear. He must have felt over-dressed because he unbuttoned his jeans and removed his pants. There he was. Ryan Reed. Lying there on my bed wearing only his boxers.

Our hands were everywhere, mine getting lost in his soft hair. I was surprised when he reached behind me and expertly unhooked my bra as if he'd done it a million times. I couldn't stop my brain from thinking about how many times he must have done that before. My body stiffened at the thought. I wanted to scream at myself for attempting to sabotage the mood.

"Something wrong?" he asked noticing I was drifting out of the moment, "Did I do something wrong?"

"Sorry, it's nothing," I lied.

"Ros, seriously." He was getting too good at this, or I was just an awful liar.

"It's just that you were pretty good at that, you must have had a lot of girlfriends." The thought made my stomach somersault. I didn't like thinking about him with anyone, especially when I was in bed with him.

"Ha! Don't I wish!" he laughed and kissed my shoulder, I scrunched up my face at him and rolled my eyes. "You really want to know? Now?" he asked.

I nodded apprehensively, did I?

"One girlfriend, lasted about six months, she said I was too moody," he said looking at me waiting for some kind of reaction, but when whatever he was waiting for didn't happen. He continued, "That's all over and done with, I'm with you. How about you then? Lots of boyfriends I'd imagine," he said changing the subject.

"Yeah right! You know the answer to that," I said thinking back to how awkward I had been with him the first time we got close.

"I do?"

"I guess I thought you could tell that I'm pretty new to all this," I said looking away.

"You've never had a boyfriend?" he asked raising an eyebrow as if he was suspicious.

"Well, I've had a couple, but it was really stupid. It was lame, mostly just hanging out together, I never felt that interested in anyone I guess. I'd always find something about them that annoyed me. It was always over before it started practically!" I started to squirm with how uncomfortable this conversation had gotten. "Let's be done talking about this, it's bad enough I'm thinking about how you were with your ex!"

"Yeah don't think about that because I sure as hell am not going to. I'm here with you, right now, and this is the only place I want to be now and forever," he kissed me passionately as if punctuating it to prove his point. He was pushing out all of the crazy thoughts from my head with the force of this kiss and it was working.

"I'm not going to have sex with you tonight," I blurted out.

"We don't have to," he said kissing me again as if I was his life source and he needed to recharge.

"It would just be too soon, you know? I wouldn't want you to get the wrong idea about me," I said feeling as though I needed to explain. His hands kept moving and his lips kept working their magic. I felt like I was under some kind of blissful spell.

"I understand," he whispered against my cheek, "We stop when you say so."

I kissed him back as if it was my turn to take charge. I pulled him on top of me wanting to feel his skin against as much of mine as possible. It felt silky, but more importantly, I loved how I felt safe being this close to him. I started thinking about how if this was the end of the world, why would I deny myself something I really wanted? There was no question I wanted to be with Ryan. I reached down and started to wiggle out of my underwear.

"Ros?" He looked confused.

"I changed my mind... if you want to?"

"Are you sure?" he asked looking at me with his serious Ryan face. I wanted happy Ryan back as soon as possible, I smiled and nodded. I was sure. I couldn't have been more sure.

We became a single tangled mess of arms and legs and kisses. It was soft and sweet. Fast and rough. So many new and wonderful feelings and sensations jolted through my whole being.

And when we came down from our cloud, we were both smiling. And nothing mattered and nothing existed except for us.

It was just me and him. For a moment in time we had become one, and it was more than I imagined it could be.

I was glad I had changed my mind. After all I think I was in love with him. I knew without a doubt I'd do anything for him. I already knew he'd do anything for me. It was the right time for us.

My eyes glanced towards the slightly cracked door. Ryan must have forgotten to close it completely, not expecting all this to happen tonight. For a second I thought I saw something move. Had someone been out there looking in? I blinked but there was nothing there.

"What is it?"

"I thought I saw something, but I guess I was wrong," I said bringing myself and my thoughts back to Ryan and this bed.

We couldn't remove the smiles that were

pasted to our faces. My cheeks felt sore. I pulled the sheet up over myself and he kissed me lightly on the shoulder, wondering if I was OK. I was. I was happy. I had forgotten about the miserable world. I had forgotten about Seth upstairs in absolute misery. And I wouldn't let myself think about those things, or about how Ryan and I would never have a normal relationship, like movies, dinners or dating. What we had right now in this moment was perfect, nothing else mattered. What our future would be like was a complete mystery, it would be so different from what things would have been like before all this. I'd worry about it later.

For now, we needed rest. Ryan would want to go on the pharmacy run early and hopefully searching for a car was on the list of things to do. Sienna, Dean and I would have to take care of Seth while they were out, and that would probably be a challenge in itself.

We drifted to sleep quickly and with smiles still on our faces. It was the best night I had since everything happened.

I wasn't sure how much time had passed when I woke up to the smell of smoke. It was still dark outside, and at first I thought I was still dreaming. Until the smell was so strong I knew it was real, and I was sitting there completely wide awake.

Chapter seventeen.

"Ryan!" I shouted, shaking him vigorously, "Ryan! Wake up!" He groaned and turned over, I searched for my clothes and quickly got dressed to see what was going on. Owen was tossing and turning on the couch, it wasn't quite as smoky in the living room and kitchen as it had been in my room. Must have something to do with how the vent system was laid out. I ran upstairs to see the blaze through a crack in the door to Seth's room. Dean's room was next to his, the door open and filling with smoke.

"Dean! Dean! Please, please wake up!" I was shaking him back and forth and pulling him up trying to lift him. "Dean please!"

"What? What is it?" he said looking at me confused and then coughing. "Smoke? What's going on?" he asked confused, his movements seemingly weak and labored.

"There's a fire in Seth's room, please get up. Help me!" I said dragging him with me. He only had on his boxers, I barely noticed and I didn't care.

He pushed Seth's door all the way open to

see the fire blazing all around the side of the bed and the wall near the window. Seth wasn't sleeping. He was looking at us, recoiling away from us back onto the bed. He looked like a crazed animal. The way he crouched and cowered made him look wild, "Seth!" I screamed at him, "What are you doing?" I felt I saw a glimmer of Seth look back at me, but most of what looked back at me was poison and evil. Whatever that dog had done to him wasn't something that any antibiotic would have been able to cure. It was like he was rabid and he put the whole house in danger.

"Seth, come with us," Dean said reaching his hand out over the fire. Seth leaped backwards putting even more distance between us and him. Dean yanked his hand back from the heat, not because he wanted to, but because it was a reflex. His arm was cooking, and he could only leave it near the heat for so long. He shook it attempting to cool it down.

The fire was growing with each second. "Seth, please! You have to come now!" I screamed, my face red with frustration and from the heat. "There isn't much time!"

Sienna came up behind us "What's going on," she said in a panic.

"Well, there's this fire," Dean said rather rudely.

"Obviously," she said, "Let's get out of here!"

"Great advice," Dean said, "but Seth is being a little stubborn right now."

Seth grinned. The fire blazed up sending us

another foot away from him. "Seth please," I begged. I didn't even know if he could hear us anymore. He opened the closet door and shut himself inside. "Noo!" I cried.

"Seth!" Dean said as he stepped forward nearly into the flames, only to immediately jump backwards from the intense heat.

Sienna was full out crying.

I saw his candle on the bedside table, tipped over, the wax poured out, and the crumpled up papers and books scattered all around the bed in a circular shape. He had started the fire. He had taken matters into his own hand, but it was going to get us all killed.

I had fallen to my knees and was sobbing for the Seth I had known. The closet doors were on fire now, it wouldn't be much longer, that is if the smoke hadn't already been too much for him. Dean pulled me over to the top of the stairs, the smoke was getting unbearable and if we didn't leave now we wouldn't have much of a chance.

"Sienna, fill a pack with clothes… whatever you need and that you think we can't get in town, hurry," he said pushing her into her room. "Ros, wake up Owen and Ryan, quickly fill your packs, GO!" He disappeared into his room covering his mouth with his hand but of course coughing anyway. I could see him moving around his room fast, which motivated me to move my feet. I rushed down the stairs and ran into Owen at the bottom about to ask what was going on.

"Fill a pack," I said.

"What is it?" he asked groggily.

"A fire, we gotta get out of here, pack your essentials and get outside," I said rushing passed him.

"My things are upstairs," he said confused.

"Shit!" I yelled, "Right, um, you'll have to get new clothes and stuff later, pack some food and water for us." Thank God for quick thinking, it didn't give him a chance to think about what he was losing and it would give him an extremely important job. That's what he was good at, getting things done.

"Ryan wake up!" I yelled as I shook his leg. "There's a fire. We need to get out so GET UP AND GET DRESSED!"

"What? A fire?" he said not understanding, it was as if I had been speaking to him in another language. "Is this a dream?"

"For the love of Pete, I wish it were, please get up and go fill a pack! Clothes, whatever you need, hurry!" I yelled while I filled my own pack with clothes and my novel. I couldn't think of anything else I absolutely needed that I couldn't find once we were safe. Water and food would be far more important so I'd just fill the rest of my pack with necessities.

Ryan pulled on his pants and left my room to see all the smoke gathered in the hallway, "Holy shit," he said covering his mouth as he coughed. He went into his room to pack his things. I slid my shoes on without socks and went to the kitchen, Dean and Sienna were making their way out the back door.

"Wait, the guns!" Owen said. "Don't go out

yet! It may not be safe." He opened a closet and took out a few guns, packed some bullets and put one of the guns in his waistband, "OK, go!" He handed me a gun, safety on, and I put it in my waistband. The fire could probably be seen from far away, at least the night sky would hide the smoke. We were not safe here, inside or outside.

I noticed Dean had his bow and arrows hanging off of him. "Let's go over by the shed," Dean suggested, and we all ran towards it. "Check to make sure we have what we need," he said looking around anxiously. I made a mental list and ran through it quickly making sure we had food, water, and weapons. I guess we were back to just the essentials.

"Where is Ryan?" I said stomping and staring at the back door. "What is taking him so long?"

"I'll go get him." Dean dashed off at top speed meeting him right as he was exiting the back door coughing like crazy. He was doubled over from the smoke inhalation. It was getting much worse. Dean practically dragged him to the rest of the group.

"Where's Seth?" he choked out also noticing one of us was missing.

We didn't know how to tell him what happened and that this was all because of Seth. I suspected Owen had a feeling it had something to do with Seth but what exactly he didn't know. Ryan was oblivious. "Umm…" I started but stopped when the words didn't come and a tear streamed down my cheek.

"The fire started in his room," Dean said, his head down. "Guys we gotta get out of here, it's not safe," he said looking around nervously.

The house was starting to really light up the night sky. We would see people coming. We would see the dogs, but the bad part is they would see us too, and they would see the five of us in bad shape. We had lost our shelter. We had lost our supplies. We lost our safety. We lost a friend. We were so far from the top of our game it wasn't funny.

"Do we have a backup plan?" I asked.

"We find a car. We find somewhere to spend the rest of the night that is safe, and then in the morning we go find a car," Ryan said walking into the darkness. He coughed again, and scratched his arm where he had his wound from the dogs.

We followed him as we always did, leaving behind what felt like everything.

Chapter eighteen.

We walked about three miles before we found another house. It was a small house with a trailer in the yard. We didn't want to waste the time doing a full check of the house, so we decided we'd just spend the night in the trailer. Owen and Ryan cleared it in a matter of minutes and we all went inside. Thankfully Owen had been smart enough to pack a flashlight, unfortunately he'd only packed one, but once we were situated he turned it off and we sat in the darkness.

The trailer was dreary and had signs that someone had stayed there recently. There was opened cans of food on the small kitchen table and blankets piled up on the couch. Whoever had been here wasn't there now, but I worried about whether they'd be coming back or not. Anything that had been of any value had been taken out. Pictures that once hung on the wall were laying broken on the floor, all sorts of things had been pulled out of the cabinets and strewn on the counters and floor. It looked as though a tornado went through this trailer with how messy it was. I had been happy when the flashlight went out and I didn't have to look at the sadness left behind in this beat up, stinky trailer.

Owen lounged in a chair with one leg up over the arm rest and was trying to sleep. He hadn't been ready to ask about Seth and I didn't blame him considering their past. Ryan sat on a chair in the kitchen near a door which I figured was probably a closet door, he liked having a wall behind him instead of open space. With a wall behind him he only had to watch three directions instead of four. Sienna and Dean shared a small couch, each lying sort of in a crunched up position trying to get as comfortable as they could manage. I stood there too anxious to sit in the recliner behind me. We all needed sleep for whatever tomorrow held, our somewhat easier life was gone. Just like that.

"What exactly happened back there?" Ryan asked when everyone was silent and possibly asleep.

"Are you asking me?" I whispered back, hoping he was talking to someone else.

"Anyone that will tell me," he said. But if anyone else was awake they didn't say anything.

"I woke up to the smoke, went upstairs and found his room on fire. He was trapped, but he had no desire to leave, we begged him, repeatedly," I said sniffing up the tears and Ryan's head dropped.

"I knew something was wrong when I went to bed." Dean's quiet voice broke through the darkness and over Owen's heavy breathing. At least Owen was getting rest since I thought this would be the hardest on him. We'd all lost someone, but Owen lost his best friend. Maybe he hadn't asked more questions because he wanted to sleep, and just wasn't ready to process what had happened. And maybe he already knew enough that the details didn't matter. "That's what I came to tell you guys."

I froze.

"Came to tell us?" Ryan questioned, "No one came—"

"That was the 'something' I thought I saw," I said to Ryan hoping that would jog his memory and I wouldn't have to spell it out.

Dean sighed.

"What were you going to tell us?" I asked feeling the heat from my embarrassment on my face and neck. It was too dark no one knew it was there but me.

"That Seth was acting weird. He'd had an episode with me, much like you described earlier, but it was worse. After a while he crouched down on the floor, like a beast and growled at me. I closed his door almost all the way, I wanted to be able to see him if I looked in and I wanted to be able to hear him if he needed me. I sat there holding my bow until he went back to sleep. I wasn't about to leave Sienna alone up there with him awake." Dean sighed again and continued, "Even when he was sleeping I didn't want to leave her alone for more than a minute, and actually even a minute was too long. But I couldn't stay awake all night again.

"By starting that fire, I think in his crazed mind, he thought he was protecting us from him," Dean said. "Seth started that fire to protect us from whatever was inside him, I think he thought he was doing the right thing. I really, really, really tried to save him Ryan… I did," he said as he sniffed, seemingly to disguise the fact that he voice had started cracking.

"He did, and I did too, he just wasn't himself. Dean, you couldn't have done anything other than what you did," I said trying to sound comforting even though I was still plenty embarrassed by what Dean had seen. If we hadn't left the door open by mistake, Dean would have knocked and told us about Seth, maybe it would have saved him or maybe it wouldn't have mattered.

"Yeah well, maybe if I would have told someone instead of just going back to bed, Seth would still be with us," he complained. I wasn't sure if he was taking a jab at me and Ryan, or if he was angry with himself for being tired. Either way I let it slide off me. After all, he had every right in the world to be upset. We all did.

Dean and Seth had been longtime friends too, maybe not like Owen, but I could tell it was hurting him — I wanted to hug him. This was hard on all of us, we had all grown to know and love Seth. He was kind and gentle, never wanted to hurt a fly. If it hadn't been for his overheating issue he still wouldn't have went on runs, he'd never use a gun he'd try to find another way and by then in some cases it may have been too late. He wasn't foolish, he was just sweet and tried to see the good in people, even if it wasn't there.

That was all that was said on the topic of

Seth. Everyone either sat in silence or drifted off into fitful bouts of sleep, which is what I had done. I tossed from side to side waking up every time I saw Seth grin at me in the darkness behind my eyelids before he'd shut himself in the closet all over again.

When the sun came up just enough over the horizon to give us some light, we ate our breakfast. I forced myself to eat something even though it was the last thing I wanted to do with how much my stomach felt like it was tied into knots. I knew I needed the fuel. I would have to be alert and aware now that we were no longer sitting safely in the nice house we had turned into a home. I couldn't afford to let myself get weak and add to what I felt was already a long list of my shortcomings.

My throat was sore from all the screaming and the smoke. We were all still coughing every now and then trying to get the putrid stuff out of our lungs. I didn't even bother volunteering to help when Ryan, Owen and Dean went to scope out the area.

* * *

I must have fallen asleep while waiting for them to come back in, because when I woke up, I heard mumbling outside. Sienna was stretched out and sleeping on the couch and I could see all three boys standing in a circle talking. I watched them through the slit between the closed curtains

215

covering the thin window. I realized quickly what
was going on. Owen kept his head down most of
the time and then he brushed away a tear. They
were telling him what happened to Seth. Both
Ryan and Dean stayed with him a bit patting his
back, but they turned to come inside to give him a
moment to himself. He had probably asked for
some time alone I guessed. I ducked back down
and pretended to still be sleeping.

When Owen came in ten minutes later I
acted as if the door had woke me. "We should get
going," Ryan said and Dean gently shook Sienna to
wake her up.

Before we left we checked the garage at the
main house for a car, it would have to be suitable
for the now five of us. They had one in the garage
but it was a small car. Too small for us and our
packs, we were going to need to find a truck, an
SUV or a van. Everyone and their uncles had
SUVs, would it really be that hard to find one? We
moved house to house staying out of the city, but it
was getting harder and harder with the heat and
with the houses all being miles apart from one
another. So it wasn't long until we decided to risk
it and go into town, staying in residential areas until
we could find something that would work.

It had taken us a good three hours to find an
SUV, it was black and one of the newer models.
The SUV had half a tank of gas which would be
enough for a while since we had no idea where we
were going. It was parked in a garage of a nice
home that hadn't seen much damage. The SUV
was in nearly perfect condition and we found the

216

keys hanging on a key rack in the kitchen, it was probably the first thing that went right for us in months. We were lucky. It started right away even though it had been sitting for so long. We headed east, merging onto I94 and just drove. There were still cars strewn about the roads, but most had been blown off into the ditch from when the storms had passed. And others had probably been pushed off to the side to make way for those who were still alive and traveling. Ryan took the first exit that had a sign barely hanging on the post that indicated gas stations.

As we pulled off the exit ramp we stopped at the first gas station we saw which was pretty obviously abandoned. Ryan pulled up to a pump and everyone started to get out of the car, "Whoa! Wait guys, I'm just getting gas," he said.

"I want to look for water," I said.

"We have to check for supplies," Owen said.

"Um, fine, Owen will take you in but be fast and stay close to him," Ryan said sounding bossy. Clearly he wasn't happy with the whole idea, but Owen was right, this was where we'd be gathering most of our supplies from now that we were on the road. Sienna and Dean came too, leaving Ryan alone, which made me nervous, but of course he insisted he'd be fine.

Owen liked being put in charge and he was quite capable, the proof of that was that Ryan trusted him enough to take care of me. I thought of him as our muscle. I felt pretty safe being around Owen, he would do what needed to be done to protect us.

217

There had been no reason to worry, once we were inside it was clear there was no one else there. In fact, the mini mart had been cleaned out. I figured it had been mostly empty because it was so close to the highway. It was an easy stop. I looked out the window to see Ryan moving the car to another pump.

There were a few dusty cans of Pinto beans on the shelf which I stuffed into my pack. I found a package of saltines which I also took. The water, however, had been cleaned out.

"I need to use the bathroom," Sienna said.

Owen led her to the ladies room. He peeked inside first to make sure it was safe and then he waited outside of the door for her. "Hey look at this," he shouted. Dean and I both rushed over and saw a sign posted on the corkboard next to old washed out business cards.

The sign read:

Come HOME
Fairbanks Alaska
"Safety awaits"

For some reason it made me think of the note that I had found in what had remained of my house. Could that have been left there telling me to go to Alaska? Could I have been in Alaska this whole time with my mom? It seemed like a stretch. HOME? I had no home. My home was destroyed with everything else, what was this HOME?

"No directions." I looked around the area to see if there was any other information.

"Nope," Dean said running his fingers through his hair, "maybe it's so obvious you can't miss it."

"Fairbanks," I said not wanting to take the sign but wanting to remember where to go.

Sienna exited the bathroom and joined us. Noticing the sign, she touched it as if she wanted to make sure it was real, her eyes lit up but she said nothing. "Are you guys ready?" Owen said looking around. He didn't like staying in one place too long. I didn't blame him and it probably wasn't the best idea to leave Ryan out there waiting in the wide open for too long.

"Let's go," Dean said throwing a lighter and an old candy bar in his pack.

We piled into the car and Ryan jumped back on the eastbound highway before we got a chance to say anything about the sign. I wasn't even sure if the others were going to tell him. I grew impatient waiting for Owen, so I took care of it myself. After about 30 questions we didn't have the answers to, he pulled the SUV over and slammed it into park. He wanted to know if we should go, and without knowing more about this HOME, we took a vote. Since no one had a better idea, we decided to go to Alaska. We weren't sure what we'd do once we got there, but we were going to head in that direction for now, and we could always change our mind. Ryan turned the car around and we backtracked, but at least we had a destination in mind.

Ryan had the AC cranked. The car was more comfortable than being outside but it was still warm from the hot sun beating down on it and perhaps the heat had something to do with how inefficient the AC was. We hadn't driven very far when he said we needed to find a car shop, something that would have window tint, his hope was that it would keep the car cooler. Mostly I think it must have bothered Ryan because his arms were on the steering wheel with the sun blasting down on them or on his face where his visor didn't protect him. I didn't like the heat but I was just thankful I wasn't outside.

He picked a town and exited off the highway. We drove up and down the bumpy streets of what appeared to have been the main drag once upon a time. He finally found a place that might have the window tint. Owen and Ryan ran inside leaving us in the car, they'd be quick he promised. Dean wouldn't be able to use his bow in the car should he need to do something, so Owen gave him a gun.

"It's hot, but it's not that hot inside the car," Dean said, "I wonder why the heat is bothering Ryan so much. It never used to bother him that much. At least I never heard him complain about it, but I suppose you'd know if it had better than I would."

I rolled my eyes and ignored him even though he was right. The heat did seem to be bothering him more than usual.

They came out of the shop with a ton of supplies and then discussed how they were going to approach the project. After a short time they came to tell us they were going to find somewhere more secluded to install the tint. To me everything felt secluded, but I understood they'd want to feel as safe as possible while they worked. We found a vacant home several miles off the highway. It would be easy to see anyone coming from a mile away. But no one came. It took them several hours to install the window tint, and once we were back on the road, Ryan was pleased with how much cooler the car was. For that reason alone it had been worth it.

We headed north at the first major highway that would take us to the Alaskan Highway. Other than that we were going to need some maps to figure out our way to the HOME. "Ryan? Can we get some maps?" I asked. I wanted to get started planning our route even though we hadn't been on the road long since our last stop. It would give me something to do.

"Sure, let's just get another hour or two of day driving under our belt. I'll stop before it's dark," he said with a forced smile. He seemed a little off. He was still pale and not talking at all, which really wasn't that unusual for Ryan but it was the far off look that went with it that made me notice it more. I offered him a drink of water and a cereal bar, thinking he was just hungry, but he refused both and just kept his focus on the road. I'd talk to him about it once we had a little privacy, and I didn't have to try to talk to him around the back of his seat.

* * *

We'd been on the road for two hours when the sun started to go down and Ryan found a large gas station that hopefully still had maps for the taking. How many people that were still out there would need maps? At this point I was more concerned with how he was feeling, he was not himself. I was going to make sure we got a little alone time before we drove off. We all needed a little break from the road to be honest and maybe that's all Ryan needed too. Maybe everything that had happened with Seth was just catching up with him, I still hadn't properly mourned him, and maybe I never would.

After the boys made sure it was safe we went inside while Ryan topped off the tank with what was left in the reservoir. I grabbed a stack of maps to sort through and sat at one of the little tables on the restaurant side of the gas station. Sienna was looking through magazines that were months old. Dean and Owen were emptying the shelves and taking things from the storage in back that most people seemed to forget about when they came to gas stations.

Ryan came in and I gestured for him to come sit by me. I passed him my water and a protein bar, "I'm so sick of protein bars," he said as he took an enormous bite.

"Aren't we all?"

"I want a cheeseburger. Or a sub," he said

nodding towards the graffiti covered sub sign that no longer lit up displaying it's plentiful menu.

"Oh, I wanted to ask, um, how are you feeling?" I asked nervously, thumbing through the maps doing my best to be nonchalant.

"Fine, why?" he said not making eye contact. I think he was looking at a picture of a sub as he chewed his protein bar pretending it was something else.

"Oh nothing, you seemed to be bothered more by the heat than usual and you've been so quiet, more than usual," I said finally looking at him longer than a quick glance. I noticed his cheeks were splashed with a hint of pink, like the cheeks of a painted doll face. Before he could even answer my hand shot out like a karate chopping temperature taker and I had the back of my hand against his forehead. He was burning up. Dammit. "God, Ryan!"

"Keep your voice down," he said a little too threatening for my liking.

I glanced at Sienna. She didn't look up at us and if she was listening in, she was doing an excellent job of making it appear as though she wasn't.

"You're sick," I said under my breath.

"I'll be OK, I just need something to get the fever down and everything will be fine," Ryan said scratching his arm. The arm that had the scratch from those rabid poisoned dog-beasts.

"Let me see it."

"No."

"Ryan, let me see it so I can help you," I

said, worried about what I'd find under the wrappings. He pulled the bandage up and I was devastated. When Ryan saw the look on my face he quickly covered it.

"See there's nothing you can do," Ryan said as my hands slid over my face. I didn't know if I was going to scream, cry, fall to the ground and just give up or what. It felt like there really wasn't a point to any of this anymore.

"We'll go to the bathroom and clean it, I'll get some peroxide if they have it, and some new bandages. Go to the women's room and wait. I'll be there in a second," I ordered, and he obeyed.

I grabbed what I could as secretly as I could, and I turned right into Dean as I stepped out of my aisle. I had been so preoccupied I didn't see him turning the corner. "Hey! Careful!" Dean said with a half-smile. Dean also wasn't himself, but that was easily traced back to what happened with Seth. He was doing the best he could, and it weighed very heavily on him. Mainly the fact that we hadn't been able to save him and he blamed himself.

"Sorry."

"Where are you going so fast?" he said looking at me with a raised eyebrow. He was suspicious and for a split second I wanted to tell him, I wanted to confide in someone how scared I was and beg for help but I didn't. Dean wouldn't have an answer any more than I did, it wasn't right of me to want to burden him with it, and Ryan would probably have never forgiven me.

"Restroom, I'll be right back, don't worry!"

I forced a smile and rushed off worried Ryan would have second thoughts and have us leave without letting me clean his wound.

He was sitting on a sink when I went in, "You think it's really bad don't you?" he asked already knowing how bad it was.

"Ryan, I'm not a nurse or a doctor, I have no idea," I said while my brain was screaming yes it's bad it's really, really, really bad!

I took the old bandage off to see the redness around the original wound had spread. It seemed pretty clear to me that Ryan had taken to scratching the wound. A lot. It must have been irritating him in some way and those scratches had torn open more skin. The original scratch now had several neighboring surface scratches that were bloody or oozing pus. And what injury would be complete without a little bit of bubbling at the widest part each wound? I poured water over it slowly until the bubbles slowed. I didn't find any peroxide, but I did find a bottle of rubbing alcohol, a tube of antibiotic cream and two bottles of a generic spray antiseptic.

I took the bottle of rubbing alcohol, "This is going to burn… a lot," I said, "But I really think we should do it because I want your wound to stop bubbling."

"OK," Ryan said looking at me intently, I thought he'd ask about the bubbling but he didn't. He must have already known.

"Keep in mind I have no idea what I'm doing."

"Noted."

225

"Still want to do it?" I asked not even sure it was a good idea myself. He nodded. "So if you can't take it anymore, tell me, I'll rinse it with water."

"Got it," and he held his arm out to me over the sink.

I poured the alcohol on his wound, and it bubbled more. He started hitting his leg with his free hand, harder and harder as he tried to cope with the burning pain from the liquid. His veins started popping out and his fingernails dug into his palms. I couldn't bare to watch him suffer through it any longer so I poured the water over it, two bottles' worth. After I had rinsed it, it didn't appear to be bubbling any more. It was still red all around. I don't think the rubbing alcohol helped with the redness at all, in fact it may have actually made it worse. I sprayed with the antiseptic and then squeezed a generous amount of the cream over the wound instead of applying it with my fingers. I didn't think it was a good idea to touch it. Lastly, I applied a clean bandage.

His fever hadn't let up. I gave him two of the fever reducers I found, unfortunately it was a kid's liquid and I wasn't sure it would be strong enough to bring down his fever. He took two shots, double the recommended dosage for kids. It was Owen's turn to drive, thankfully, so Ryan could get some sleep. Maybe that's all he needed to fight off the infection. We had decided earlier that we were going to drive straight through, only stopping if there wasn't anyone awake enough to drive. Owen drove while Dean sat in the passenger seat helping me figure out our route with the atlas I'd found. Sienna was bunched up beside me, head against the window sleeping with a little smile on her face. I loved when people forgot where they were and had a smile on their face, like I had when I was with Ryan those few nights before we had to leave our nice little home. Just him and I being there together, safe, well relatively safe, was nice. The thought of it almost made me smile... almost.

Ryan was sprawled out in the backseat having a fitful rest. He held his bad arm over his head and would groan every so often when he'd try to twist into a new position to get comfortable. The SUV wasn't the best for sleeping.

I was worried about him, very worried, but all we could do was drive on towards this HOME place. I hoped more than anything else that HOME would have help for Ryan.

Chapter nineteen.

Ryan took the night off from taking his turn driving, and slept in the backseat. Owen and Dean didn't mind since we all knew he needed the rest. I thought the most the others knew was that Ryan wasn't feeling well, but I didn't think they knew why.

We stopped at another gas station when the sun crept over the horizon, and filled up the tank. Lucky for us, this gas station was pretty far off the beaten path. So far off that it had full gas tanks and plenty of food and water on the shelves. Best of all, it had a working gas stove in a little kitchen area in the back. It appeared as though it had been used to warm up big batches of soup. Maybe for truck drivers who'd pass through wanting something hot to eat, at least that is what I envisioned.

There wouldn't be any semi trucks coming through here anymore, so I decided to make a warm breakfast of oatmeal. I had to make it with water but it was still good. Or maybe it wasn't and we thought it was because it was a hot breakfast, different from the normal toaster pastry. I put a dollop of jam on top and everyone commented on how good it was. If only that's what it took before all this happened to please people, a warm, mildly OK breakfast. I thought of extravagant breakfasts of Eggs Benedict, cheesy omelets, crispy hash browns and thick cut bacon. If there would have been a pig wandering around at this gas station I'm not sure he would have survived very long. Someone would have been out back butchering him up, and not a single one of us would have complained. Since all this happened I would have bet that all of us had lost at least fifteen pounds. We could all stand to eat some bacon.

Before we left I checked Ryan's wound again. It was bubbling. I didn't let the tears that were threatening to fall leak out.

"No rubbing alcohol," he begged.

"No, not today," I said even though I wanted to douse it again, I wanted it to sit in a vat of rubbing alcohol until all the poison in there was gone. Instead, I washed it and applied more of the healing gel and passed him two more pills for the fever. After cleaning it I searched the shelves for medicines so I could start a stockpile, but if they carried anything here, it was gone. I'd have to look at the next stop. I wasn't even sure the medicine was working to reduce the fever, it didn't seem to be, but I had no way of measuring without a thermometer. He felt hotter each time I felt him. The heat that radiated from him made the air outside seem cool. Today, when I had bandaged him up, I had to use extra gauze on the wound because it was spreading, the redness was larger and the wounds themselves seemed to be getting bigger. Eventually we'd have to tell the others.

I tried to hide it but Ryan could tell by my face or my body language that it wasn't good. "I don't think you should drive," I said, "I'll take an extra turn. We'll just say you're too tired, no one will care."

"They don't want you to take an extra turn, you drive too slow," Ryan smiled at me.

I smiled back trying my best to keep the sadness and worry out of my eyes, "I drive safe."

"We are the only ones on the road," he chuckled.

I kissed him on the lips. "Please get better," I whispered.

"Well OK, but only because you asked so nicely," he joked. He let out a loose cough, probably still from the smoke. Although it was only Ryan who was still coughing. It was torturous to watch him get worse. The sooner we got to Alaska, the sooner he could quite possibly see a doctor. That's what I was holding on to. Help may be in our not so distant future.

I told the others I'd drive but Dean laughed. "You're one turn was more than enough, I'll drive. That way we can actually get to Alaska in this lifetime." He was trying to stay upbeat, but he was worried about Ryan too, and he was worried about me worrying about Ryan. He didn't say as much but I could tell by all the secret looks that came my way when he thought I wouldn't notice.

Ryan lowered himself onto the backseat again. I sat with him letting him rest his head on my lap while I stroked his hair and stared out the window. He looked pale but peaceful. I told him how I had wished there would have been a pig wandering behind the gas station so I could have served up some bacon with breakfast. He curled his lips into a weak smile before he drifted off into what was, thankfully, a restful sleep.

I watched the world pass by and with each mile I felt Ryan slip further and further into the sickness. Worst of all there wasn't anything I could do about it but sit here and try to make sure he was comfortable. With how hot he was, there was no such thing as comfortable. At least he wasn't alone, I was with him, and I wouldn't leave him, I would do what I could to help him through this. I had to.

* * *

This was our second day in Canada and the further north we drove the more tolerable the temperatures became. It wasn't 100 plus degrees outside any more. During the daytime my guess was that it was more like upper 80's or lower 90's when the sun was out. At night it was actually quite comfortable. That was another thing I noticed more of, clouds. Pretty, white, fluffy clouds floating through the crystal blue sky. Further south, clouds had been much more rare, and when there were some they were thin and gray.

The bad part was the cooler it got outside the hotter Ryan felt under my touch. At the last stop I'd found more medicine and packed it all away. I became a clock watcher and gave him a new dose at precisely the right time. Not allowing it to wear off. At every stop I'd clean his bandage. Even if he didn't want to leave the SUV I made him at least get out so I could clean the wound without soaking the seats. He had developed noticeable dark circles under his eyes and no matter how much rest he got, they didn't go away.

Ryan's wound was twice as big tonight as it had been yesterday morning. Each day it seemed to be getting worse and I didn't know how much more he would be able to take. I had found a thermometer at the last stop but it hadn't been very accurate. We had all tested it and everyone got a different reading each time we tried it. His range was always between 103.5 and 105.2, but I had no idea if the 105 really translated to a real 105 reading. Either way, it was clear he had a fever and quite possibly a dangerously high one at that. But I hadn't needed the thermometer to tell me that.

At the last stop we saw a sign posted on the front door and near the bathrooms. It was another one about HOME. We didn't learn anything new.

Family - Friends - Community
Come HOME
Fairbanks Alaska

I wondered about a place where people would come this far south to put up signs advertising their wonderful community. Maybe they had planes or helicopters. I couldn't imagine someone had driven all this way just to put up signs, and I'm sure it wasn't just this route that had the signs. It seemed like it would be a lot of work and trouble to go to just to catch the eye of a random passerby.

It was getting dark quicker the further north we traveled, and it didn't take much darkness to put me into a light sleep, riding this much was both tiring and boring. I was out before I could offer to take my turn that would end up with me getting teased for my grandmotherly driving speed. Most of the time Dean and Owen had been switching off, but they had to be tired. They'd tried to teach Sienna to drive on one stretch of road but she didn't like it. It made her nervous and the lessons ended up taking too long, so they gave up and didn't make her try again. Ryan was physically incapable of taking his turns but the least I could do is continue to take mine and do my best at driving faster. They probably wanted to get help for Ryan just as fast as I did and knew that would mean not letting me drive.

I was certain that everyone knew something was wrong with Ryan but still no one had asked about it. Maybe because of the fever they just thought it was a stubborn virus, but as far as I could tell they hadn't guessed it was related to the wound. I knew it was only a matter of time before I'd have to tell them.

I didn't even realize I had fallen asleep until the rough swerving of the car had woken me. Owen was in the passenger seat and he too must have been jostled awake by the movement. "What's going on?" he demanded. Owen had sort of taken over as group leader while Ryan was incapacitated.

"An animal or something, sorry about that," he said focusing on the road. He swerved again and the SUV rocked. "Jesus! Stop running into the road," he yelled at the windshield after another animal darted across the road. He pounded the steering wheel with his palms.

"What was it?" I asked.

"I'm not sure," he said.

Then there was another, and another. Dean slowed the car and then the whole car jumped to the side when one of them ran into the front fender with a solid thud.

"Oh God!" Dean said peering out the window seeing something I couldn't.

"Christ," Owen said seconds later when he saw what Dean had seen.

"What?" I asked.

"Stampede!" Dean said, "Hold on!" as he drove off of the road and into the ditch, sort of using a tree as a shield.

The animals ran across the road heading northwest, they ran like they were running away from something fearing for their lives. Our car was parked just at the edge of their pack, we'd get hit by one every so often and it would feel like the car might tip. I watched the herd of beasts running and jumping over the hood of our car and hoped they wouldn't do any major damage. It would be an absolute disaster to get stranded out here without a

234

working car. Cities were farther apart the further north we traveled. We could drive an hour or more without seeing a gas station.

"Are they deer?" I asked. I was seeing them a little clearer now that the majority of them had passed and the dust they were stirring up was settling, but I still wasn't sure.

"Yeah," Owen confirmed.

"Why are they all going north?" I wondered out loud.

"Maybe they are going to HOME too," Dean joked.

"Or maybe just to escape the heat," Owen suggested.

There was a big thud as one ran smack into the side of the SUV. None of us were expecting it as the herd had thinned so much. Sienna and I screamed. I glanced at Ryan, his eyes were half open, but rolled back and closed when the car stopped rocking.

"Let's get going," Dean said as he put the car into drive and got us out of the ditch moving us forward once again. I was curious to see what the car would look like after all those deer had hit us. I imagined it was pretty beat up, several of the hits were very hard. It was running fine though, and that's what mattered.

I breathed heavily, glad it was over and that we were back on the road towards HOME, which hopefully had a team of medical professionals.

* * *

235

On our third day on the road Ryan was officially staying in the backseat. With his fever he spent most of his time sleeping or groaning. He was getting worse fast. Ryan was still able to eat a little and drink water which I thought was good. He was fighting with everything he had, but today his whole arm from his shoulder to his fingertips was covered with the deep red of infection. The wound had grown larger, but with him being out more often he was scratching at it less which seemed to have slowed it down. I still cleaned it with water and antibiotic cream even though it clearly wasn't making any difference. At least it made me feel like I was doing something and maybe the clean bandage every so often was what was keeping the infection from raging and taking him over.

At one stop I had talked to Ryan about wanting to tell the others what was going on. He gave me his blessing to talk to them about it with a small nod. So I did. They didn't react. Perhaps they had sort of expected it all along as they knew Ryan had gotten bit by the dog. That hadn't been a secret, we all had been there. Or maybe they had overheard him and I talking one time or put one and one together. It didn't matter. What did matter was that everyone wanted to get him help as soon as possible. No one said it, but we desperately, me especially, didn't want to lose another of our own. Hell, it was likely none of us would even be here if it hadn't been for Ryan. We owed him.

They would give us alone time when I cleaned his bandage, and I'd talk to him about whatever popped into my head, the only topic that was completely off limits was Seth. I'd try to keep his spirits up even though he barely responded to me. Most of the time, the best I got was him looking at me through his half closed eyes or just a small squeeze from the hand on his unwounded arm.

After I'd spend time with him, I'd leave the car and crouch down beside the wheel and let my tears flood out of my eyes. The others would give me space, let me get it out, until it was time to go and then they would usually send Sienna for me, to look for supplies or use the bathroom. It was something to take my mind off of what was happening to Ryan and even though they felt awful about it too, they refused to show it in front of me. They stayed strong for me. I didn't say anything but I appreciated it.

I'd always look at the medical supplies hoping we could find something, a magical solution to the problem. Something I hadn't thought of trying. But the gas stations never had anything. A few different medicine brands, different kinds of bandages, but nope, none of the gas stations had carried miracles. It had gone beyond anything I could do for him.

"Let's go," Owen said when we were all gathered around the car. He was taking the next driving shift to give Dean a rest.

Sienna climbed in the car first and I started to follow until I heard the extra footsteps behind us.

They were running towards us, something grabbed the back of my shirt and I was pulled backwards. Out of the corner of my eye I saw Dean being aggressively pushed down against the cement. Owen ducked down on the other side of the car. I hadn't had time to grab my gun. Whoever had me had his arm wrapped around my neck so tightly I was gasping for air and clawing at his arm.

"You guys can't just come here and take stuff, this is our place," the guy holding me said.

"You have to pay for that stuff one way or another!" the other guy yelled at Dean as he punched him in the ribs. The guy with his knee pressed down on Dean's spine had a big sheathed knife in his belt and a gun pocket on the other side of the belt. I didn't know what the guy holding me had, except for exceptional strength. At least he had eventually eased up enough for me to get a few solid breaths.

I heard Dean coughing and choking out, "OK, OK!" Sienna was pounding on the door and yelling for him to stop from inside the van. I was hoping she'd quickly close the door and lock it keeping her and Ryan safe but she didn't. The punching guy realized there was someone in the van and he went for her, even though he hadn't done anything to restrain Dean. He must have thought the beating would be enough.

Dean acted fast and grabbed the guy's foot tripping him, which took Punchy by complete surprise. He hit the cement hard. This gave Owen an opportunity to come around the front of the SUV with his gun drawn at the guy on the ground. It made me think the guy holding me must not have had a gun, or Owen would have likely pointed it at him, at least that was my best guess.

"Let her go," Owen said to the guy holding me but never taking his eyes off the guy on the ground. When he reached for his gun, Owen shot the ground ten feet away from his head, but close enough to scare Punchy. "I wouldn't do that if I were you… stay down. Don't move," Owen said putting his foot on top of the man's hand. Punchy squirmed and cried out in pain.

The guy holding me tightened his grip again. I couldn't speak. All I could do was claw at his arm with my fingernails hoping he'd let go, or at the very least loosen his grip so I could get some oxygen.

"Take his weapons," Owen said instructing Sienna. She quickly followed his order. Dean had managed to get to his feet with one hand holding his middle and the other holding a gun. Blood dripped from his nose and mouth. He stood next to Owen, "Get him up," he ordered, and Dean obeyed. He kicked him in the side, harder than I would have imagined Dean was capable of, then he pulled Punchy to his feet. Dean held him there by twisting his arm around his back, it almost looked as though Dean could snap it like a twig if he wanted to. A move I wondered if he had learned from his survival books and magazines.

"Trade?" Owen said to the man holding me.

"You'll just kill us," he said, "The second I let her go, you'll pull that trigger!"

"I don't want to kill you. I didn't want any

239

trouble… you two idiots started this. I want her back and if you don't give her back well then I can't make any promises," Owen said. Maybe it was from the lack of oxygen but I had an out-of-body experience as if I was watching everything play out like a movie in the theater. Everything around me was dark and quiet, the sound was loud and the screen almost too bright. "Let her go, and you can have your friend back and no one gets hurt."

He hissed like a scared cat and pushed me towards Owen. He turned and ran like his life depended on it. He ran until he was far enough away to pull out his gun from his ankle holster and take a shot in our direction. The bullet whistled somewhere past my left ear. He missed by a mile thankfully, but would I be so lucky on the next one? Owen held Punchy out in front of us like a shield while we started to climb into the SUV. He shot at us again, another miss. The third bullet, however, didn't miss.

Chapter twenty.

I screamed when I heard the little thud of the bullet hitting its target. Owen dropped Punchy unable to hold all of his weight. Blood pooled out around his shoulder and soaked into his clothing.

Dean shoved me into the SUV and slammed the door behind me. He moved as fast as he could to the driver's side, which was much slower than normal because he hadn't had a chance to recover from the attack. I wondered what kind of damage had been done, but I was glad he was able to move albeit slowly. Owen kept his gun drawn until Dean was sitting down and ready.

The man shot at us again. The bullet made a ping noise when it hit the SUV. Sienna and I both screamed. She ducked down and I looked Ryan over to make sure he hadn't been hit. I sucked in air when I heard the bullet whiz out of Owen's gun. I'm not sure why it had surprised me that he shot back. He was protecting us, and I've known for months that something like this could happen. I guess I never really thought about why or how it would happen. We'd probably been lucky it took this long for something like this to happen. But other than the guns being used to kill those horrible dogs, I never actually imagined them being used on a real live person. I looked out the window and saw both men lying on the ground.

"Owen you hit him!" I yelled at him from inside the SUV.

"I know," he said, his voice lacking any emotion as he jumped inside the SUV. "GO!" he ordered, and Dean sped off down the highway driving way too fast. Leaving the two men behind. One that we had killed, or injured and left for dead, or worse, left for the dogs.

"We have to go back!" I said feeling confused and conflicted. "We need to help them, we can't just let them die!"

Owen turned around looking at me like I was crazy, and maybe I was, at least temporarily, but it all felt wrong. "He was shooting at us Ros, we can't go back and put ourselves back into that kind of danger! Don't be stupid! You want Ryan to get shot through the side panel? Or someone through the window? Jesus Christ Ros, pull it together!"

"We can't just let people die," I said. I couldn't get my feelings in check. I didn't know what to say or how to say it. Everything I was feeling was a jumbled mess. I just knew that killing people was wrong, but obviously it wouldn't have been right to put any of us in danger either.

"We can and we will, drive Dean," Owen demanded, even though Dean had absolutely no intention of not continuing to drive away from the men.

"Ros you're in shock or something," Dean said glancing back at me.

"I'm not in shock," I said.

"Well, you sure aren't thinking clearly," Owen added.

We drove in silence for miles and miles and miles. I waited for someone to freak out like I was freaking out on the inside but it didn't happen. Owen may have just killed a living, breathing human being and we were all accomplices for helping him. There was no longer any policemen enforcing any kind of laws. Did it really matter Owen had defended us? We had been in danger, but I was having trouble finding within myself that place that believed that this was the right way. I would have to carry this with me the rest of my life. That we hadn't gone back, that I just let someone die. But another part of me thought I was being ridiculous, he was shooting at us, and he could have killed any one of us. Owen did the right thing, I had to suck it up, who knows maybe one day I would have to pull that trigger myself... killing one to save another. Perhaps that part of me was right, it's just that shooting and possibly killing someone was a pretty big thing. It was hard for me to just shrug off.

After everything that had just happened, Ryan was a little more alert for a short while. Maybe he could sense how upset I was. He watched me through little slits that threatened to stay closed with each bump on the road. At one point, he weakly asked if I was OK and all I could do was force out my best attempt at a brave smile.

243

Once he fell asleep, I tried to get some rest as well, my brain needed the down time, my body needed to recover from the surge of adrenaline. Every ounce of me needed it. Sleep would help me process and move forward, at least that's what I told myself. Forward was the only way to go in this new world anyway. Dwelling was not an option.

* * *

        The next twenty-four hours passed without a hitch. It had been an unusual stretch of smooth sailing, and thankfully much needed for everyone's peace of mind. The others all seemed to return to what was our normal, it was as if nothing had even happened. It was like Owen never even shot anyone. When my thoughts weren't about Ryan, they were about Owen pulling that trigger. I'd hear that gunshot and scene play out over and over again, trying to figure out what I should have done, like it was a puzzle I had to solve. I should be happy he was protecting us, cut and dry self-defense and all, but it was still a human life. I couldn't shake this guilt of being party to murder. What if he laid there shouting for help for hours before he bled to death? A long painful death just for shooting at us and accidentally hitting his friend in the process. As usual my thoughts became overwhelming and I'd have to stuff them deep down inside me hoping they'd get stuck with all the rest. Then I forced myself to change my thoughts and put them back on Ryan and his desperate need for help.

Today was a productive drive. We stopped only when necessary and made really good progress. Owen and Dean switched on and off and they both drove long and fast before needing a break. I knew they were doing it for Ryan. They saw his increasing need for help. It's not like it was a secret, it was obvious to anyone who saw him. We all saw the wound spreading, the infection growing. They listened when I'd read his temperature from the inaccurate thermometer. It stayed a pretty solid 105, but what it would be on a better thermometer was anyone's guess. Maybe it would have been higher, or maybe it would have been lower, but it didn't matter. Either way he had a bad fever and needed help. They didn't say much other than a 'Sorry Ros,' or maybe just a hand on my shoulder with a simple 'let's go.' And then we'd be back on the road in no time, going as fast as they felt was safe. As for Dean, I'm sure his thoughts went back to seeing Seth close himself in the closet, burning down our shelter, leaving us helpless. It was a terrible thing to happen, although, if he hadn't burned down the shelter we wouldn't have ever found out about this HOME place in Alaska. Thankfully Ryan's mind hasn't turned to that awful place Seth's had, at least it hadn't yet.

We all wanted to help Ryan any way we could, but there wasn't much we could do other than try to get him to HOME and hope there was help there. We all owed Ryan and we all cared about him. If it hadn't been for Ryan none of us would probably be alive right now. He was the one who pulled us to safety in his family's shelter. In my case literally. He couldn't die. We couldn't let that happen. That would just be wrong on so many levels. A person who does something like that doesn't deserve this. It wasn't fair.

He only had the wound because he was trying to save the rest of us, again. He shouldn't have to be in this pain and, on a selfish note, I don't think I could get by without him. I need him. I love him. He needed to get well.

* * *

We had passed cars before on rare occasions. I could count on both hands how many cars we'd passed on our journey so far. They were few and far between. We'd pass, maybe look at each other to see what the others looked like, guess at what they were doing or where they were going, but everyone would go about their business not interfering with the other. Maybe out of fear, or maybe something else, I didn't have a guess. That's why I didn't think anything of it when I saw a pair of headlights in the darkness coming towards us down the road.

I think we had just entered Alaska about an hour or so ago. It had to be around midnight when we saw the headlights in the distance. As it got closer I could see it was a big, beefy pick-up truck raised up high on its unnecessarily big wheels. It had four blindingly bright lights lined up on top of the cab. It was a noisy truck, not a bad kind of noisy like it was dying but the kind some people would do on purpose. We passed each other, and they appeared to slow down as they watched us go by, attempting to see into our tinted windows, a feat that would be quite difficult during the night.

This time meeting another car was different. This time they didn't keep going on their own way. They made a big U-turn and came up behind us fast, shining their big lights into our SUV. Dean adjusted his side mirror so he could focus on driving.

"What are they doing?" Sienna asked nervously.

"I'm not sure," Dean said with both hands on the wheel, not changing his driving in any way. He maintained his same speed, not slowing down as one might naturally do. I thought he was trying to make it appear as though we wouldn't be phased by a big truck trying to bully us. Owen slid his gun onto his leg, trying to keep it hidden but I saw the light from their headlights bounce off of it. I wanted to scold him and tell him to put it away, that he was only going to hurt someone, but I didn't.

The driver tapped the accelerator. The engine roared as it jerked at our rear bumper making an attempt to intimidate us. There was no doubt about what they were doing. It seemed like they were sizing us up, and they would be able to count our heads through the tinted windows using their overly powerful top lights. Then they sped up jerking forward again, only this time they tapped our back bumper causing us to lightly jolt forward.

"Did they just hit us?" I asked rhetorically.

"Yeah, yeah they did," Dean said.

"What did we do? Why are they doing this?" Sienna whined.

And they bumped us again. And then again. Then they backed off a little, only to speed forward to hit us again, harder this time. We weren't prepared for such a big hit, none of us were ready and our heads jerked forward with the force.

"Everyone have their seat belts on?" Dean asked. I figured he expected it would get worse, and I did too.

"Yeah, everyone except Ryan," I said with a frown, knowing there wasn't much we could do about that.

The truck had backed off a little, following still much too closely. My whole body was tense. One thing I was thankful for was having a nearly full tank of gas. If we would have had to stop for gas things could have gotten bad. For all I knew they still might, but it was one less thing to worry about. They zoomed up again and hit the left side of the bumper causing Dean to swerve, but he managed to keep control and stay on the road.

They weren't letting up. The truck sped up and pushed our SUV forward, pushing, pushing, pushing. They were being aggressive, trying to run us off the road, but what I didn't know was why they were terrorizing us. We hadn't done anything. I had my gun, but after what had happened at the last stop, I knew I didn't want to have to use it. It was bad enough that I felt I'd have to carry around all these bad feelings from having witnessed what happened. But to actually have to do something like that myself was unfathomable. Even when I threatened the biker with the gun, I had no intention of actually using it, I wasn't capable. It was just that simple.

The truck came to an abrupt stop and flicked off their lights but I could feel they were still there. I was certain I heard the noisy truck, but they were quite a bit behind. Then it gradually got louder and louder as they sped up alongside of us with their lights still off.

I couldn't see inside their truck it was too dark. It was unfortunate that we didn't know who we were dealing with. They swerved at the side of our SUV causing Dean to jerk away in an attempt to avoid them, but they pulled back like they were toying with us. They swerved at us again... this time they hit us. Dean turned the wheel left and then right and managed to steady us and keep the SUV on the road. They swerved into us again right after Dean had corrected the car from the last hit. This time was harder than the last. When Dean lost control I heard Sienna scream, though she sounded miles away. My body was tensed up so tight bracing for impact that my ears had muffled all sound and possibly put them on a time delay. He was steering and counter-steering, doing everything he could to keep us from rolling. He managed to stop the SUV in an upright position, however we were in the ditch facing the wrong direction. The car was fine, and we were fine. Well, we weren't fine but we were alive, and the car was probably pretty dented up.

We sat there in the dark in complete silence, no one had even taken a breath yet, the truck appeared to be gone.

"Everyone OK?" Owen asked. I made some kind of quiet breathy noise to show that I was alive. The others grunted out their own noises, Ryan said nothing.

I sucked in air when the truck lights popped on only a few feet in front of the car. It was like the truck itself was staring at us with its big headlight eyes. I was temporarily blinded from the unexpected bright lights. They revved their engine at us and jerk forward a few times as if they were going to ram us head on. I noticed out of the corner of my eye two vehicles honking and speeding down the other side of the road. It looked as if they were in a big hurry to get somewhere and were trying to get the attention of the truck, maybe alerting them to something. The truck blew its horn back, some sort of southern tune and sped out of the ditch down the road after the other cars leaving us alone.

I turned to check on Ryan. He was still laying in the seat but his leg had flopped down, he didn't have the energy to pull it back up himself. His eyes were closed but I could tell part of him had been with us. He didn't have the strength to keep his eyes open, much less talk.

"Is he OK?" Owen said looking back at me over his shoulder.

"I think so," I whispered back. I took my seatbelt off and reached over the back of my seat to pull his leg up and try to reposition him. Sienna could tell I was struggling a bit and without a word turned and helped me get him back into a comfortable position.

Dean didn't wait for anyone to tell him to go, he started the car and put it back on the road driving as if nothing had happened. He drove the rest of the night not asking for Owen to take a turn until we stopped in the morning.

In the light I noticed that the terrain was different the closer we got to the HOME. There were actually patches of green grass, shrubbery with buds and leaves that were actually green, even the trees were starting to sprout leaves. Things were growing and there were colors of life around, it wasn't just the faded earthy browns of dying plants. I hadn't really given it a lot of thought until that morning, but the air was crisp and much cooler. The further north we traveled the cooler it was getting. Seth would have loved it.

It wasn't just dry dust and dirt anymore. Although there were still patches of it scattered about, enough to remind me that it hadn't been some sort of awful dream, and that all the destruction really had happened.

I opened the car windows so Ryan got some fresh air during his bandage changing time. For the brief and random moments he was somewhat present with me, he seemed to enjoy the brisk air. He didn't try to talk about what had happened last night, I couldn't decide if he hadn't remembered, didn't have the energy, or just didn't see any point in talking about it.

251

Dean came bouncing out of the gas station, "Sign inside says HOME Checkpoint 60 miles. I have no idea what that means exactly but I guess we are getting closer to finding out. Closer to help." He was in pretty good spirits considering he hadn't gotten any real sleep in some time. Maybe it was the thought of possibly finding help for Ryan in less than an hour that fueled him.

I smiled at him from my lonely spot behind the tire. The place I went to feel sorry for myself while watching for approaching vehicles.

"We'll get him help," Dean said, promising something he couldn't promise. He was trying to make me feel better, to keep my spirits up, but he and I knew all too well what would happen to Ryan. We'd seen it before. As far as I was concerned this virus, disease or whatever it was would eventually take over his brain. Seth had been weak, but when he lost it that night he suddenly had the strength to do what he did. Ryan was still himself thankfully, probably because his wound started smaller, it was just taking longer to take over.

"I hope so," I said burying my head between my knees.

"I have a good feeling… I think he'll get taken care of." He sat next to me which was unusual. They usually like to leave me alone during my break downs, but this time Dean just sat with me. Letting me feel whatever I wanted to feel and just stayed with me. It actually felt kind of nice, really nice, and I rested my head against his shoulder. I felt the tears fall out from my eyes like giant rain drops of sadness, I wiped them away quickly.

"Ros, he saved me. He saved all of us, I'll do what I can, OK?" he said lifting my chin so my eyes would see the seriousness in his.

"Yes, I know," I said letting my head fall weakly back on his shoulder. He wrapped his arm around me and just kept me in that half hug until Owen and Sienna were ready to be back on the road.

"If this weather keeps up, we are going to need jackets!" Sienna said with a bright smile. "Isn't that funny?"

I smiled at her, it was kind of funny until I let my mind wander back to the shelter and what happened when it got too cold. What we had seen through those cameras gave a whole new meaning to what a blizzard was. We wouldn't survive a blizzard like that in our SUV up here in Alaska.

"Let's find that checkpoint thing," Dean said as he hopped in the passenger seat.

And just like that, we were off, flying down the road as Owen drove at whatever speed he felt like.

Chapter twenty-one.

There were several signs posted along the way indicating how many more miles left until we reached the checkpoint. The signs were neatly hand-painted on wooden slabs nailed to wooden posts, nothing fancy. My nerves caused my muscles to tighten as we got closer and closer. I felt both excited and uneasy at the same time. My gut was giving me mixed signals, get there fast, turn around, hurry up and get help already, beware. I wasn't comfortable simply committing to being part of the HOME without knowing anything about it. It could be some sort of scam for all I knew, and that's what made me worry even more. Then again we didn't really have any other options. Ryan needed help and fast.

When we pulled up to the checkpoint there was another car stopped ahead of us. There were two guards posted outside, a large man with an even larger gun near the driver side of the car, and a second average sized man with a similar gun who stood near the passenger side of the car wearing dark sunglasses. He didn't seem to pay much attention to the car, perhaps it was just the sunglasses hiding his eyes that gave the illusion of not caring. He seemed to be more interested in scanning the horizon, so much so that I turned to see if I could find what he was searching for.

"Here we are," Owen announced, and Dean woke up in an instant. There was no in-between, it was either awake or asleep. He instinctively reached for his gun, but stopped himself when he realized we weren't in danger. It was just a natural reflex, well, natural to him now.

The big guy with the gun was doing all the talking to the car ahead of us. I couldn't hear what he was saying to the small black vehicle with Florida license plates. Of course that didn't mean they were from Florida but if they had been, that would have been quite the drive. I wonder how hot it had gotten in Florida. He pointed them towards a road that forked off in two directions, left or right. The right road turned behind a building, and I guessed that was the way they had directed them to go. But they didn't. They turned left and floored it heading back down the road away from the checkpoint.

"What the heck?" Dean said looking confused.

The second gunman raised his gun slowly and took aim at the fleeing car. It seemed as though he was going to take a shot at the car until the big guy said something to him and he lowered his gun. The car sped off back into the desolate world choosing that world over the HOME.

The big guy quickly said something into his handheld two-way radio and pointed his thick fingers at us and then curled two of them indicating us to pull forward.

After seeing the other car speed off, I think Owen was a little more apprehensive about pulling forward. I felt my stomach twist. The only thing that made us pull ahead was the possibility that Ryan could get help. He eased the car forward and rolled down the window.

"Hello," the guard said cheerfully while his face remained straight. "How are you folks today?"

Owen shrugged, "Uh, OK?"

"Could I get your names please?" he asked poised to write.

"I'm Owen. That's Ryan, Sienna and Ros," Owen said gesturing towards us as he said our names.

"I take it you aren't familiar with HOME? You're first timers. No problem. We just need to ask you a few basic questions and you'll be on your way in no time," the guard said looking around. The name sewn on his shirt, whether it was his or not, was Duncan, the other guard was Merlose. "First I need to know where you are coming from."

"North Dakota," Owen answered quickly like he was being quizzed and fastest answers got the most points.

"Long drive," he cleared his throat before the next question, "How did you hear about HOME?"

"We saw a sign posted in a gas station, decided to check it out," Owen said. In my head I was thinking he should say as little as possible, keep his answers short and sweet but I had no way to transmit that message to him, although I tried to telepathically.

"Great. Word is getting out then. Perfect." He made some quick notes and flipped through pages on his clipboard. It felt like a telemarketing phone call, like it was all perfectly scripted and they would have a stock answer for anything we might ask. All he'd have to do was scroll through his handy what-to-say-next guidebook.

"Next I have to ask, if you are carrying any weapons on yourself or in your vehicle?"

This is when Owen got really nervous and so did Merlose. "Yes," Owen said short and sweet just as I had hoped. I saw Merlose's fingers tighten on his beefy gun, he didn't trust us, and I sure as hell didn't trust either of them. My stomach twisted the other direction, I was afraid it was trying to tell me something. Maybe the same thing the driver of the other car's stomach told them. I reminded myself that Ryan needed help, we'd have nothing for him if we left. At least here maybe there was a chance. Maybe it was a small chance but there was no chance at all if we drove off. We would have to watch him get even worse until what happened to Seth, happened to Ryan too.

"What exactly are you carrying? How many of each?" Duncan asked.

"Four guns," Owen said while the guard wrote that down. I could tell he circled it a few times on the papers based on the movement of the pen. Owen had completely forgotten about the knives and the bows, hopefully that wouldn't be a problem.

"What other types of goods do you have in your car? Food, water, clothing?"

Owen listed what he could think of, "Yeah, I don't know, your basic necessities," he said with a shrug.

"That's fine, fine. We just need to make sure you declare your goods and don't bring anything to HOME that could put it or any of the people here in any kind of danger."

Off in the distance I could have sworn I heard a gunshot. If the others heard it they made no change in their expressions or body language. I glanced at Merlose and I could have sworn the corner of his mouth tilted upwards just a hair. Satisfied.

"Can we look around and inside your car please?" Duncan said, "Don't get out, but please slowly open your doors, this is for our safety as well as yours."

Our safety? How so? If anything, this exposed us even more and made us less safe! But I kept thinking of how close to getting help for Ryan we were and that I needed to keep my mouth shut no matter how hard it was. No matter how much I wanted to tell Owen to zoom away just like the other car did.

Duncan looked in by Owen first then behind him on Sienna's side. He used a flashlight even though it was daytime to check her over and the area around the seat before he spotted Ryan in the back. Merlose had done the same first with Dean then by me and noticed Ryan at the same time

Duncan had. I saw the two look at each other before they continued and viewed the back of the SUV. They closed the back hatch and Merlose whispered something to Duncan before they came back to the front of the car, closing our doors on the way. I wasn't expecting it and jumped so hard I felt the whole SUV shake. Both Merlose and Duncan looked at me but I pretended not to notice.

"I think we have all the information we need, for now. I'll forward this ahead. You'll be driving to the decontamination center next, they'll explain more. But basically it's just a cleaning facility to make sure you don't bring anything into HOME that could harm anyone." Duncan skimmed over the papers making sure he'd filled out what he needed to. "Oh, just one more thing before I can let you go, what happened to him?"

"Dog bite," Owen said.

"Oh, hmmm. OK, one second. Wait here." Duncan went inside a little booth and took the radio off his belt. He started talking to someone, while Merlose waited for him to return standing next to Dean's door. Merlose must have been able to hear what they had talked about. He tapped on Dean's window and gestured for him to roll it down.

"Was anyone else attacked by this dog?" he said stressing dog as if the word disgusted him and I wondered if they had seen this sickness before.

"No, not anyone else with us anyway," Dean said reminding himself of Seth, "I mean we are fine."

Merlose shook his head back and forth to Duncan, and he set down the radio and came back to the driver side of the car. "All right, everything is set except for just one small detail."

"Which is?" Owen asked with a raised eyebrow.

"He can't go to decontamination. He must be taken to the infirmary and seen by one of our experts. When he heals he'll be released to HOME but for now we cannot risk the chance of him spreading anything to others at HOME. I hope you understand, it's the rules there is no way around it," Duncan said, and waved to two men inside the larger building behind him. They were dressed in white suits that covered them from head to toe.

"Wait!" I said. "I need to go with him!"

"I'm sorry ma'am but we cannot allow that. It would be risking your health."

"I've been with him since it happened and I'm fine! I can't…." My hands shook as panic started to set in.

"It's just temporary, I assure you," Duncan said with a fake smile. I've seen first-hand what this rabid dog disease is capable of doing to a person, so my hope in this infirmary being the answer to Ryan's problem wasn't very strong.

"I think this is probably the best place for him," Owen said.

"He needs the help," Dean chimed in.

I turned around trying to reach out to some part of Ryan that might still be able to hear me. "Ryan, I hope you hear me. They are going to take you, and make you better but they won't let me come with you!" I said, hoping he'd suddenly be better and refuse to go, but he was too weak.

Ryan moved his lips and airily whispered, "I'll be fine, I promise." He used his last bit of strength to mouth, "I will find you. I love you." It took everything I had not to break down and cry in front of him.

He was passed out before I could say it back, but that didn't stop me, "I love you too!" The men were pulling him out of the car. I thought I heard one of the men say to the other something that sounded like 'he's almost gone' but I wasn't sure what I had heard. They were talking to each other through some communication device inside of their suits. "What did you say? What did you just say?" I asked and started to pull on his suit to get his attention. "What did you say to him?" I yelled. Merlose rose to attention quickly while the men in suits ignored me.

"Ma'am don't touch him," he said repositioning his gun into a slightly more threatening position. My thoughts went to my own gun, but that would just be stupid and potentially dangerous to us all. It was obvious these guys had plenty of weapons training, or were really good at making it appear that way. For all I knew they were in the military back when we had one. I had barely even used my gun other than to kill a rabid dog and to threaten a dumb biker. That wasn't going to work with these guys and I couldn't justify putting the others at risk.

The two men put Ryan on a bed and then wheeled him into the building, within seconds he was gone. He was no longer with me, I couldn't see him, I couldn't feel him. He was just gone. A hot tear rolled quickly down my cheek and dropped onto my pants leaving a large wet dot. Sienna put her arms around my neck and held me tight. I wasn't certain but I think she was crying too.

"Great!" Duncan said, and I thought of nothing other than the fact that I wanted to spit on him. "Now if you folks are ready you can proceed to decontamination. Your friend will be joining you in no time," he added for my sake. "Just take this road..." he said pointing to the one that led to the right, "...and follow it until you hit a large three story building. You can't miss it," he forced a smile.

"OK," Owen said putting the car in drive.

"Oh and welcome HOME," Duncan said with a sickening fake grin that made me hate him more than I already did. I was happy when Owen pulled away because a few more seconds there and I might have told both of those creeps what I really thought of them.

The road we took was dirt covered and curvy. I waited several minutes before I whispered to the others how I thought we'd made a big mistake. I told them I regretted leaving Ryan and putting him into the hands of complete strangers. We had no idea if they could even really help him. Were there even any real doctors at that place? Did they have other patients? Then we heard another gunshot, this one closer, sounding to me as if it had come from inside the building we'd just drove away from.

"RYAN!" I screamed as I clawed at my door to get out, "Oh my GOD! They killed him! They

262

killed him!" My fingers weren't working, I couldn't figure out how to work the door.

Dean had managed to move to the middle row and with the help of Sienna they were trying to pull me away from the door before my crazed hands actually found the door handle. He pushed me into the backseat where Ryan had just been laying and held me down using most if not all of his body weight. The seat was still warm from Ryan's body heat which added fuel to my outburst. "Settle down Ros," Dean said pressing half of his body down on mine as I struggled to get away.

"Let me go! They killed him! I'm going to kill them!" I screamed at him. "Let me go!"

"I can't do that," Dean said getting my arms and pinning them down above my head so I couldn't push at him anymore. "You need to freakin' calm down before we get to that decontamination building. Just stop and think for a second, JUST THINK. Do you really think any of us would just give up on Ryan? We'll find him. You aren't alone, you have us. We care about him too for Christ's sake!"

"YOU don't care about him," I snarled as a montage of all the dirty looks he gave Ryan played in my mind.

"Don't be stupid, of course I do! I can be mad at and jealous of someone and still care about them!" The fact that he was admitting to the jealously slowed me down, it made me think that Ryan had been right about how Dean felt about me. What would Owen think of what he said? Or Sienna? Neither of them questioned it, maybe they already knew, or maybe it didn't matter to them that they didn't understand. My adrenaline was slowing.

"You heard the gunshot," I said a little more calm, but I still had little bursts of trying to get myself out from under Dean's body. I thrust my hips up trying to get him off-balance and then attempted to pull my hands loose, but Dean was stronger than I was. I was getting tired, weaker, and I gave up when I saw the building come into sight.

"Pull it together!" Owen ordered from the front.

"It's OK Ros, we'll find him again," Sienna said trying to sound reassuring.

"But they killed him," I screamed at her. I was sure of it. The timing. The men in suits saying he was a goner. I had little to no doubt they'd killed him. They weren't going to risk their people to one diseased person who maybe didn't have a chance in hell at survival. Maybe Seth never had a chance either and he knew it, and that's why he did what he did. Maybe those men knew Ryan didn't have a chance. Maybe this isn't the first time they've seen the disease, that's why they didn't want me inside. Not because of Ryan, but because of all the other diseased people they had inside.

"We will figure it out Ros, I promise you! Please! You have to compose yourself, if they kick us out of here, it'll be much harder to find Ryan. The best place for us to be is here where he is. Even if he is not in this building, he is in this area, with these people, THIS is where we have to be to get Ryan back," Dean said and even though I didn't want to admit it, he was right.

"Was. This is where he was."

"Huh?"

"You said where he is, I corrected you. This is where he was."

"We don't know they killed him and we can't assume that they did. Step one, get inside. Step two, learn as much as we can and step three, find him," Dean said, as we pulled into a parking spot. Before Owen had even cut the engine, someone was walking out to greet us. "You can do this. We can do this. We'll get him back."

I wanted to start screaming or crying or pounding on this woman's face until I got some answers but instead I wiped my tears and forced myself to wear a pretend smile. I'd do what I was told and follow their stupid directions, but only until we found Ryan. And if I didn't find Ryan someone would pay. I wouldn't stay here any longer than I had to. I didn't care how wonderful it might be on the inside. Anywhere else would be better. There were four other cars in the lot, one was parked close up to the building and the others were parked in seemingly random spots.

"Hi!" the woman said as Owen stepped out of the car. "Welcome! Glad you've come, hopefully it wasn't a difficult journey HOME!" She wasn't much older than we were. She held a clipboard against her large chest and smiled at us with a perfect toothy smile. She gave us each a good once over while she spoke, "So... I'm Ms. Deezil and I'll be your guide through d-con as we call it. First your car stays here for two weeks before it is taken away. The reason it remains is just in case this isn't a good match you are allowed to leave during probation at any time. You can leave with all the things you came with, nothing more, nothing less. I do, however, need to take your keys in the meantime. They will stay here because we always go on the assumption it will be a great fit and you'll be here for the long haul. Like most everyone who comes HOME does," she said smiling the whole time. "Ah, before we go on, you are Owen?" Deezil said reaching her hand out to him as if she already knew.

"Yeah, that's me," he said a little confused how she knew but figured it must have somehow identified him in the papers she had on her clipboard.

"Lovely, nice to meet you. And that means you're Dean," she giggled.

"Right," he said unimpressed by her, even though she was obviously really impressed with him. I consciously stopped my eyes from rolling beyond halfway point, so instead it looked as though I was looking up at the sky.

"Perfect," she said holding on to his hand longer than she should have, and I could have sworn she was blushing. I couldn't blame her, Dean was very attractive and tall and solid. All the things that made most women get goofy. "That makes you Ros and you Sienna," she said guessing correctly.

"Yep," I said giving her a nice fake smile back, one that closely mimicked her own. She scrunched up her eye and looked at me strangely. I could instantly tell she saw right through it and the smile melted off my face. It was then I saw something in her eyes. There was something she was trying to communicate back to me, her expression had changed, she wasn't being fake, and it only lasted a split second. But I just couldn't get her message. I couldn't understand what it was. I wanted to take her aside and ask. Deezil knew something. Deezil wanted me to know something.

As we followed her into the building, I wanted to ask her, make her tell me, but I could tell she didn't want me to utter a word. She had practically pleaded with her eyes for me to keep my mouth closed. She almost looked scared, and I could tell she regretted whatever it was she had tried to say with her eyes. Before I knew it the moment was gone and she was her fake-self again. If I said something to anyone about it she'd deny it. What did she know? What was it she wanted me to know?

"Boys this way and girls that way," She said once the big glass doors behind us closed and we were inside d-con.

Owen and Dean walked down one hallway with Deezil, while Sienna and I, hand in hand, slowly walked down the other looking back at them. Sienna watched her brother, and I watched the two guys that had taken care of me until this point, walk away from us. Ryan was gone. Dean was gone. Owen was gone. Seth was really gone. Everything and everyone kept disappearing.

It took all that I had not to just drop to the

floor and get myself into their mental institution if they had one. I grabbed Sienna's hand tighter as we pushed open the big metal door.

Chapter twenty-two.

Inside there was a man sitting behind a desk who asked our names, just our first names. I guess the likelihood that there would be more than one Ros here at any given time was pretty unlikely. After confirming who we were he directed us to the first station, and we were separated. They had me go first. I undressed and then proceeded to the next station for what they called 'the cleaning.' I was told that my clothes would be burned but that new clothing would be provided. After a scalding hot and overly soapy shower, I was given a lightweight cotton robe to wear.

I was led to a waiting room where I sat for awhile alone until Sienna was brought to the same room. She sat next to me and took my hand. It felt like we had been sitting there for hours before they called her back. I stood up with her, nervous about being separated again, but the woman dressed like a nurse assured me she'd be fine and we'd be back together before I knew it. I let go of Sienna's hand and she walked off with the nurse.

"Hold tight hon, you're next," she said smiling as if I had been told what I was next for.

Only about five minutes passed when the same nurse-like person came and called my name even though I was the only one waiting. I looked around the waiting room and then back at her, but she just smiled.

I followed her down a hallway where she weighed me, wrote down my height, shoe size and a few other measurements for clothing. At least that's what I assumed they were for. It was just like being at a doctor with a few extra measurements. I thought it was strange when she wrote down my hair color and eye color, she didn't ask me she just wrote them down with the other measurements. I wanted to ask to see the form so I could see what else had been documented.

"Right in here Ros," she said opening the door and pointing to a little bed just like the ones they had in doctor's offices. "Have a seat, Dr. Rose will be right with you."

I hopped up on the bed holding my robe closed. I wrapped my arms as tightly around myself as I could in an effort to keep myself warm. The whole building was freezing. I was surprised icicles weren't hanging off of the ceiling. They had electricity. I couldn't figure out why they used air conditioning instead of the heater. Maybe it was another way to keep us here. We couldn't get away fast if we were frozen. I wondered where the electricity was coming from, the building was so large I doubted it had a generator. Maybe there was a windmill or something I hadn't seen. I figured that meant HOME would have electricity and maybe the infirmary did too.

The room didn't have a computer on the desk like you'd expect, but I figured computers must be pretty much useless if no one else used them. There was a calendar hanging on the wall, showing it was September, whether or not that was accurate I didn't know. Maybe they had been keeping track of time here since this all went down. Something we probably should have attempted to do too.

The door opened and a tall thin woman with over-sized glasses slipped in. She set down the clipboard and looked at me, "Hi Ros, I'm Doctor Rose," she smiled at me.

"Oook," I said. I wasn't really sure what to say.

"Oh sure, I suppose this is all very confusing to you. I'm just going to check you over to make sure you are healthy and ready to go to HOME. It won't take long I promise. When I finish Nurse Silar will take a blood sample and you'll be on your way," she said pushing her glasses up.

Dr. Rose gave me a basic physical and determined I was perfect for HOME pending the blood test results. The nurse came in and drew my blood. Before she left she handed me a folded up bundle and asked me to change. I was led out to another larger waiting room where Sienna was already waiting.

"You'll wait here for your results and further instructions," the nurse said before she walked out. Eventually Dean and Owen were brought into the waiting room, and we embraced as

271

if we hadn't seen each other in years.

We sat stiffly in our new clothes partially due to the cold and the other part was from the stress. We all matched in our light blue jump suits. Our names were written on our suits along with a sewed on patch with the word "Probationary" stitched on it. Right now none of us cared how we were dressed we were just happy to be together again. Dean hugged Sienna again and then me. At first I thought it might be awkward but it wasn't, I welcomed it. Ryan wouldn't be jealous he'd be happy there was someone there with me and he'd be happy it was someone like Dean, and Owen too, that actually cared about me. Owen seemed nervous and was giving his full attention to our surroundings. I could tell that he felt overwhelmed and powerless and it was causing him a great deal of anxiety.

Dean, Sienna and I sat down on a couch close together and Owen sat down in an arm chair. His eyes darted around the room quickly, scanning and memorizing everything.

"Did they take your blood?" I whispered to Dean.

"Yeah."

"They took my gun," Owen said clenching his fist, "why didn't I leave it in the car?"

Obviously they weren't going to let us keep our weapons, but thankfully I had left mine in the car. At least I knew where one was, not that I could get to it easily but who knows, just knowing where one was could come in handy. Maybe once we were gone they'd take our weapons from the car, after all they did have the keys. Eventually a heavy, metal door at the back of the waiting room opened silently and Deezil stepped out closing the door behind her.

"Great news! You are all set for HOME!" She smiled at us as if we should be elated by the news, but all I could do was stare at her and wait for that glimmer. The one that made me think she was trying to tell me something telepathically. I wanted another chance to try to read her telepathic message. "So, again, your car will be held temporarily in case you need to leave. You can leave one of two ways, one if you aren't a good fit, and two, by your own choice." Did she say that last part weird? Strange inflection? "Next you'll be taken by helicopter to HOME as it's still quite a while away. We have to keep its location as secret as we can for the safety of our family at HOME. A family you are all now part of, so, congratulations!" She gave us each a brief hug to make it official, of course her hug with Dean was a solid five seconds longer and she kind of lingered. She needed to get out more. "So if you have any questions for me now is the time," she said looking at each of us. When none of us spoke she continued "Great, let's go."

She walked us out back to where a helicopter was loudly idling with the pilot sitting inside waiting to drive us off to our new blissful future. Deezil waved enthusiastically at the pilot and he gave her a simple nod back, her shoulders seemed to sink. She shook our hands one by one. When she got to Dean she put her hand on his chest and let it linger there for just a moment while she shook his other hand. Of course the message she was trying to send him was loud and clear, but the one she was trying to get to me was dreadfully subtle. I looked at him out of the corner of my eye to see his expression when she moved on to Sienna. He looked back at me with a wink and a smile, and I couldn't help but smile back at him. I guess he'd gotten her message too. The mood shifted when she took my hand and looked me square in the eyes, she mouthed something at me that looked like "he's gone" but I wasn't sure.

"What?" I said as I was getting ushered away by someone dressed in orange. "Wait, what? What did you say?" I yelled back at her.

"I said, welcome HOME!" she shouted but her eyes were serious and I knew that wasn't what she said.

"No, no!" I said getting pulled further and further away. "Wait, I—"

"Sorry ma'am we have to go now," the man in orange said. "Everything you could possibly want or need is at HOME. You'll see," he grinned. I wasn't even sure his smile was authentic. There was no one I could trust except for Owen, Dean and Sienna. I just felt like they were trying to tell me something but that they couldn't. And maybe the reason they couldn't, was because they were being watched, maybe we all were. Maybe that's what they were trying to tell me, that we were always being watched. Or maybe I was being paranoid.

* * *

The helicopter ride was disorienting. I assumed that was done intentionally. Right when I was starting to feel nauseated from the bumpy-twisty-turny ride, I saw what appeared to be an old modified military base being used as the location for HOME. I couldn't be sure but I think we traveled mostly west and somewhat north from where we had been. The pilot had made numerous strange turns that didn't make sense and threw me off from trying to memorize the route.

We watched the land get closer as the helicopter swooped down and landed abruptly. The pilot told us to exit the helicopter, and once we were far enough away it flew off. There was no one outside waiting for us, just a single path with bright orange arrows painted on it. We followed the markings to the entrance of a huge facility.

"I don't like this," I said so quietly I wasn't even sure any of them heard me.

But Owen had. "Me either," he said feeling it too.

"Just think of Ryan," Dean said to try to keep us focused. "We can't leave without him, so this is it. Be smart, say as little as possible and for Christ's sake try to fit in," he reminded us, but I think it was mostly directed at me. We had to keep it together, me especially, and stay here for Ryan. It was the best place to be if we wanted to get him back, or in my mind, find out what happened to him. Although I was pretty confident I knew what had happened to him, but I wasn't going to give up hope completely until I knew I was one hundred percent sure.

I hadn't even been away from Ryan for a full twenty-four hours and I missed him terribly. A small part of me had faith he was alive, and that he was being taken care of, getting the treatment he needed and he'd be fine. But then I'd think back to that moment, the one where I had heard the gunshot. And I'd convince myself all over again that the bullet had been for Ryan. Maybe that was the only cure for the poison in him. Either that or fire, like Seth chose. Both resulting in the same final outcome. Death.

The door opened and two guards stepped out. They were dressed the same, and they were both armed. They each had a name patch on their chest, just like the ones on our jumpers. One was named Arnold, a first name I assumed, and the other was Slade. It took me a minute, but I knew Slade. He looked slightly different from the last time I saw him, but I knew his eyes. When his eyes locked with mine I knew he recognized me too. He was the guy I should have helped back when the storms had started. The one I had left behind to follow Ryan to his grandpa's shelter. And no thanks to me he had survived and had joined up with the circus freak gang who had taken our gear. Now here he was at the HOME. I figured he must have been here for a while to be working the door since that seemed like it would be an important job to hold. Would he be high enough up on the chain to know where Ryan was? Maybe he could help

276

us?

They looked us over one by one and frisked us to make sure we weren't bringing anything into HOME we weren't supposed to. First they checked Owen and let him in, then Sienna and then Dean. When they got to me, Slade whispered something to the one named Arnold and then they checked me.

"She's got a knife!" Slade said pointing his gun at me.

"No I don't!" I said.

"Don't move!" he shouted, and I raised my arms up. The one named Arnold secretly placed, then removed a knife from by my ankle. There was nothing I could do. Slade had set me up. My friends were inside, and I was alone on the outside being accused of concealing a weapon.

"Dean!" I screamed, uselessly reaching out for him as Slade grabbed at my flailing arms and pulled them behind me. "Dean help me!"

He appeared in the doorway briefly. Confusion instantly washed over his face, "Ros?" When he noticed my expression, he knew something was wrong. He tried to come to me, a look of panic on his face. But before I could say anything, someone roughly shuffled him along.

"They set me up Dean! DEAN! Oh God, Dean!" I screamed. I heard a small scuffle and then nothing more. He was gone. I didn't even know if he could hear me any more. In fact, I was fairly certain he couldn't.

Slade nodded and Arnold went back to the door. He pressed a button on the intercom and called for a return flight, a 'code W,' I think he had said. Slade kept his gun on me the whole time staring at me, "You don't deserve to be here," he said to me under his breath.

"I don't know why you are doing this to me," I said.

"Really? You don't?"

"If this is about the storms, it's not like I abandoned you on purpose," I said looking him straight in the eye. "In fact, I tried to go back for you, but they pulled me away."

"Ahhh! So you do know why. I'm sure you put tons of effort into trying to help me," Slade said with a sneer.

"I tried," I said, knowing he wasn't going to believe me or care what I had to say. He would always perceive things his way. The way he experienced them. I didn't think there would be anything I could do to change his mind.

"You don't know how easy you had it," he said.

"And you don't know what I had and what I didn't have."

"I know Ryan's family had a bomb shelter, I remember when the builders were there putting it in. I'd bet you had it pretty good and I know you all could have taken me with."

"Of course we would have if we could have!" I said frustrated with him.

He spit on the ground near my feet and laughed, "You know, the whole neighborhood laughed at that bomb shelter, made jokes, thought the family was crazy... not me."

"I don't know what you want me to say!

I'm sorry!" I felt my tears start to fill my eyes, and the last thing I wanted was to shed a single tear near either of these two. There was no way I could let them know how bothered I was by all this.

The helicopter landed and Slade ushered me towards the helicopter with his gun pressed between my shoulder blades. I knew it wouldn't matter what I did or said he wasn't going to understand and he wasn't going to change his mind. What's done is done. I felt helpless. There was nothing I could do but get on the helicopter and go back to d-con for the car. Then what would I do, just drive right passed the infirmary were Ryan was? Leave him and the others here and just keep going? What could I do? What choice did I have? Where was I going to go? I was truly alone, and this was what Slade wanted. He wanted me to suffer as he had. For him it was a challenge, but for me it was a death sentence.

The ride back was absolutely terrifying. I was scared about what they would do to me. My hands shook uncontrollably. I didn't think they would let me go easily. The only people I could trust were inside HOME, they were gone and I had no way to communicate with them.

When I got out of the helicopter, Deezil was waiting for me. She quickly stuffed the keys in my hand, "Take these and go, do not look back." She wasn't joking around. I thought that she might be breaking protocol.

"OK." I took the keys and held them tight. I wanted ask her all sorts of questions but I knew she wouldn't answer, and I knew I needed to get out of here.

"I don't know how to say this, but they don't like when people have even a general idea of how to get to the main base. Go and don't stop until you are completely out of this area. Go far and go fast," she said waving me towards the SUV. When I didn't move she yelled, "Go!"

I hesitated for one second. I was tempted to ask her to come with me but based on the anxious look on her face I knew she couldn't, or wouldn't. But my guess was that she would have liked to. Dean's sweatshirt that he wore when he slept was draped over the passenger seat. I grabbed it, and covered up my jumpsuit. It smelled like Dean. One day this jumpsuit might come in handy. It may be the only way I'd ever find my friends and Ryan again. I pulled my gun out of the back pocket of the passenger seat and set it in the cup holder. I left the safety on and locked the doors before I sped off. The tires squealed against the pavement as I turned down the winding road and away from this hell.

Chapter twenty-three.

As I sped down the road I imagined the SUV getting shot at but it didn't happen. I think I passed through quickly enough, before they had even been alerted to my departure, likely thanks to Deezil. She probably walked back inside as slowly as she could, gave me some time and then radioed it in. At least that is what I imagined. For all I knew they really did just let the rejected probationary people go. They probably figured I was as good as dead on my own, and sadly, I probably was. How was I going to survive by myself?

I didn't know exactly where I would go or where I would find food or water in this world. With no help. No one to watch my back. I was a girl, alone, in this broken down world with potentially dangerous people everywhere. I knew this would not be easy. I didn't even know how I wasn't bawling my eyes out at this moment, but somehow I stayed focused and kept my thoughts on Ryan.

I thought that if he was still alive, he would need me. Maybe I was his only hope because I was on the outside. I made up my mind as I drove away from the HOME putting more and more distance between the people I loved, the people I considered my family, that I would find a shelter. I would search for something as close as I could but far enough away that I wouldn't be in any more danger then I already was in. But I couldn't get too far from Ryan, Dean, Owen and Sienna. Dean had gotten a glimpse of what had happened, he knew I wasn't on the inside. I knew he wouldn't give up on me and he would tell the others. If they got out they'd come looking for me. I couldn't go too far, they'd have to know I wouldn't. There was no way I would just lie down and die no matter how much easier that would have been. Not now, not after everything I've been through.

I'd find a way to leave a message for them and post it as many places as I could, hoping they'd see it. I'd find a shelter, secure it as we'd done before, although it would take longer on my own and it was clearly more risky, but I knew what to do. At least it was a plan. It was the best I could think of doing, and a plan was better than no plan at all. I'd build another fortress. I had the weapons, ammunition, a small stock of food and water. As long as I could find somewhere to hide myself, I would be all right.

I remembered the seed packets I'd saved in my backpack, there was life around here, things were growing. I'd start a garden. Of course I didn't know if the seeds I had would grow here, but with the change in climate maybe no one would know what would or wouldn't grow. At least I had the seeds so I could try.

There hadn't been any traffic as I drove away, and very little when we had driven up this way only a short time ago. I'd find somewhere far off the main roads but still close enough to the HOME that the cars coming and going from HOME wouldn't see me. Or so I hoped. I'd find the perfect place, something small, something hidden away, maybe this could actually work. I felt determination set in, and it felt good.

Once I was far enough away from the checkpoint, I stopped at the first rest stop I came upon. I ripped a piece of paper out of Sienna's notebook, something with a drawing that hopefully they'd recognize, surely Sienna would, and wrote, "I'm still here - R." I only wished I knew the exact date. I put down the year and my best guess at the month.

* * *

It was three weeks later, sometime in October I guessed. I had started keeping track since remembering about the calendar I saw in the doctor's — or whatever she was — office. It was a way to measure time even if I wasn't sure how accurate my estimate was.

I'd secured a small home near a little but beautiful stream with drinkable water, although I always boiled it first. I had been lucky enough to find a home with a fireplace. It even had a little metal stand and a pot next to it that I could use to boil the water and heat up canned food that had been left in the cabinets. This place must have been used as some kind of hunting or fishing cabin. Or maybe just some place someone went to get away from society.

The little house had a fair sized basement that was more than adequate for storing my supplies. It also had a second floor with a small bedroom, and a closet. From the windows in that upstairs bedroom I had a good view of all directions. I'd see someone coming as long as I was paying attention. But no one had come this way. I was secluded which meant if the others had left HOME and were out looking for me, they probably wouldn't find me. I was completely alone. Isolated from everything, which is exactly what I wanted, that was, until I could come up with a plan to find my friends.

I had started a little garden, to see if anything would grow. I saved most of the seed packets so that when it was spring or summer I could try again. But for now I crossed my fingers that the potatoes would grow. There was a sprout from one of the tomato seeds, but I still didn't know if my plants would thrive. Since the seasons were all messed up I didn't know the right time to plant anything, not that I would have anyway. There were some brief instructions printed on the packet on how and when to plant, so I did the best I could with what I had available to me.

Any time I left the little cabin I drew detailed maps. I'd start at my house and walk out in all directions documenting what I'd find, hoping that one of these times I'd come upon the HOME base. So far I haven't. I mapped out several gas stations and would take home gas, food and water. My supplies were generous and even though it was getting colder I didn't worry too much about not having enough. I used a semi-sharp ax to stock up on wood for my fireplace. I started piles inside and in the basement and when those were full I made stacks outside. If any of the others had seen what I'd done, I knew they'd be as proud of me as I was of myself. I was impressed with how prepared I was, but after having done this for as long as we had, it shouldn't be that surprising. Although doing it alone is much more difficult and lonely.

There were several things that kept me going. But one of the big ones that was keeping me alive was the thought of seeing everyone again. I'd left signs everywhere for them — on trees, rest stops, gas stations, little shops, light poles, anything I could find to leave my little messages on. The only thing I hadn't been able to leave was directions on how to find me, that would just put me in immense danger. I felt I was already putting myself in danger leaving the notes all in this general area, but I needed to. Once they traveled further and stopped seeing the notes, they'd come back and check the area thoroughly. At least that's what I hoped.

As for now, I had a feeling they were still inside HOME. They probably couldn't leave, I imagined that they weren't really free to come and go as they pleased. I hoped they'd found Ryan or at least found out what happened to him. And if

Ryan was alive, that they were all together again, working on a plan to get out. I didn't even let myself consider the possibility they had given up on me, or that they wouldn't be able to find me. Instead, I knew it was as simple as they couldn't come, not yet, but they would as soon as they could.

So for now I had to figure out my own plan to get back together with them. They were my friends, the only people I trusted. They were my family, and all I had left in this world. Not getting back to them was just not an option.

I would find it.
I would get in.
I would find them.

***

About the Author

Kellee L. Greene is a stay-at-home-mom to two super awesome and wonderfully sassy children. She loves to read, draw and spend time with her family when she's not writing. Writing and having people read her books has been a long time dream of hers and she's excited to write more. Her favorites genres are Fantasy, Sci-Fi and Romance. Kellee lives in Wisconsin with her husband, two kids and two cats.

Coming Soon

Book two in the Ravaged Land series is expected early 2016. Please 'like' Kellee L. Greene on Facebook to be one of the first to know when it's available!

www.facebook.com/kelleelgreene

Mailing List

Sign up for Kellee L. Greene's newsletter for new releases, sales, cover reveals and more!

http://eepurl.com/bJLmrL

Made in the USA
San Bernardino, CA
27 February 2016